2nd Michigan Cavalry Chronicles: Book II

The Perils of Perryville
by

Cody C. Engdahl

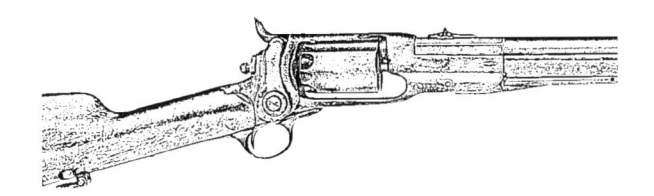

Copyright Cody C. Engdahl 2020

All rights are reserved. No part of this publication may be reproduced, stored, or transmitted in any form, or by any means, without the prior written permission of the copyright owner.

Cover designed by Stephanie Churchill, who is also an author. You can find her books on amazon.com as well

Contents

Preface	5
Acknowledgments	7
Glossary of terms	9
Dedication	13
Epithet	14
Part I: Corinth	15
Chapter One: The Traitor	16
Chapter Two: Visitors	29
Chapter Three: Hearts of Fire	40
Chapter Four: Boats and Letters	53
Chapter Five: The Fall of New Orleans	66
Chapter Six: The Death of a Giant	82
Chapter Seven: Waiting for the Federals	95
Chapter Eight: A Familiar Face	112
Chapter Nine: The Siege of Corinth	129
Part II: Perryville	139
Chapter Ten: The Battle of Memphis	140
Chapter Eleven: The Return	153
Chapter Twelve: Back in the Saddle	166
Chapter Thirteen: Munfordville	183
Chapter Fourteen: Forgiveness	199
Chapter Fifteen: The Offensive	214
Chapter Sixteen: Punishment	229
Chapter Seventeen: Into Darkness	244
Chapter Eighteen: Home	258
Chapter Nineteen: Two Ceremonies	272

Historical Note	279
Preview of *Blood for Blood at Nashville*	286
Sources	398
Works from Cody C. Engdahl	301

Preface

Thank you so much for your interest in this novel. I hope you enjoy it as much as I did writing it. This is the second book of the *2nd Michigan Cavalry Chronicles* series. It picks up pretty much where *Rampage on the River* left off, however: YOU DON'T NECESSARILY HAVE TO HAVE READ THE FIRST BOOK TO ENJOY THIS ONE. Although, I hope you do, mostly because I'm proud of it and I'd like you to read all of my work. But you may have found this book first, so I wrote it with that in mind, giving you just enough information about what had happened previously so you understand the context of my characters' actions in this story.

The series follows the 2nd Michigan Voluntary Cavalry through the American Civil War. The main characters and their stories are purely fictional. However, the historical events that happen around them are true. It was extremely important to me to get the actual history right. For some, this may be the only place you'll learn about these events, so I believe it is my duty to be correct. You, may also be a Civil War buff who can easily pick me apart if I'm not. I wrote this for both of you.

This novel includes real historical characters as well. You may recognize many of them. I tried to be as true to their real selves as possible, even using actual quotes at times. The only exceptions are the men in H company of the 2nd Michigan. Captain Chester E. Newman, Sergeant George Barth, Private Charles

(Chucky) Scott, and Private Max Bates are all names that I pulled from the 2nd Michigan's roster at the beginning of the war, but this is where the similarities to the real men end. If you happen to be related to any of the real men, I'd love to hear from you and please, I mean no offense with the way I portray them. The only thing I know about Captain Newman is that Marshall Thatcher describes him as having a "stunning hat" at the beginning of his memoir, *A Hundred Battles in the West*. To me, that speaks of a man with great bravado and panache, so I went with it.

The American Civil War is still hotly debated today. People argue over the cause, the reason people chose to fight, and the conduct of both sides. It is not my intention to make arguments either way. I wanted to write about what it was like to be human and caught up in the madness of this war. I also wanted an entertaining and adventurous story that is also historically accurate. I hope you enjoy it.

Cody C. Engdahl, Nashville, Tennessee, 2020

Acknowledgments

I should start by saying I could not have done this work without my girlfriend, Laura Reinert, who not only is my editor but patiently listens to me as I go on and on about my work and has given me support and guidance along the way. I also want to thank my mom, Nancy Thompson, for also helping with the editing and giving me a life full of encouragement in all my creative endeavors.

Stephanie Churchill designed my cover. She's also an author. She writes historical fantasy, so if you like *Game of Thrones* and *Lord of the Rings*, you should definitely check her out. You can find her books on Amazon as well.

I want to thank J.T. Thompson and the staff at the Lotz House Museum in Franklin, Tennessee. This was the first brick-and-mortar place to carry my first novel, *Rampage on the River*. I also want to thank Parnassus Books, the Robertson County History Museum, and Fort Negley who also carry my first book.

I have benefited quite a bit from the Civil War Podcast. Rich and Tracy do an excellent job researching and narrating the war. Their descriptions of battles have helped me see them clearly. civilwartalk.com is also a great resource full of very helpful people. I'd like to thank all the authors and historians whose work I consulted to write this book. I have a list of sources in the back.

I'd like to thank all of my friends and family in the real world and on social media who have supported me through this journey. I'd also like to thank you, dear reader, for picking up this book and giving it a go. Thank you.

Glossary of terms

Abattis: an obstacle, like a felled tree, used as a field fortification.
Bayonet: a long knife or spike-like weapon that can be attached to the end of a rifle turning it into a spear.
Brevet: a rank, like "brevet captain" for example, is a promotion for outstanding performance
without the raise in pay that would normally come with that rank until it is confirmed and made official.
Caisson: a wagon used to carry ammunition for a cannon.
Canister: a cannon shell filled with smaller balls meant to disperse upon firing.
Contraband: an ex-slave behind Union lines, often working for the army.
Carbine: a shorter version of rifle designed to be fired from horseback.
Earthwork: a tall mound of dirt piled up as a defensive wall.
Enfilading Fire: shooting into the flank of a line of men where the maximum potential targets are exposed.
Feint: a false attack meant to distract the enemy from the real attack.
Grapeshot: like canister but with larger projectiles often resembling grapes.
Hardtack: a hard cracker-like bread issued as rations.
Laudanum: an opioid in liquid form.
Minié ball: a conical shaped bullet as opposed to its spherical shaped predecessor.

Mortar: a large, cauldron shaped artillery piece that lobs its shells instead of shooting directly.
Musket: a muzzleloading black powder long gun.
Orderly: an aide assigned to do menial tasks for officers.
Reveille: a bugle call meant to wake troops in the morning.
Picket: a small group of men set out from the main group as a lookout or a guard.
Rifle: a long gun with groves in the barrel that causes the bullet to spin. Rifles can still be muzzle-loading muskets. Rifles eventually replaced smooth-bore muskets.
Saber: a single-bladed, curved sword designed for slashing from horseback
Sharpshooter: a sniper, marksman, or a soldier trained to shoot targets from a distance as opposed to a regular rifleman who provides volley fire.
12-pounder: a cannon that shoots a 12-pound ball. Cannons are often called by the weight of their shot.
Vedette: like a picket but on horseback.
Volley: multiple muskets or cannons firing in line at the same time.

Civil War Ranks for both Armies
-Enlisted
Private
Corporal
Sergeant
Major Sergeant
-Officers
Lieutenant
Captain
Major
Lieutenant Colonel
Colonel
Brigadier General
Major General
Lieutenant General
General
All officers with the rank of brigadier general or higher are typically referred to simply as "general."

Typical Civil War Military Units:
Company or a troop: about a hundred men, but varies greatly. Typically commanded by a captain.
Regiment: made up of several companies, typically ten, commanded by a colonel.
Brigade: made up of several regiments, typically three, commanded by a brigadier general.
Division: made up of more than one brigade, commanded by a brigadier or major general.
Corps: made up of more than one division, commanded by a brigadier, major, or lieutenant general

Army: the largest field command made up of more than one corps, commanded by a major general or higher.

Dedication

This book is dedicated to my father, Larry Engdahl, who taught me the love of reading and then read the books which that love produced.

Epithet

"It is well that war is so terrible, otherwise we should grow too fond of it."
General Robert E. Lee, CSA

Part I: Corinth

Chapter One: The Traitor

"Not only are we taking our horses on this boat," Confederate Lieutenant Lathan Woods growled at the poor, gray-clad private trying to stop him, "but you're staying here. It's your choice whether as a corpse or amongst the living."

The private put up his hands and stepped away. He'd gotten used to officers yelling at him during the chaos of the last few days, but this was the first one to shove a gun in his face. "Sir, Colonel Cook says no horses. The boats are for men only," he pleaded.

Lathan cocked his pistol, "Shove us off."

With a sigh, the soldier pushed the small boat that held Lathan, his two companions, and their three horses into the darkening waters of Reelfoot Lake. Lathan glared at the hapless soldier on the shore as other men fought for space on whatever they could find that would float in order to flee the Yankee advance.

After weeks of artillery duels and stalemates, the Federals finally got the gumption to move on Island No. 10. It was called that because it was the tenth island on the Mississippi south of the Ohio River. For the Rebels, it was the last line of defense to keep the Yankees from pouring into the South by way of the Mississippi. It sat on the first of two hairpin turns. Union ships would have to slow down in front of it before making the hard 180° turn. That made it the perfect place to amass artillery and destroy any ship trying to get through.

But the Union forces with their overwhelming numbers had surged into the area where Missouri, Kentucky, and Tennessee all met and took New Madrid. That city sat on the Missouri side on the second bend in the river. With the loss of New Madrid and the two forts that defended her, it was only a matter of time before the Union Army would flood into Tennessee from below and then move on the island from the south while their navy attacked from the north.

It was a trap and General Beauregard had seen it. That's why he started stripping the forces that were clustered on and around the island and sent them south to Fort Pillow, which sat along the river just north of Memphis, and to Corinth, Mississippi. That's where the retreating Rebel forces were amassing to make a stand against the Yankee invasion. That's where Lathan needed to go. He had a lot of questions for someone in particular there, someone who, Lathan believed, had sold them out to a Yankee spy. Now after this crushing defeat, he was going to find that traitor and make him pay for their losses.

Lathan had never liked Kyle Bethune. To him, he was an overprivileged son of a plantation owner. He had only been cordial to Kyle because Lathan had eyes for his sister, the beautiful red-headed Kathryn. Lathan was the mere son of a working man, a blacksmith who died before Lathan had grown into a man.

While Kyle was off in the North getting a Yankee education, Lathan was making a living doing what he did best: tracking. Negro slaves were expensive, more than what he could afford. That's why owners paid dearly for the recapture of runaways. Lathan was good at it, probably because he enjoyed it so much. There was nothing better than putting an uppity runaway negro in their place. Their cries and pleas meant nothing to him. He wanted to make sure they had plenty of horror stories to tell the others who might think they're too good to work for a white man and take to running.

But what was more despicable than an uppity negro, was an overprivileged, Yankee-tutored, negro-lover, especially one that was a traitor. It made sense. Everyone knew Kyle had eyes for the help. His years at a Yankee private school was probably where he was indoctrinated into their disgusting abolitionist cause. Those Northerners were so detestable, they even hated themselves. They despised their own whiteness and wanted nothing more than to raise the negroes to be their masters. It all made the sense. Kyle had gone to the dark side.

Kyle had conveniently missed all the work. Because he was worthless as a soldier, Captain Gray had sent him to Bowling Green, Kentucky, to beg for more men and supplies while Lathan and the rest worked frantically to build the defenses at New Madrid and Island No. 10. Kyle disappeared for weeks.

Instead of seeing him return with the supplies and the men that could have held back the Yankee invasion, Kyle's sister, Kathryn showed up with the man she called "Cousin Carl." This Carl had the look of a typical mix-mongrel from the North: olive skin, wavy black hair, and a listless demeanor. His stolen

Confederate uniform and the story that he was from Texas didn't fool Lathan. Once "Cousin Carl" opened his mouth it was all too clear that he was a filthy mixed-breed Yankee.

Lathan had caught Carl, if that was his real name, trying to run off with a negro that had belonged to Kyle's family, a runaway that Lathan had captured himself and brought to New Madrid to do his part in building the walls. Lathan had made short work of the cowardly Carl, but then the black giant blindsided him with a sucker punch. Lathan cringed in humiliation. He'd never drop his guard again. He'd also make that unruly negro pay dearly. Twice that big farm animal had run away. Carl and his negro had tied Lathan to a tree and then scurried away on a rowboat. Lathan grimaced to think that was exactly what he was doing now: running away on a boat.

Lathan had freed himself from the poorly tied ropes, got his men, and rode the two cowardly dogs down. He intercepted them halfway between New Madrid and Point Pleasant. He was going to saw off one of the runaway negro's legs for starters, and then hang the Yankee mongrel, but Union cavalry had overwhelmed his small squad, killing two of his men. Lathan spat into the lake in disgust at having to run from Yankees.

The Federals had surged into Point Pleasant with little resistance from Lathan's superiors. It was barely an inconvenience for Yankees. Surely they were well informed because of the Yankee spy and his negro lackey. And then finally, daddy's boy, Lieutenant Kyle Bethune showed up in New Madrid just clean as a whistle as if he had spent the last month on holiday instead of working like the rest of them. Lathan certainly wanted a word with the pampered prince about his sister and "Cousin Carl," but the arrogant fop of a boy was immediately ushered into General McCown's headquarters. The story that came out was that the Yankees had easily taken Fort Henry and Fort Donelson. With complete control of the Tennessee and Cumberland Rivers, they then had their sights set on the Mississippi. Island No. 10 and New Madrid were the last defense.

Lathan waited for his chance to catch Kyle alone. They were equal in rank, but Kyle was his social superior because of his family. Lathan had to be cautious before denouncing him outright. He had to probe. Kyle seemed very popular after his return. All the other dandies wanted to hear about the battle at Fort Donelson and Nathan Bedford Forrest's daring breakout, all of which Kyle claimed to be a part of.

Lathan had to wait for days until his opportunity came. Finally, having had their fill of Kyle's self-glorifying stories, the other junior officers left him alone. Kyle stood by himself in the street, staring at the river as if lost in thought while others hustled to and fro around him. Lathan made his move. He walked steadily towards the wealthy fellow officer, approaching him from behind while trying to control his own internal rage. He had to be careful.

"Lieutenant Bethune, might I have a word with you?" Lathan heard a voice come from his periphery. An artillery lieutenant approached Kyle from Lathan's left. Lathan changed course as if he suddenly had a different destination in mind. He walked away slowing, trying to hear as much as he could before walking out of earshot.

"Ah, Michael, how are you?" Kyle replied.

"It's Lieutenant Davis now," Davis said flatly, "I'm afraid I have some serious concerns to speak to you about your sister, Kathryn, and her cousin Carl."

"I beg your pardon?" Kyle took a step back from his fellow officer.

"I believe your sister has taken advantage of my trust and goodwill. Furthermore, I believe your cousin stole my…" Davis's voice faded away as Lathan walked farther from them. He found a shadow under an awning along the street to hide and watch the exchange. The two young men spoke with much animation that drew a few turned heads their way. Eventually, Davis walked away leaving Kyle standing alone looking stunned.

Lathan decided to bag his own designs for a while and watch this play out instead. *Let the fops do the work for me*, he thought. Lathan observed the two officers at odds as much as he could in-between his own duties. The two didn't speak to each other again after that first confrontation.

It was in the officers' mess a few days later when Lathan spied Kyle lingering alone after supper. Two artillery officers approached him curtly. One of them handed him a folded piece of paper and then waited for Kyle to read it. Lathan smiled to himself as he watched the blood drain from Kyle's face. Kyle looked up from the letter at the two officers and said something that looked like, "I accept."

Lathan's interest in the quarrel increased ten-fold. He carefully monitored the two during the days that followed. He enlisted two of his most trusted men, Bill and Tom, to watch the two and report everything they saw. Mostly what they observed was that Kyle and Davis never spoke to each other directly, instead, they spoke to their separate sets of friends. Those friends would meet and then discuss among themselves. What his spies were able to glean from these quiet meetings were a set time and place. Lathan was determined to be there too.

Lathan and his two men got to the grounds before anyone else did in the early morning darkness. Soon, the two separate parties arrived carrying lanterns. Kyle and Davis stood apart from each other in their shirtsleeves. Their collars were opened and unadorned. The separate set of friends convened in the middle then retired to their respective sides. Davis pulled his saber and handed the scabbard to his second. Kyle did the same. The two combatants placed their left hands on their back hips, sank into their postures, and advanced.

Davis attacked first thrusting his saber forward, then flicked his wrist downward trying to score a quick cut on Kyle's forehead. Kyle was quick to parry, raising his sword over his head to intercept the cut, and then slid it around and under Davis's blade to swipe at his extended arm. Davis quickly drew his arm back and deflected the blow with the side of his blade. The loud clangs of steel from the rapid exchanges had the seconds looking around nervously. Being caught dueling could get them all in trouble.

But then, a different noise took their attention. Lathan could hear it too. Those weren't small field cannons lobbing shots at each other, those were siege guns. The two combatants continued clanging their sabers together frantically as if to get the duel over with as quickly as possible. The seconds looked around nervously as it seemed that a full-on battle was breaking out with the morning light, a battle from which they were all absent.

An explosion from the direction of Fort Bankhead caused Davis to flinch and turn his head away from the fight and towards the flames that erupted in the twilight sky. Kyle saw the opening and quickly slid his blade between Davis's sword and bicep, cutting him on the upper arm. Davis hissed in pain as he clutched his arm and snapped his eyes back at Kyle.

"Are you satisfied, sir?" Kyle said, panting. He stole quick glances towards the sounds of the battle.

Davis scowled in pain and irritation. He looked to his seconds on the sidelines. "Come on, man! We mustn't tarry here! We'll all be absent from duty!" one of them pleaded.

Davis looked back at Kyle, "Fine, I'm satisfied!"

"Good! Come on! We've got to go!" Kyle replied.

The artillery barrage continued all day. By the afternoon, the top brass determined that they could not hold New Madrid from the overwhelming Federal numbers. Only the darkness and pouring rain gave the Confederates the respite they needed from the Federal bombardment to begin the evacuation. Lathan watched Kyle ride through the masses of soldiers loading onto the transports. He was yelling orders to the men over the hissing rain. Lathan was momentarily stunned when the young upstart caught him watching. "Lieutenant!" Kyle shouted through the rain. Lathan raised his eyebrows in surprise. "Your men are next! Form them up here with their horses and prepare to board once we get these men in front of you loaded!"

Lathan smiled slowly at the impertinence of this uppity daddy's boy, "By all means, Lieutenant Bethune." Kyle paused for a moment as if he had sensed the threat in Lathan's tone, but then turned his horse and rode off to corral more men onto the transports.

It was sickening to see Southern men run like rats in the rain before the cowardly Yankees. Lathan and his men were deposited on the Tennessee side of the river along with several other cavalry and infantry units. The cannons that they were able to save and their gunners went to Island No. 10 or to the mortar rafts that clustered around it. They tried to disable the rest of the big guns before they fell into Yankee hands.

In the days that followed came more sickening news. The Confederate high command had decided to cede the river at Island No. 10 to the Northerners. They were pulling most of their troops from the defenses, leaving just a token force to fool the Yankees into thinking they were making a stand. This was in hope of delaying the inevitable defeat in order to buy time to fortify Fort Pillow and Corinth. This would open up the floodgates to the Yankee invasion, allowing them to penetrate over a hundred miles into

Southern soil uncontested. The Yankee ironclad gunboats would then be able to sail almost all the way to Memphis. Lathan spat into the water in disgust.

Then more bad news came. Before Lathan could corner and confront the man he thought had sold out New Madrid to the Yankees, General McCown sent Kyle off with dispatches to the high command at Corinth along with many of their troops. It seemed the commanders were giving up on Island No. 10. Once again, the overprivileged daddy's boy got out of doing any real work or fighting. He had slipped through Lathan's fingers as well. But Lieutenant Davis was still around and he was easy pickings.

"Might I have a word with you, Lieutenant?" Lathan startled the popinjay of an artillery officer who was coming out of the woods believing he had been alone while relieving himself. Lathan saw his face change from surprise to loathing as he recognized an officer of inferior social standing.

"I'm sorry, but I'm quite busy," he huffed as he made to walk off.

"I see," Lathan said with a slight bow, tapping the visor of his hat, "but certainly not to busy to aid a Yankee spy…"

Davis froze on the spot and then turned slowly, "I beg your pardon, sir…" Lathan smirked at the man's attempt at sounding surprised and outraged.

"Are you missing a uniform?" Lathan purred, "I think I may have seen the man who was wearing it."

"I assure you I do not know what you're getting at, Lieutenant, but I do not like your tone. Who is your commanding officer?"

"Why, General Jeff Thompson, sir," Lathan smiled at how easily this fop fell into his trap. "I'm sure he'd be interested in the subject as well, and how you got that nasty cut on your arm." Lathan delighted as Davis involuntarily clutched at the wound hidden under his sleeve. "You know dueling is strictly forbidden, even amongst true gentlemen like yourself."

"I don't know what you're talking about…" Davis came back with.

"Don't play daft with me. Me and my boys watched you and your friends engage in a duel while absent from duty…right when you were needed the most. I'm sure this will not do well for your career and reputation," Lathan finished with a rise of an eyebrow.

Davis paused, not sure of what to say next, "What do you want?"

"Just information, my friend. I mean you no ill will," Lathan said warmly.

Davis complied. Once he got past his natural distrust for the snake-like, lower class Lathan, he poured in his own sense of betrayal and humiliation into his story. He had been duped by the beautiful Kathryn Bethune and her *cousin* Carl. Davis had merely tried to be a gentleman by offering them, and her servant, his room at the inn while he slept among his men. When he returned, he found his expensive, new uniform had been stolen and that the three had run up his tab at the inn with expensive food and wine. He said he knew Kathryn was Kyle's sister, so he demanded an explanation as well as satisfaction when Kyle had returned from his courier duties.

Lathan listened to the man whine, disguising his own disgust at the man's weakness. His story seemed to confirm his suspicions, however: Kyle and his sister had brought in a Yankee spy to scout the Confederate fortifications at New Madrid and then smuggled out the runaway slave that had come from their plantation. It made sense. The slave they called Elijah was as big and probably as strong as an ox. Lathan knew this well as the oversize slave had knocked him out with one punch. Lathan grimaced at the indignity of that. But moreover, the boy had a gift with horses. It was like he was a beast himself and could speak directly to them. The Bethunes made a fortune off of horse breeding just like they did with their cotton. They selfishly didn't want to give up their magical pet negro to help with the war effort.

The war came on hard once the Federals finally found their courage. Their ironclad ships pummeled what was left of the Confederate batteries at Island No. 10 to the north, while their infantry and cavalry poured into the narrow strip of land between the river to the west and Reelfoot Lake to the east. This effectively trapped the fleeing Rebel troops between the two bodies of water and the two Federal forces.

Lathan saw hundreds of men captured, most of them surrendering readily to the overwhelming surge of Federal troops. He took great pleasure in seeing Lieutenant Davis's shore battery overrun. The last he saw of him, Davis was wearing his second-best uniform with his hands in the air. *Good! One less rival to get in my way.*

Lathan lost most of his squad to the rush of Federal troops. He and his two most trusted men, Bill and Tom, slipped away, leaving the rest of his men to the mercy of the Northerners. They made their way south, staying off of main trails and far away from Tiptonville where surely the Yankees were planting their flag. Instead, they made their way to the shore of Reelfoot Lake where many were trying to escape. Men splashed into the water, some tried to swim, some even drowned. Others fought over any boat they could find. Lathan had commandeered a skiff large enough for him, his men, and their horses from a hapless fool of a private left to guard it. As they poled their way across the lake to safety, his last view of that private was him putting up his hands as blue-uniformed men surged in around him. Lathan spat into the water and looked ahead to the far shore. He had places to go and people to see. His first stop would be the Bethune Plantation.

Chapter Two: Visitors

The distant booming softly rattled the china at the Bethune Plantation. It was driving Kathryn crazy. "Good heavens! Is there anything we can put between those plates to stop all that racket?"

"We'll be far away from all this noise soon enough," Liza answered as the two young women worked to pack up most of the home's valuables and hide them where they could.

"I wish we could take it all with us. It's a terrible shame that we have to run from those horrible Yankees like a couple of refugees," Kathryn shook her head.

"It seems you don't think all of them are so horrible," Liza quipped, raising an eyebrow as she looked for a reaction from her friend.

Kathryn blew strands of hair from her mouth as she lifted a stack of plates to carry to the cellar. "Don't get lippy with me, missy," she said with humor.

Life had never been the same since her brother had shown up with his Yankee classmate just over a month ago. Kathryn had written to her brother for help. Liza's brother had run way, got caught, and then got impressed into hard labor as the Confederate fools tried to build a fortress around New Madrid. True, Liza and her little brother, who was actually quite an enormous young man now, were slaves, but to Kathryn and her brother Kyle, they were family.

Liza had been assigned to serve Kathryn before the two had even understood that one of them was a slave. The result was that they grew up like sisters. Liza used her position in the main house to secure a cushy job in the stables for her brother Elijah. It turned out to be a boon for the plantation. The big gentle giant seemed to have a way with horses that made her father very happy. Daddy's well-bred horses fetched high prices at the market and served as a secondary income to his cotton crop.

 Of course, the war had thrown everything into chaos. The Confederate army commandeered most of the horses, Mama and Daddy had to take their cotton to New Orleans to try to find a smuggler, and Liza was sick with grief over her baby brother. Then Kyle showed up with the stranger in a Yankee uniform. Yes, he was as uncouth like the rest of the Northern devils, but his big green eyes held a sweetness that drew her to him. Kathryn scoffed at her own lapse of judgment. With her beauty, she was used to bending men to her whims. But Carl, with his silky black hair and smooth olive skin, was pretty like no man she had seen before.

 Thankfully, he was a sucker like the rest of them. She and her brother convinced him to help them smuggle Elijah out of the labor camp at New Madrid. When it came time to part ways, Elijah went with him to be free among the Yankees instead of coming home. All the better, she supposed. Everything was falling apart and most of the slaves were gone now anyway. Nothing would ever be the same again.

 Kyle had returned to his army as well after their adventure, but he came back again within a few weeks. Kathryn smirked at her foolish brother as he came charging down the lane on his horse like he was some gallant errant knight. To a girl like Kathryn, it was all too easy to see that he had had a crush on the beautiful Liza. It made for an intriguing childhood. When he had first come home with the war on and their parents gone, the two finally succumbed to their childhood romance. With no one to see but Kathryn and Carl, they were openly affectionate to each other. Now the fool just couldn't stay away.

"Kyle, whatever are you doing here? You're going to get yourself in trouble," Kathryn had greeted him on the veranda as he leaped from his horse and handed the reins to a slave.

"Come inside, Kathryn," Kyle said breathlessly, "I'm afraid it's serious." The two sat in the main parlor. Kyle waved off her offer to call for refreshments. "I can't stay. I shouldn't even be here."

"I'm quite sure that's true," she smiled.

"Look, New Madrid has fallen."

"Oh, my goodness!" Kathryn drew herself up, placing her hand on her chest.

"General Beauregard has called for most of the troops to move south to Corinth. We're going to make a stand there. It's only a matter of time before the Yankees blow past our defenses at Island No. 10. When they do, there will be no stopping them from here all the way to Memphis. You, Liza…all of this will be behind enemy lines. You must get out as quickly as you can. Go to Ma and Pa. I've already written them in New Orleans; I don't know if my letter will get through."

"Wait, where are we going…?" Liza's voice broke through Kathryn's stunned silence.

Kyle stood from his arm chair to watch her as she came down the stairs. "Liza…you are absolutely radiant…" he stammered at the girl who had stolen his fancy since childhood.

"Yes, she certainly seems to have a certain *glow* to her since your last visit…" Kathryn said slyly.

"You must get out quickly. I can't be here to protect you. I have dispatches that must get to Corinth, and that's no place for you either," Kyle said worriedly.

"What about the slaves? Many of them have already run off ever since Overseer Johnson left to join the army. We can't take them all to New Orleans with us," Kathryn said.

"That's another matter I must attend to presently," Kyle said rising from his chair, rubbing his face with anxiety. Without another word, he walked outside and found Old Man Enon whittling on his stump near the slave cabins. "Enon, if you'd be so kind, please gather the workers and bring them to the veranda steps?"

The old man squinted at Kyle, then drew himself up from his perch. "Why sure, Master Kyle. Some done run off. I think you ought to know."

Kyle sighed, "I'm sure they have. I don't think it matters much anymore." Enon looked at him with wonder as the young man made his way back to the big house.

Within fifteen minutes, a few dozen workers gathered around the steps of the grand house. There were men, women, and children of various ages. Their clothes were worn but patched and clean. They stood straight and held themselves with dignity. Kyle looked at their dark, clear faces. Their brown eyes were wide with nervous wonder and anticipation.

"As you may know, things are changing rapidly," he said to them. A murmur of acknowledgment rolled through the crowd. "The Yankees have blown through our defenses on the river. It won't be long until they make it all the way here." That got a few gasps and a small number of contained cheers. "I don't believe you have anything to fear from them if you're still here." There was a ripple of shock and raised eyebrows among the workers. "We can't hold you here anymore. We certainly can't take care of you if you stay. I don't have the ability to give you all manumission papers at the moment, but I can't stop you from leaving either, so…you're all free to go."

The effect took a moment to sink in. Then a mixture of emotion swept through the people gathered before him. Some threw off their hats and leaped into the air, others sat down and cried. It was a mix of elation and fear.

"But where will we go?" a mother asked clutching her child.

"I don't know, Sally. You can stay here as long as you need to. I know that some of the slaves that have run north have found work with the Yankee army. We'll be shuttering up the house until it's safe for us to return. I ask that you be kind to my sister as she prepares to leave."

"Of course," Enon said straightening himself, "your sister will be safe so long as I'm here."

"I'm glad of it, Enon," Kyle said gripping the old man's shoulder, "I'm glad of it." Kyle's voice broke as he fought back against the emotions washing over him. Kathryn and Liza stared at him in stunned silence as he walked back into the house.

"Liza…" he said, fighting for control, "you're free." Kyle trembled, then fell to his knees, holding his face as he sobbed.

Kathryn turned to her lifelong friend with wide-eyed fear. Liza had never seen her mistress lose the veneer of confidence like she seemed to have now. Liza looked at her with pity. She reached out and squeezed Kathryn's hand, "You think you getting rid of me that easy?" Liza said, looking into best friend's eyes. Kathryn sniffed in a sob and steadied herself.

Liza knelt next Kyle and put her arm around him. "Come on, let's get you up." Kyle stood up weakly. He allowed her to walk him to an armchair and set him down. "I'll get you a bourbon, Kyle."

Within an hour, Kyle had pulled himself together. The girls packed him some food and walked him to the stables. He took Liza's hands and held them, "Stay close to her. Protect each other and when this is all over, I'll come for you," Kyle said, looking deep into her eyes. He paused for a moment and then said, "I don't care what anyone says is right or wrong anymore. I've seen enough. I've seen enough of this awful world and the terrible things men do to each other. All I know now is that you are my home, Liza. My home is with you, wherever you are."

Liza's eyes softened as she looked at Kyle's earnest face. She put her hand softly on his cheek, "Stay alive, Kyle. I'll be waiting for you." They kissed and then held each other's hands for a moment before Kyle leaped onto his horse and rode off to Corinth.

The days that followed were frantic. Kathryn secretly wished Kyle had at least waited until after they had packed up the house to free the slaves. It was so much work! The slaves dwindled as the days went on. Some walked off immediately after Kyle finished speaking. Some lingered, not knowing what to do next. It didn't seem right to ask them to help so she and Liza worked to cover the furniture, pack the valuables, and seal the house by themselves. Kathryn wondered if it was even worth the trouble. She could only imagine the Yankee marauders breaking in and doing as they please with her family's home and property.

The constant booming of cannon off in the distance became a mind-numbing drone over the days. It was the rattle of dishes that drove her crazy. Then at some point, it must've stopped. Katherine realized she hadn't heard a cannon, perhaps all day. Did she hear them the day before? She was still wondering when a knock at the door startled her. "Who in the world…?" Kathryn mumbled looking up from the wooden crate that she was arranging.

"It looks like Confederates, just two of them in gray uniforms," Liza said, peering out of the window.

"Oh, thank goodness! Hopefully, they're here to escort us to the river," Kathryn said opening door. She was startled by the cold green eyes and clean-shaven face that stood waiting for her on the other side. "Why, Lathan, what a surprise!" she gasped.

"I'm sure it is. I'm looking for your brother," he smiled cooly.

"I'm afraid he's not here. He left for Corinth days ago. I'm sorry, but we're very busy at the moment," she said attempting to shut the door.

"I understand," Lathan said stopping the door with his hand and setting a foot inside, "still, I have some questions about him. May we come in?"

"I'm sorry but that would be highly inappropriate…" Kathryn started.

"So is aiding a Yankee spy," Lathan said coldly as he shoved the door open and stepped into the foyer.

"What in the world do you think you're doing?!" Liza shouted as she tried to shove him back outside. Lathan's swift backhand sent her to the floor where she lay stunned. She reached to her face and felt the trickle of blood that began to form on her lip.

"Next time you touch me, I'll have you strung up and whipped like your masters should have done with you long ago," Lathan spat on the floor.

"Get out of my house!" Kathryn stood between Lathan and her friend.

"Don't you get lippy with me, missy," Lathan poked her in the chest. Kathryn slapped him across the face. Lathan's head never moved. He held his gaze on her. "You need some taming yourself, Kathryn. Once your brother is hanged as a traitor, your parents will need to marry you to a capable man like me. You better start learning your place."

"You're an animal!" Kathryn screeched as she tried to claw his face. This time he caught her hand.

"Don't think I'm above giving you the whipping you need too," Lathan smiled. Kathryn spat, hitting him in the face. Lathan shoved her into the arms of his companion and wiped the spittle with a handkerchief. "Hold her down, Tom. I'm about to do the work her daddy should have done years ago," Lathan said, removing his belt.

"Jesus Christ, Lathan..." his man, Tom, stammered.

"You wouldn't dare!" Kathryn screeched.

"You'd be amazed, Kathryn, just how daring I am," Lathan said, snapping his belt in his hand.

"Okay, fellas," an older voice broke through the room followed by the cocking of two hammers, "that'll be enough for today."

Tom let go of Kathryn as Liza slowly rose to her feet. All of them turned to see the old man holding a double-barreled shotgun step fully into the room.

"Now you boys go on and get on your horses. It's time for you clear on out now. That'll do for today," Old Man Enon said calmly.

"Put the gun down, old man," Lathan growled with his hands up and open, one of which still loosely held his belt. "I'll shoot you dead if you miss." Lathan motioned to the pistol on his hip with his head.

"Maybe," Enon offered, "but I've got two shots worth of trying."

Lathan let out a chuckle, "Okay, okay...Let's all just calm down a bit here."

"Just as soon as you and your friend step back outside," Enon said.

"You're getting in way over your head, old man," Lathan said as he and Tom backed out of the front door and onto the veranda. Liza darted quickly across the room to slam the door and lock it.

"Kathryn! Kathryn, come on!" Lathan shouted from outside. "You know I wasn't going to hurt you! I just need to know what you and your brother are involved in! I might be able to save Kyle from the noose if you help me! Kathryn!"

"That man is a monster," Kathryn hissed as the three worked to barricade the doors.

"Kathryn…?!" Lathan shouted as he returned the belt to his waist. "Come out and talk!" The house responded to him with silence. "I can wait all day! You and your negroes can't hide in there forever! You'll have to sleep sometime!" Lathan continued to call from outside.

"Another one's coming," Enon said peering out the window. The girls ran to the window to look themselves. Another gray-clad horseman came barreling down the lane towards the house.

"There must be a good reason why you left your post, Bill. You're supposed to be the lookout. What's going on?" Lathan asked him.

"A squadron of Union cavalry," Bill said breathlessly, "still a few miles out, heading this way…"

"Damn it…" Lathan hissed to himself. "Alright, boys, hang tight," he then said to his men. He turned back to the house, "Did you hear that, Kathryn?! Union cavalry heading this way!" Still, he got nothing but silence from the house. "Come with us, Kathryn. You can bring your negroes too. We'll keep you safe!"

Lathan stared at the silent house in frustration. "These Yankees will do more than ransack your house! You've got a lot more to fear from them than you do from me!" Still, no response came from the house. "They'll do more to that sweet behind of yours than tan it!"

"That man is such a pig…" Kathryn whispered to her companions as she peered through the lace of the window dressing.

Lathan turned to his men. "Okay, we've got a little time. Let's make sure those Yankee raiders find nothing of use when they get here. Start gathering up some kindling and place it around the house."

Chapter Three: Hearts of Fire

Carl could see the smoke ahead. His stomach had been in his mouth all morning as his patrol had taken a route into familiar ground. Since the fall of New Madrid and Island No. 10, he had been on several patrols foraging, or as it seemed to him, robbing farms. They were also searching for bushwhackers. Those were civilian partisans who'd attack Federal forces, seemingly out of nowhere, and then disappear back into the dark, swampy woods from which they came, leaving a few dead Federals in their wake.

But it wasn't the fear of Southern guerrillas that had him on edge. They were coming closer and closer to the home of the girl that had him completely infatuated: Kathryn Bethune. She was the sister of his best friend, who happened to be fighting for the other side. Carl had gotten tangled up in helping them rescue their runaway slave, Elijah, from the labor camps at New Madrid. Carl and Kathryn had had their romantic moments in the midst of the adventure. He told her he loved her and that he'd come back for her after the war. But she just laughed at him and told him to go back to the girl he had left behind in Detroit.

That was Anna, the girl in the locket he carried that Kathryn had found in his pocket. That was a whole other story. A simple kiss with Anna had ended in a duel with her maniacal brother, Klaus. That duel led to Klaus losing a hand and Carl's arrest. Carl was given a choice of jail or the army. Then, to make matters worse, Klaus reappeared months later with a brass claw for a hand and the gold bar rank of lieutenant on his shoulder. Carl was nothing more than a private. They fought a second duel which was interrupted. Since then, Carl had done his best to avoid the revenge-seeking son of a German immigrant.

But it was the redheaded beauty, Kathryn, that haunted his dreams. Now after bidding her farewell weeks ago, his patrol was drawing nearer and nearer to her home.

"That doesn't look good," Captain Newman said, putting his hand up to call the column to a halt. The signal was repeated along the line. "Sergeant Barth."

"Yes, sir," Barth nudged his horse up next to Newman's.

"Send one of your boys to see what's smoking up there. That sure ain't a campfire."

Barth looked back and motioned forward with his head, "Scott," he hissed lowly, "ride up there and see what you can see, but be quiet."

"Yes, Sergeant," the diminutive Chucky gulped. He gave Carl a worried look and then pulled out his pistol before nudging his horse forward through the woods. Carl let out a sigh. He had hoped it would have been him going to investigate instead. He was dying to see the home, to see if Kathryn was there. To see her once again. Maybe she had changed her mind and realized she loved him after all.

"Spread them out, Sergeant, and set up a rear guard. I don't want any of these squirrel-hunting yokels sneaking up on us," Newman said, stroking his pronounced mustache.

"You got it, Captain," Barth said. He then started directing the men to their positions.

Newman turned to his two lieutenants next. "Boys, go take up the flanks and keep the men ready."

Carl remained in the center just behind his captain. He gave Bess a pat to calm her as she gave out an agitated snort and pawed the ground. The wait was killing him. The sound of heavy hooves broke the silence as Chucky came barreling back. "Sir, there's a big house on fire, just up the way!"

Without thinking, Carl spurred forward, only to be stopped when Newman grabbed his reins. "Whoa there, son! Just where do you think you're going?"

"I'm sorry, sir…" Carl stammered, "there could be people in there!"

"Yeah, people that might shoot us, you fool," Newman said with a small hint of humor. "Nice and easy, boys, let's move up to the edge of the trees and take a look before we start offering them targets." Carl was beside himself with frustration. He wanted to tell them that it was his friends that could be in house, but how was he going to explain that his friends happened to be Rebels.

Carl could hear the crackling as they drew near. A warm breeze blew floating pieces of ash past them and carried the smell of burnt wood. Then through the trees, he could see the enormous conflagration. Flames licked high into the sky. Carl looked agape as the once beautiful home he had stayed in was now engulfed in flames.

The order to dismount came. The horses were brought back and left with the rear guard. Carl and his fellow troopers took their Colt revolving carbines with them as they waited in the tree line and watched the enormous home burn. A detachment swept around the perimeter of the house looking for an ambush. Once they gave the "all clear," Captain Newman ordered the rest of the men forward with his hand. The men moved cautiously into the open, many in a crouch, expecting bullets to start flying at any moment. None came.

A pane of glass exploded in the flames, causing many of them to jump. A nervous laugh rippled around the ring of men that stood before the burning home.

"No one's here," Private Bates said.

"Yeah, but someone did this on purpose," Sergeant Barth replied. "Look at the charred wood pushed up against the house."

"They didn't want to leave us anything useful," Captain Newman added.

"Captain!" one of the lieutenants called, "there's an open cellar door around back. But it's too hot to go in there."

"Okay, let's not then. Take a detachment and check the barn for anything we can filch. Sergeant, set up a perimeter to watch those woods. I don't want any of these bushwhackers taking potshots at my boys."

"Captain," Corporal Hans Becker called in his German accent, "there are fresh hoof tracks heading south into the woods. Maybe three horses."

"*Ja*," his constant companion, Corporal Dieter Housman interjected, "Shall we follow them?"

Captain Newman chewed on his mustache for a moment, "Nah, they're probably just frightened. It's a damn shame about their home. It just doesn't seem necessary."

Carl felt sick to his stomach. His patrol had uncovered a boon of supplies, grain, and livestock to carry back to camp. He had to give up Bess, his horse, so she could help pull one of the wagons laden with foodstuff. Instead, he was part of small detail tasked with driving the hogs and cattle they found on foot. His best friend's house crackled and smoldered behind them as they made off with everything of value they could find. Would he ever tell him about what they did that day? Would he ever see him again? Where were Liza and Kathryn? Did they make it out? Carl hoped that the open cellar door meant they did, but who would intentionally burn their house down? Certainly not Kathryn or Liza.

They were heralded as heroes when they got to camp. Men hooped and hollered at the great haul Company H had brought in from patrol. Carl wanted nothing to do with it. Once Bess was free from pulling a cart, he walked her back to the stables. He was full of dread at having to explain what had happened to the one person he knew he might meet there.

"Ah, my Bessie!" Elijah called with glee. "There's my sweet girl! He didn't hurt you none, did he?" Elijah took her reins from Carl. Elijah and Carl had formed a bond ever since Carl had helped him escape from a labor camp at New Madrid. Elijah's gift with horses put him in charge of the stables. The large man's empathy for the creatures extended to his friend as well. "What's troublin' you, Carl?"

Carl looked up at the big brown eyes that held him with sympathy and kindness. "I don't know where to start. Your old plantation, it's…gone…"

Elijah furrowed his brow as concern washed over his face.

"I think the girls got out…" Carl stammered under the scrutiny of the big man. Carl fumbled through his story, ashamed at what they had taken.

Elijah's eyes softened at that shame. "You did what you had to do," he said, laying a big hand on Carl's shoulder. "I don't think any of that stuff would have done anyone no good just sitting there anyhow."

"Where do you think everyone went?"

"I don't know," Elijah said rubbing the top of his head, "but if I know Liza, she's taken good care of Miss Kathryn. If something happened to her, I would have felt it." Elijah dropped his eyes to the floor with those last words. Carl wondered just how confident he was with them.

The orders came and everyone was excited. They were on the move again. A large battle had been won at Pittsburg Landing. It was off the Tennessee River near Alabama. Now General Pope's army at New Madrid was to join with the other forces there and finish off the Rebels who were licking their wounds just across the Alabama line in a town called Corinth.

But it didn't sound like much of a victory to Carl. Stories and rumors ran through the camp that thousands had died in just the first day of fighting. Soldiers were saying that Grant's army had been caught sleeping as a horde of screaming Rebels hacked them to pieces in their beds. The rumor had it that Grant's men had been nearly pushed into the river by nightfall. They said that it was the arrival of General Don Carlos Buell's army overnight that allowed the Federals to push the Rebels back all the way to their base in Alabama. To Carl, it seemed like they were merely going there to replace the dead bodies that were probably still lying on the field.

However, most of the other men didn't share his gloom. They were excited to board the ships once more. They would have to go back up the Mississippi to Cairo, then east on the Ohio River, and finally down the Tennessee to Pittsburg Landing and on to the battlefield that surrounded a little church called Shiloh. This meant no marching and a few restful days cruising on the rivers. But a lot had to be done before they could embark.

General Pope's Army of the Mississippi was over twenty-thousand strong. The 2nd Michigan Cavalry alone needed more than two ships to transport its men, horses, and equipment, all of which had to be packed and stowed aboard. Carl and Chucky were carrying a crate across the gangplank when they saw it.

"What the hell…" Sergeant Barth mumbled.

"Is that one of ours?" Chucky asked to anyone that could answer.

The boys set their load down on the deck and ran to the other side of the boat. They leaned over the guardrail to get a better look. An armored ship with her gun ports open and her cannons out crept around the bend and was coming their way. Alarm bells started clanging as sailors scurried to their battle stations.

"Jesus Christ, that's a Rebel boat!" Sergeant Barth exclaimed.

"We don't even have our guns!" Chucky said in awe.

Carl watched as the sailors on one of their escorting gunboats tried to signal the approaching enemy with flags: no response. A naval officer came out onto the foredeck and called out through a large speaking-trumpet, "Stop your ship or we will fire!" The Rebel ship continued to crawl towards the Federal fleet. The officer looked back at the men peering out of one of the forward gun ports. "Send one across her bow to show her we mean business," he told them.

Bam!

Smoke and fire exploded from the gun port, breaking up the tense quiet of the afternoon. The cannonball whizzed over the Rebel ship's smokestacks and smacked into the water behind her. The men inside the gun port scurried to swab, reload and move their gun back into position. Still, the enemy gunboat crept on. "Put one in her hull," the officer told the men. The next shot punched a hole in the Rebel ship near the waterline. Still, she kept on.

Next, a small boat full of armed men rowed out and boarded the silent vessel. Moments later one of them called out through his cupped hands. "She's empty sir! Must have slipped her mooring!"

Carl and Chucky watched as the Rebel gunboat floated past and then lodged itself onto a sandbar. There it slowly started to sink.

"Come on, boys," Sergeant Barth clapped them on the back, "back to work. She's no threat to us now."

The rumble of the steam engines and the churn of the paddlewheel put Carl to sleep almost immediately once they got underway. The men talking and even walking over him couldn't rouse him from his deep slumber as he lay on the floor of the main deck. It was only when Chucky roused him for dinner that he got up, feeling thick-headed from his long afternoon nap. Carl tried to seem interested as Chucky went on and on about whatever adventure they'd be off to next with unmasked glee and excitement.

The clang of spoons on tin bowls created a din that blended with the chug of the engines and the churning of the water. Men sat where they could and enjoyed stew with pieces of bread on the decks of the big paddle boat. The soft glow of lanterns and the cool but pleasant spring air was comforting as the dark countryside crawled by. Carl felt as if in a dream. He could see the blur of lights from the other ships in their convoy as they chugged along in the mid-spring evening. A man came into his focus as he made his way through the men sitting on the floor. He was calling out names to which men answered and were then rewarded with envelopes and small packages.

"Smith! Private Smith!" the man called out.

"Um…that's me," Carl held up his hand.

"Here you go son," the man handed him an envelope.

Sudden excitement ran through Carl as he looked at the letter. It was from home. His friend, Francis Beauchamp was the only one who wrote him. Carl's mother had not spoken to him since before the duel that had gotten him into this mess. She was upset with him for leaving her. Carl understood. She feared she would lose him just as she had lost his father in the Mexican War. Still, Francis dutifully checked in on her and wrote for her in his letters.

Francis wrote about the ongoings at school that Carl and Kyle were missing out on. But Francis still insisted that he was the one missing out. There was talk of a colored regiment forming in Detroit. Francis thought surely, with his education and family's prestige, he would be an officer. *The fool*, Carl thought. He would write him as soon as possible to tell him to stay as far away from the war as possible. Francis was more fit for the ballroom floor than the muddy battlefields.

News of their victory was the toast of the town. Francis had included a clipping from the *Detroit Free Press* exalting their very own Michigan boys' exploits at Island No. 10. and New Madrid. So many young men were now itching to get in on the glory before it was too late. Carl hoped it would be.

Francis next wrote about Anna Schmidt, the cute and curvy girl with golden locks and big blue eyes that was smitten with Carl. Carl sighed in annoyance, yet he was still excited to read on. Her family had forbidden her to write him ever since their little tryst ended in the duel in which her brother lost his hand, and Carl got shipped off to war. Like his mother, Anna wrote Carl through Francis, or through whoever may bring her news of the boy who had stolen her heart.

The heavy clank of boots and spurs roused him from his reverie. "Oh, shit…" Carl mumbled as he saw the German lieutenant march with hard purpose towards him. Clamped in his brass prosthetic claw was a letter. His reddened face looked as if it would explode with rage. His blond hair stood on end with static electricity as his icy blue eyes bored into Carl.

Was he coming to propose another duel? In front of everyone like this? Clearly, Klaus would know that dueling was illegal. Carl felt that his luck in their first two duels would soon wear out. He may not survive a third. Chucky made to get up and salute the staff officer. Carl started to as well.

"Stay seated," Klaus said coldly. He stood over Carl, fuming, taking a moment to collect himself. Carl could not have felt more awkward sitting on the floor with this furious officer towering over him. Other men started to take notice of the odd scene. Carl looked around as if for help. Finally, he met Klaus's glaring eyes.

Klaus was breathing loudly through his nose with such rage that it fluttered his wispy bangs. He raised the letter in his claw to peer at it and then returned his glare to Carl. "Are you fine?" he asked with barely controlled rage.

"What…?" Carl blinked at the ferocious German.

"I asked," Klaus looked at the letter again, and then back to Carl, "are you fine, sir?"

"Um…yeah…I'm ah…great," Carl stammered.

"Thank you. Then I shall report that you are," Klaus said curtly, turning on his heel and walking away.

"How are you?" Carl called out.

"None of your business," Klaus said as he disappeared into the officer quarters.

"What was that all about?" Chucky asked with his jaw agape.

"Girl trouble…" Carl replied. He was tempted to take out the locket he kept with him that Anna had given him when he left for the war. It held a portrait of her and even though he didn't like to admit it, he found comfort in looking at her from time to time.

"Private Smith!" the postmaster called out again.

"Here!" Carl called out raising his hand.

The postmaster grunted as he recognized that he had given Carl a letter earlier. "Here, you've got one more." He handed Carl a small envelope. Carl could smell it before he even saw the handwriting.

My God, that's her smell! he thought. He felt an unexpected stirring in his pants as he recognized the sweet smell of Kathryn's perfume. The envelope simply read:

Pvt. Carl Smith, H. Company, 2nd Michigan Cavalry

There was no postmark or return address. Carl held the envelope to his nose drawing another draft of her scent before opening it. Inside was a small note.

Lathan suspects Kyle. He's in trouble. Warn him if you can. Last known to be at Corinth.

*Regards,
K.*

Carl quickly tucked the letter into his jacket. *She's alive!* he thought with excitement and relief, *and she wrote me!* He smiled but then realized the implication. Kyle had been part of the plot in which Carl had sneaked into the Rebel-held town, stole a Confederate uniform, and freed Elijah from the work camp. Furthermore, it was Carl's inside intelligence that the Federals used to attack New Madrid. If Lathan had figured that out, it meant he could denounce Kyle as a traitor and a spy. *Good heavens!* Carl thought. That could easily put his best friend in front of a firing squad.

Worry ate away at his stomach. Carl felt miserably useless sitting on the deck as the big steamboat chugged lethargically up the dark river.

Chapter Four: Boats and Letters

Kathryn finally had a moment of peace to herself on the upper deck of the big paddleboat as it chugged its way down the Mississippi River. She had just shooed away the last would-be beau and was now taking a moment to look at the stars that were just beginning to pop out in the evening sky. The last days had been harrowing. She still couldn't believe her home was gone. She was able to take one last glimpse of the old plantation house as it roiled in flames before Liza tugged on her arm to urge her on.

It was amazing how servants knew so much more of a house than those who merely lived in it. Kathryn never had much reason to visit the musty old cellar. It was merely a place where food and wine were kept in cool dark corners that were more suitable for spiders than ladies of the house. She never knew that there was an outside door to the cellar that allowed servants to come and go quietly to do their work without disturbing the family.

They first had to wait and watch from inside as Lathan and his men pushed stacks of firewood against the house, splattered them with pitch, and then lit them on fire. It didn't take long for the flames to start licking the sides of the home. Lathan and his men stood outside for a moment, admiring their work, then took to their horses before the Federal troops arrived. Kathryn, Liza, and Enon had to time their own escape. They waited until they were certain that Lathan and his boys were far enough away to not see them exit, but still have enough time to flee themselves before the Yankees saw them as well.

In the meantime, she gathered up what money she could find, her stationery, and whatever else that might be useful before the house was too full of smoke to continue searching. "Come on!" Liza had yelled as she grabbed her arm and guided her through the haze. The stairs to the cellar in the kitchen looked like they ended in black nothingness, but Enon and Liza navigated the darkness with routine familiarity. The cellar was a welcomed cool to the rising heat of the ground floor. In the darkness, Kathryn could see daylight frame the outside door. Enon shoved the doors open with his shoulder. Brilliant sunlight spilled into the room. Kathryn could see they had emerged in the backyard. They darted quickly into the trees before the first of the blue-uniformed men stepped into the open ground in front of the home.

Enon led them through the marshy woods with the shotgun gripped firmly in his hands. Kathryn's shoes were soaked almost immediately. They spent that night shivering in the wilderness, huddled together for warmth. She was sure that every sound they heard had to be the marauding Yankees or Lathan coming back to finish his work. Enon sat up clutching the shotgun as the girls slept fitfully.

They made their plans in the morning. They would go to Tiptonville. "It's got to be crawling with Yankees," Liza said disapprovingly.

"Certainly, but there'll be officers too. Surely they won't allow their men to harm two girls and an old man," Kathryn said looking at Enon who had since dozed off, cradling his shotgun now that the girls were up. "I have to get a message to Mama and Daddy. They must know what happened. I must try to warn Kyle, too. Lathan will be quick to denounce him once he reaches Corinth."

Liza sighed, "We don't even know if your other telegrams have reached them. They may not even know we're coming. They might not even be there anymore. For all we know, the Yankees have taken New Orleans too."

"Certainly not!" Kathryn protested. "New Orleans is the jewel of the South! Our boys would never let it fall!"

The girls decided to let Enon sleep as long as they could while they freshened themselves up. They felt bad at having to rouse him from his slumber.

"Hey," Liza nudged him.

"Hmmm?" Enon popped an eye open.

"It's time to go. We're going to Tiptonville."

"Alright then," Enon said, using the shotgun to help himself up.

It took them all day to get to Tiptonville. They kept to the woods and made sure to hide themselves every time they heard horses. Enon hid the shotgun in some bramble before they approached the first picket.

"What the hell do you guys want?" one of the blue-clad soldiers who was guarding the road into town said. He spat on the ground.

"Well, some manners to start with," Kathryn snapped back putting her hands on her hips.

The second Yankee soldier burst into laughter. "She sure told you, Bob!" he said, slapping the first man on the back.

"I'm sorry, sir," Liza stepped in using her practiced subservient tone. "We just need to buy some things in town, if you don't mind."

"Sure, go on in," the second soldier said, still laughing at his grumpy friend's expense. They could hear him go on as they walked away. "Bob, you sure got a way with the ladies!" he laughed.

Kathryn swallowed hard as she saw blue-uniformed men seemingly everywhere in town. Many of them leered at her and Liza with lustful eyes, "Good heavens, these heathens are uncouth!" she whispered to Liza. Men dressed in officer uniforms crowded the telegram office.

"Excuse me, miss," one of them stepped in front of them, blocking their entrance, "may I help you?"

"Why, yes," Kathryn fluttered with her practiced sweetness, "I must send a message to my parents in New Orleans."

"No civilian communications right now, General's orders. I'm sorry," he said flatly.

Kathryn could see she'd get nowhere with this cold-hearted Yankee. "Can I post a letter, then?"

"No."

"Hmmm…" Kathryn thought for a minute as the Union officer looked her over. "Can I write to my cousin who's in your army?"

The officer blinked at her in surprise, "What unit?"

"Ummm…The Michigan unit…sir" she tried. He furrowed his brow.

"The 2nd Michigan Cavalry, sir," Liza stepped in, "H company."

The man looked back and forth between the two women and then to Enon. Enon shrugged at him and then looked off as if anything else was more interesting.

"Sure, write his name and unit on the envelope. I'll be sure to hand it off to the postmaster," he said finally.

Kathryn curtsied and flashed her best smile, "You are too kind, sir."

"My goodness, they have no adherence to charm, do they?" Kathryn whispered to Liza as they hurried away from the Yankee officers as quickly as they could without drawing suspicion.

Kathryn was able to buy ham, biscuits, and blankets from the sutlers that had set up shop on the outskirts of town. The prices were abusively high, but the men who ran their mobile shops to fleece soldiers of their pay were more than willing to be charitable to a pretty redheaded Southern belle.

"Planning a picnic, darlin'?" the merchant winked at her as he twirled the end of his mustache, "might I join you?"

"I don't think my fiancé would enjoy that," Kathryn said curtly.

"I don't suppose he would," The man tipped his bowler to them as she left with her items.

The three ate quickly and then packed the rest away for their journey. Enon fetched his shotgun as they hurried out of the Yankee-controlled town before the evening curfew was imposed.

Yankee transports and gunboats dominated the river. Thousands of troops waited to board the big ships that would carry them to Pittsburg Landing. Kathryn and her companions cut a wide path around them. It was apparent that there'd be no civil transport to take them to New Orleans, so they hiked along the river looking for an opportunity. The darkness helped hide them from Yankee patrol boats, but the nearly full moon was just enough to light their way.

It was near midnight when they found what they were looking for. An abandoned fishing shack had a small rowboat beached on the shore. Liza and Kathryn stepped in as Enon shoved them off and hopped in. Soon they were adrift, carried by the current downriver. Enon guided the small boat with a long stick he had found on the shore as the two girls huddled together under a blanket.

At dawn, they spent several frustrating hours trying to flag down a steamboat that could carry them to New Orleans. Finally, a small side-wheeler pulled alongside them. A grizzly looking man with a heavy black beard caught their boat with a spar and helped each one aboard.

"Something tells me you three are up to something you ought not be," he said, looking at them with their muddy clothes and worried faces.

"Nothing could be further from the truth," Kathryn said haughtily.

"Don't worry, missy, we're up to no good too," the man smiled. "I've got a hull full of guns that the Federals would love to confiscate if they caught us.

Hell, they'd probably hang us, too." The man laughed at the startled looks on their faces. "I'm Dan, that's Paul up in the pilothouse. Welcome to the *Lunette*."

The two-man crew of the small cargo boat agreed to carry them to Memphis. That's where they were taking their load of rifles and cannon. Kathryn had to pay them more than what she thought should have been legal, but the men were obviously smugglers who were out to make big profits under the wartime conditions.

They leered at the girls as they made their way downriver. But they shared their food freely, which was the only reason Kathryn allowed them any friendly conversation. Still, she was happy to be under Enon's watchful eyes in case these rough river men tried to take advantage of the two young girls' predicament.

"So, do you girls have sweethearts in New Orleans?" Paul asked that evening as they were finishing their bowls of butter beans and cornbread. Liza immediately got up, ran to the side of the boat, and vomited into the water. "Jeeze, I didn't know I was *that* ugly!" he exclaimed with humor which got a full-belly laugh from Dan.

"You best stick to ones you got to pay for, Paul!" Dan laughed slapping his friend on the back.

"I'm sorry, she's not accustomed to traveling on a boat. I should go attend to her." Kathryn said getting up from her meal leaving Enon with the two boatmen.

"The girls are spoken for," Enon said to them flatly.

Paul and Dan's laughter died down. Paul regained his composure. "Of course, sir," he said earnestly, "I meant no offense."

"None taken, sir," Enon said, dropping his eyes to his bowl as he worked to mop up the last of his beans with his cornbread.

"Are you alright?" Kathryn asked, softly placing her hand on Liza's back.

"Yes." Liza wiped the spittle hanging from her mouth with her sleeve. "I think the stress of all we've been through the last couple of days has wreaked havoc on my constitution."

"I'm sure that's it," Kathryn said with a smirk. "Come. Let's get you to bed."

Kathryn was relieved to see the city of Memphis come into view. She was anxious to finally get off the little steamer. Liza had been sick for the remainder of the trip. Kathryn thought it would be good for her to get back onto solid ground.

Paul and Dan wished them well as they helped them off the boat onto the busy wharf. The activity there was dizzying. Men were fortifying boats with iron plates. They stuffed the space between the plates and the wooden hulls with cotton. This was in hope of absorbing the blows that would be made by Federal guns. Along the shore they were placing cannons anywhere they could get a clear shot at the river. Boats were constantly pulling in or casting off. Many of them were unloading supplies and men or sending them north to Fort Pillow or south to Vicksburg.

Kathryn and her companions needed to find passage on a boat that would take them all the way down to New Orleans, and for that they needed money. Thankfully, she could draw upon her family's account at the Memphis Farmers' and Merchants' Bank. That bought them a small cabin on a riverboat that would leave in the morning. Kathryn had to claim that Liza and Enon were her personal attendants in order for them to be able to stay on the top deck with her, but they would not be allowed to roam the upper decks or enter the dining room unless they were performing their duties.

Once their passage was secured, she sent a telegram to New Orleans hoping it would reach her parents to let them know that they'd be there in a few days. After buying fresh clothes and food to make an evening meal, the three snuggled into the family townhouse her father kept in Memphis for his extended business trips. Kathryn wrote to her brother as Liza and Enon slept. She would post it before they got underway in the morning. She hoped it would reach her brother before Lathan did. Once finished, she looked at the single flickering candle set next to her stationary. She wondered what more could she do. It occurred to her that there may be one more person that could help her save her brother. She pulled out a leaf of paper, and then after pausing for a moment, began to write:

April 14, 1862

Dear Lieutenant Michael Davis, CSA

I must beg your forgiveness and plead for your help. My brother, Kyle, is in great peril and you may be our only hope…

Kathryn scribbled on, each word draining her of her composure until she signed her name, dropped her head into her arms, and sobbed.

Clean, rested, and ready to move on, the three boarded the big riverboat that would carry them to New Orleans after Kathryn posted her two letters to Corinth. The trip wasn't entirely unpleasant. Kathryn was only able to purchase a tiny cabin, so the girls had to share a bunk while Enon slept on the floor with his shotgun cuddled in his arms. He had to keep it wrapped in a blanket to hide it from anyone concerned about an armed black man. That was strictly forbidden by law.
He and Liza spent their days in the open air on the main deck where Liza had quick access to the guardrail when the nausea became too much for her. Kathryn mingled with other well-heeled travelers who remained on the upper deck. That area was reserved for their race and class. There Kathryn learned of the harrowing state of affairs in New Orleans.

"It's no place for a lady," a Confederate officer who had latched onto her since dinner said. "The Yankee ships have blocked off all routes to the sea. Forts Jackson and St. Phillip are the only defenses stopping the Federal Navy from steaming up the river from the gulf. If they get past them, there'll be nothing keeping those pirates from flooding into the city. I'd hate to see them get their hands on a pretty young lady such as yourself."

"I'm sure our brave boys will stop them," Kathryn said dutifully.

"Well, our boys couldn't stop them at Shiloh," he said with a shrug.

"What?"

"Haven't you heard? Our forces at Corinth tried to surprise the Yankees at the Tennessee River before they could organize their own attack. It didn't go well. Thousands of our boys are dead, captured, or missing. I believe their commander himself was shot. What's left of them crawled back to town. Corinth and New Orleans are no places for a lady."

Kathryn blanched. Kyle was supposed to be at Corinth. Was he among the dead? She cleared her throat and she pushed the thought out of her mind. "Well, I appreciate your concern, sir. I'm sure my father will keep me safe." She hoped this bearer of dreary news would just go away. The man had followed her out to the guardrail from the dining room. Kathryn had merely been looking for a moment to herself.

"I hope so. If I can be of any assistance, please don't hesitate to ask. I am at your service, madam," he said nobly, handing her a card.

"Thank you, Captain Dunston."

"James, please."

"Thank you, James. Now if you don't mind, I'd like a moment alone with my thoughts."

"Certainly," he replied, trying to hide his disappointment. "Perhaps we could take a stroll around the deck tomorrow before we come to port?"

"I would like that, James," she smiled grandly, flashing her big green eyes.

Captain Dunston blushed and bowed as he retreated, "Thank you, madam. Satisfied, I shall leave you in peace."

Kathryn gripped the guard rail and looked up at the early twinkling stars. She wondered who else was looking at them. She wondered if her parents knew she was coming, if her brother was safe from both the Yankees and Lathan Woods. Was she safe? Was there any stopping the Northern invasion? It felt like the world was closing in her. She could imagine masses of blue-clad men rolling across the landscape like a giant millstone crushing everything laid before it. She could see the hordes of hard, cold faces like the ones she saw swarming Tiptonville.

She let out a sigh and shuttered. Then from the masses of faces that cluttered her conscience, she could see just one. He was pretty. His skin was smooth and reminded her of coffee with cream. She thought about what it felt like to run her fingers through his silky black hair, what it was like to look into those big green eyes that had held her with such awe and naive adoration: sweet, lovely Carl.

She shook her head to clear it of these invading thoughts. *Good heavens, what's wrong with me?* Still, she wondered if he could see these same stars above as well.

She wasn't sure exactly when it was that she became fully awake or when she was aware of the sounds. She had been dreaming that the Yankees were relentlessly bombarding her home and she and her family couldn't get out. The sounds of the cannons pulsed on and on, driving her mad until she finally realized she was only dreaming.

Sunlight was creeping into their cabin. It spilled through the cracks between the door and the frame. It poured in around the curtains that covered the small window. She was snuggled up next to Liza who seemed to be radiating with heat as she slept soundly. Kathryn felt clammy under the covers. She pushed them off to cool herself. She lay there listening to the water pass by and the hum of the big steam engines below. Then she noticed it. First, it was more of a feeling than a sound, maybe even imagined. But as she lay there, it became more clear. It was a pulse, a distant thump that she felt in her chest. It began to come into focus as the glass window began to rattle. Somewhere off in the distance, someone was firing cannons.

Chapter Five: The Fall of New Orleans

Kathryn's parents were waiting for them as they came down the gangplank at New Orleans. Kathryn immediately threw herself into her father's arms and sobbed, "Oh, Daddy, it's all gone! It's all gone!"

He held her for a moment feeling the pulse of the distant cannons shake the wharf beneath his feet. "Come, child, I've got a carriage waiting for us. Let's go back to the hotel," he said finally.

Kathryn quietly cried on her father's shoulder for the whole ride back to the St. Charles Hotel. Her mother stroked her arm softly. Liza and Enon sat in uncomfortable silence. They weren't sure how to hold themselves in front of the people who had recently been their masters. Liza wondered if they even knew they had been freed. Mr. Bethune had given Enon a nod of acknowledgment and a friendly smile to Liza when they first sat down in the open carriage, but then spent the trip comforting his daughter with an occasional, "Shhhh…there, there."

Once settled in their suite, Mr. Bethune poured whiskey into two crystal glasses and handed one to Kathryn. She sat in one of the ample armchairs next to her mother. Mr. Bethune sat behind a desk. Enon and Liza, not sure what to do with themselves, stood next to the wall.

"Overseer Johnson wired me a few weeks back," Mr. Bethune sighed, holding up a telegram. "The damn fool said he was leaving to join the army."

"Roger!" Mrs. Bethune chided.

"Sorry, Martha," he said with a sigh, then took a drink from his glass before looking back at Kathryn, "I see you've brought Liza, but Enon? No offense, Enon." he added quickly, glancing at the old man. Enon put his hand up to wave off any sense of offense, then looked away as if something else in the room was suddenly more interesting. "…But, who's watching over the slaves?"

"They're gone," Kathryn said and then took a drink from her glass. She shuddered from the taste of the whiskey.

"All of them?! Christ, I knew I should have brought that runaway kid back and made an example of him!" Mr. Bethune slammed his glass down. "Now they all think they can do what they want!"

"Roger!" Mrs. Bethune exclaimed.

"Not now, Martha! Can't you see we are bleeding money here?! Those negroes are worth thousands of dollars! Thousands of dollars have just run off our plantation! We could at least have tried to sell them!"

"Daddy, they didn't run off," Kathryn said. "They're free."

"They're what…?" Mr. Bethune asked flatly.

"Kyle freed them all before he left for Corinth," she answered

Mr. Bethune sank into his chair, "Oh, that foolish boy…"

"He freed Enon and Liza, too."

"The hell he did!" Mr. Bethune slammed his fist on the desk making everyone in the room flinch.

"Daddy, please listen. So much has happened," Kathryn pleaded. Mr. Bethune sighed, drained his glass before pouring another.

"Go on," he said, slumping back into his chair.

His face contorted between changing expressions of anger, surprise, and sadness as Kathryn told him the events that brought them to New Orleans. He glanced up at Enon several times as Kathryn told him how the old man had intervened when Lathan and his boys attacked her, how Enon had led them through the cellar during the fire, and how he had watched over them during their journey that took them into a Yankee-held town and then onto a smuggler's boat.

Mr. Bethune flinched and grimaced with each detail. Once she was finished, he remained silent for a moment. He scowled at her and then glanced back up at Enon. Without a word, he jerked open a desk drawer, pulled out two sheets of paper, and started writing furiously. Once finished, he bolted out of his chair startling everyone in the room. He marched over to Enon, making the old man cringe as he approached. He handed him one of the papers. "Thank you, Enon, for looking after my baby girl," he said softly.

"What's this, Master? You know I can't read," Enon asked.

"It's your manumission paper," Liza said, wiping back a tear as she peered over his shoulder at the paper in his hand. "You're free."

"Alright then," Enon said. His eyes, which were now almost blue with age, glistened over with the threat of tears, "Thank you, Master."

"Well, you need not call me that anymore, but who am I to tell you what to do now?" Mr. Bethune smiled at the old man that had been a part of the plantation since before he himself had even been born. "Here's yours, Liza," he said, handing the second piece of paper to her. "You've always been like a daughter to us."

Liza could do no more than cover her mouth with one hand to hold back a sob as she accepted the paper with the other.

"Come, bring them to the desk," Mrs. Bethune smiled, "Kathryn and I ought to sign them as witnesses."

"Enon, I also relieve you of your oath to me," Mr. Bethune straightened himself, trying to hide the sudden shame that started creeping into him, "You may tell your granddaughter the truth."

The room went suddenly silent.

"Granddaughter!?" Liza gasped.

"Tell her," Mr. Bethune said softly, looking at the floor.

Enon looked to him for a moment and the back to Liza, "You look just like yo mama."

"My mama..?! I thought Elijah and I were bought as children…"

"Nobody buys children, child…" Mr. Bethune continued to stare at the floor in shame.

Mrs. Bethune put a hand on her husband's shoulder, "Sit down, my love, I'll tell her." Mr. Bethune sat down and drained his glass. His wife took Liza's hands and smiled kindly through her own tears.

"You and your brother were born on the plantation just like our children were. Your father was a troubled and difficult man. We always tried to be kind and treat our slaves well, but James just would not be tamed by anyone…" She looked away for a moment and then swallowed hard before continuing.

"The overseers tried everything to bring him under heel. They threatened him, they beat him, nothing would make that boy do right." She sighed and then sniffed back a tear, "I suppose I now understand why…nobody wants to be a slave…" She paused for a moment, looking down at her hands and then continued.

"But he loved your mother, Abigail, dearly. She was the only one that could tame his wild heart. She was a sweet thing and when she gave birth to you, James finally had a stake in the farm. He tried to shape up for a while, for her…for you, but in the end… he just couldn't tolerate being anyone's slave."

"James ran away after your mother got pregnant with your brother, Elijah. Word was that he wanted to find a place where they could be safe and free, then he was going to come back for her and you children…so you could be a family…" Mrs. Bethune stood up, covering her face with a handkerchief to muffle her sobs. Mr. Bethune stood up and put an arm around her. He offered her his glass, from which she took a drink and then let out a sigh, "I'm so sorry…" she sniffed.

"Sit down, dear," Mr. Bethune said to her softly. He looked back to Liza, whose eyes were filled with bewildered tears.

"We never saw James again," he continued, "It's our understanding that he died fighting a slave catcher. I suppose he preferred to die a free man than live as a slave." Mr. Bethune looked down at the floor and then back to Liza. "Your mother died shortly after giving birth to Elijah. I suppose it was over a broken heart."

Liza let out a sob and quickly covered her mouth.

"We promised your grandfather we'd always keep you, and not sell you off to anyone else. My father always respected and trusted Enon, and so have I."

Mr. Bethune looked at the old man and smiled sadly, "We just asked him to keep the secret about your parents from everyone, so that the other slaves wouldn't get any ideas of running away and then expect to come back for their kin." Mr. Bethune looked down and then smiled at Liza sadly. "I'm sorry…sorry for…God knows all the things I should be sorry for…I don't expect you to forgive us, but I want you to know, we've always cared about you and your brother like we do our own children." With that, he dropped his head into his hands and cried.

The soft tears mixed with the distant booming of cannons. Liza walked over to Mr. Bethune and crouched down. She took his hands and looked into his face. "You have always been kind to us, Mr. Bethune. I thank you for that," she said. Mr. Bethune let out a sob.

She walked over to Enon. The old man looked at her as she gazed at him in new wonder. She reached out and gently touched his face. His old blue eyes watched her as she regarded him. "Can I call you grandpa?" she asked and then immediately crumbled into a sobbing mess. She buried her face into his chest.

Enon, uncomfortable with the amount of emotion in the room, slowly put his arm around her. "I suppose so," he said patting her shuddering back, "you look just like my sweet Abigail, and her mama too."

It took a while for the room to recover from the moment. Mr. Bethune ordered dinner to be brought in once he splashed his face in the washbowl.

"That leaves other matters for us to talk about." Mr. Bethune said with a hint of trepidation. For a moment, all that could be heard was the distant booming of cannons and the noise coming off the street. Mr. Bethune cleared his throat. "We wanted to tell you before, but we had to be careful about communicating our intentions before we got out."

"Got out?" Kathryn repeated.

"The war has destroyed the cotton business for us. We can't even make money on the horses we raise. The army appropriates, or steals, rather, every mount they can get their hands on. Your mother and I have friends in Liverpool. We have an opportunity to go into business with the English. My expertise is in much need as they look to cultivate cotton in Egypt and India. We've found a blockade runner that will carry us, as well as our cotton, to the Bahamas. It's a small but fast ship that has made the run before. Once in Nassau, we can get passage for us and our cargo to England. I can arrange for you to come with us. Enon and Liza will have to stay behind, of course."

Kathryn stared at her father in stunned silence. She finally managed to speak. "What about Kyle? He's in dire trouble. We don't even know if he's alive. Have you heard about Shiloh? He most likely was there."

"I'm sure he's fine. We would have gotten word by now for sure if he wasn't. As far as this mess with his schoolmate from the North, he'll have to work it out himself," Mr. Bethune said firmly. Kathryn looked at him with open-mouthed disbelief. "Sweetie, I can't help him anyway. If I'm financially ruined, I'll be of no use to anyone. This is the best way I can save our family. Once we get this sorted, we'll take care of whatever trouble he's in."

"He'll be dead, Daddy!" she stated.

"Nonsense, you'll just have to trust me," he replied.

"I can't leave not knowing, and I can't leave Liza in her condition!" Kathryn blurted.

Liza's eyes widened in fear as she shook her head and mouthed the word, "No."

"Condition?" Mr. Bethune asked.

Kathryn looked at Liza's pleading face and then back to her father, "She's not been feeling well."

"I'm fine," Liza said. "Your father's right. You should go while you have the chance."

Kathryn looked at her and then her father.

"Look, you've been through a lot," Mr. Bethune said. "Let's have dinner and sleep on it. I'll speak to the captain in the morning. Maybe we can work something out."

Kathryn and Liza shared the second bedroom of the hotel suite as Enon slept on the couch. They fell asleep to the pulse of the distant guns. The booming became louder and louder in the early morning hours. So did the noise from the street and the hallway of the hotel. Mr. Bethune tried to fall back asleep as frantic voices and footfalls outside added to the din. Finally, he gave up and stepped into the hallway. There he found a chaotic scene. Military couriers raced back and forth with dispatches and pounded on the doors of their commanding officers who kept rooms at the hotel.

Mr. Bethune grabbed a young lieutenant by the arm, stopping him as he tried dash by. "What on earth is happening?" he asked. The young man looked at him with wide eyes full of shock and fear.

"Sir, the Yankees have blown past the forts guarding the entrance to the river. Farragut's fleet is steaming up from the gulf as we speak. We cannot hold the city once he gets here. All military personnel is to evacuate immediately. I suggest you and your family do the same!" He yanked his arm free with those last words and dashed off.

Mr. Bethune stared in stunned silence, watching the chaos of military personnel scurry around like angry ants out of a destroyed anthill.

"Get up!" he ordered as he burst back into the suite.

"Roger, what in the world…?" Mrs. Bethune sat up rubbing her eyes.

"No time to explain, Martha. The Yankees are attacking. We've got to get out now."

The dark streets were filled with chaos. Soldiers galloped through on horses. Men fought over carriages. Women and children wailed in terror. "Damn it! There's no chance of us getting a carriage!" Mr. Bethune bellowed. This time his wife merely squeezed his arm in fear instead of protesting his language. "There!" he yelled, pointing to a carriage that had just arrived to drop off several officers in front of the hotel. The five of them dashed to the carriage and started climbing in.

"Oh, no, you don't." A young man in civilian clothes grabbed Mr. Bethune by the collar as he tried to mount the steps into the carriage. "This carriage is for me and my family!"

Mr. Bethune looked in shock at the young man's face that was full of malice and violence.

CLICK

The man's face went from fury to flinching as a double-barreled shotgun suddenly pressed against his face.

"It is not, sir," Enon said. The blanket he used to hide the gun was lying at his feet.

The man threw his hands up and stepped back to where his wife held their baby. The child was wailing in fear. Mr. Bethune looked at their young and frightened faces. "You can ride with us to the docks at Lake Pontchartrain. There you can take the carriage wherever you wish," he told them.

"Much obliged, sir…" the man said softly, still staring at Enon and his gun. Enon uncocked it and gave him a nod.

L'étoile filante's engines were already running when they got to the docks. Steam billowed out of her smokestacks into the night air. She was a long and lean English-made schooner sporting two masts, but her main propulsion came from powerful steam engines that turned her side-mounted paddle wheels. Her shallow draft made her nimble and light enough to skim across the low waters of Lake Pontchartrain, through the narrow Rigolets into Lake Borgne, and then out into the Gulf of Mexico. There they hoped she'd be able to slip past the Federal Navy which was currently focused on blasting its way up the Mississippi River. Once past the blockade, she'd steam to the British-owned Bahamas where they and their cotton could switch to a cargo ship that could make the crossing to England.

The captain hailed them, waving his cap from the gangplank. "Good heavens, Roger, another few minutes and we would have had to leave without you!"

"I know, I know. We had a hell of a time getting across town. Everyone is panicking," Mr. Bethune said, helping his daughter out of the carriage.

"Who are all these people? There's no room for them," the captain said.

"This is my daughter, Kathryn, and our servants. We can't leave them behind." Mr. Bethune said.

The captain paused for a moment and then spoke, "The girl can come, but the negroes have to stay behind."

Mr. Bethune paused for a moment and then turned to his daughter, "Come on, Kathryn. It's what's best." He put his arm around her and tried to guide her to the gangplank.

"I'm not going, Daddy," she said, peeling off his arm.

"Kathryn, don't be ridiculous! There's no time for this! They'll be fine," Mr. Bethune said, grabbing her wrist.

"And what about Kyle? I can't just leave him to his peril!" she said, yanking her arm free.

"We really don't have time!" the Captain called. "We're leaving now!"

Mr. Bethune realized there was no winning. When Kathryn made up her mind, there was no budging her. "You're as stubborn as I am," he smiled sadly. "Get back to our place in Memphis. You can draw on our accounts there to live until we return and start rebuilding. We'll write to you there."

"Oh, Daddy!" Kathryn cried as she threw her arms around him.

Mrs. Bethune joined the hug. "Write us any news you get about your brother," she said.

"I will, Mama," Kathryn sobbed.

"It's now or never, Mr. Bethune!" the captain called from the gangplank as the crew was throwing off the mooring lines. The couple kissed their daughter one last time and then made their way up the gangplank with the few bags they managed to grab.

Kathryn watched as the *L'étoile filante* moved across the calm waters of Lake Pontchartrain and into the early morning light. Her parents were gone, and for the first time, she truly felt alone.

"Come," Liza said putting her hand on her shoulder. "We need to get out of the city."

"Come with us," the young man who had fought with her father earlier said. "There's plenty of room." Liza guided Kathryn back into the carriage. Enon climbed in behind them. "You may need that shotgun still, old man," the young man smiled at him. "I'm Duncan, by the way, and this is my wife, Sarah."

"Hello," Sarah smiled, trying to be pleasant despite her distress, "this is our baby, Duncan Jr."

Kathryn could see the child's bright blue eyes matched his father's. "He's so cute," Kathryn sniffed through her tears. Liza smiled at the child as well, unconsciously rubbing her own belly.

"Look, they're evacuating the militia to fight another day. With any luck, we might be able to tag along."

The first drops of rain splattered on the cobblestones as the carriage reentered the city. Flames licked the sky. The docks and several ships were on fire. Mobs of men pushed burning bales of cotton into the river. The bales burned as they floated downstream giving an eerie glow in the morning twilight. In the distance, Kathryn could see the enemy warships silhouetted by the flicking light.

Lightning lit up the smoky air as thunder rumbled across the sky. Panicked people began to crowd around their carriage. Some tried to climb in as Duncan and Enon fought to push them off.

"I can't get through this crowd!" the driver called back to them. His lead horses began to rear and neigh, causing some of the people to disperse momentarily.

"Can you get us to the train yard?" Duncan shouted above the noise.

"I can try!" the driver shouted back. He cracked his whip with a "Hyah!" The horses, anxious to get themselves out of the crowd, responded with a jolt. Duncan fell back into his seat as the carriage lurched forward. The crowd parted to get out of the way of the horses stomping their way through. Duncan raised the carriage's canopy. The rain started coming down steadily.

They got to the train yard as the last of the militiamen were loading into an over-filled boxcar. Duncan paid the driver and hurried to the platform.

"Sorry, sir, no civilians," was the answer he got from the sergeant overseeing the loading.

"I'm an officer with the regular army. I'm on leave for the birth of my son," Duncan explained as the rain plastered his hair to his forehead and ran down his face.

"Sorry, sir. There's no room. Militia only." And with that, the sergeant slammed the boxcar door shut, abruptly ending the conversation. The rain was coming down hard as Duncan now watched the train begin to creep forward.

"Come on!" he shouted as he took his wife's hand. The five of them ran along the tracks, Sarah clutching her baby with her other arm. "Here!" Duncan indicated at a flatbed car loaded with caissons and cannons. They were chained down with canvas tarps stretched over them with ropes to cover them from the rain. Duncan handed the baby to Liza and then lifted his wife onto the car. They jogged alongside as he then handed her the baby. One by one they climbed on as the train picked up speed. By the time Duncan climbed aboard himself, he was at a full run.

The canvas pulled tightly over the guns created tents under which they could shelter from the rain. "This train runs all the way to Jackson," Duncan said, "at least I hope it does today. From there we can find a way to Vicksburg. That's where we're going. You're welcome to come with us."

"Thank you," Kathryn said, "but we're hoping to get back to Memphis."

"You'll be able to pick up a steamer to Memphis from there for sure," Sarah smiled and then kissed her baby's head. Duncan smiled too, wrapping his arm around his wife to draw her closer into a snuggle. Kathryn and Liza couldn't help but smile at the couple and their child.

The train rumbled on through town as rain pattered on the canvas above them. Kathryn and Liza sat watching the city turn into countryside as they chugged along. The sun started to peek out among the raindrops. The others were dozing to the hum of the train.

"How did you know?" Liza asked rubbing her tummy.

"I'm a woman and your closest friend, Liza, how could I not know?" Kathryn smiled slyly at her.

Liza dropped her eyes and laughed shyly.

"It's certainly going to make for an interesting war," Kathryn quipped.

The two girls snuggled up next to each other for warmth. They dozed off as the sun shooed away the rain. Liza slept with both arms wrapped around her belly.

Chapter Six: The Death of a Giant

"This, by far, is the stupidest thing we've been asked to do in this God-forsaken war," groaned one of the men standing in formation behind Kyle. They were waiting for the arriving train to come to a full stop in front of them. Kyle let out a sigh. He put the alarming letter from his sister back into his pocket. He was about to turn around to address the man who had spoken when another voice stopped him.

"Shut your damn mouth, Roberts, or by God, I will shut it for you," growled one of the sergeants.

Kyle was relieved he didn't have to be the one correct the man himself. He was uncomfortable with his new rank, but as a newly breveted captain, he knew he had to be tougher with the men. But he certainly could see just how silly it must have seemed to them. How could they be expected to understand what they were doing? General Beauregard purposely kept them in the dark. He didn't want his true intentions to leak out to the Yankees who sat ready to crush their sick and weary forces at Corinth. So time and time again, throughout the day and night, the men who weren't sick, or already on the march, formed up at the platform and awaited the arrival of a train. The band was playing a jaunty rendition of "The Bonny Blue Flag" as some of the men sang along. They were encouraged to do so more for the benefit of the Yankee scouts than the men's own threadbare morale.

This was the second time many of them had retreated to Corinth. Kyle first came to the little

Mississippi town as a lieutenant, over two months before. It was just south of the Tennessee border. There wasn't much to the place except that it was the crossroads of two important rail lines. One ran north and south from the Gulf of Mexico at Mobile, Alabama, to the Ohio River that separated Ohio from Kentucky. The other line ran east and west. It connected Memphis on the Mississippi River all the way through Chattanooga, and then to Charleston on the Atlantic coast. Losing this hub would isolate many of the western Confederate states from the East.

Corinth was also easier to defend. It was too far from the Tennessee River for the Federal ironclad ships to shell. Its two creeks and surrounding swampland also created natural barriers that would stymie any approaching army. These were the reasons General Albert Sidney Johnston chose it to consolidate his forces after losing Fort Henry, Fort Donelson, and the City of Nashville. Once New Madrid had fallen on the Mississippi River, Johnston's second-in-command, General P. T. G. Beauregard, called for most of the remaining troops at the nearby Island No. 10 to come to Corinth as well. Kyle was sent as a courier ahead of those troops. Johnston had eyed him suspiciously when Kyle showed up with a handful of envelopes. Johnston scanned them quickly before returning his eyes to Kyle.

"If I'm not mistaken, Lieutenant, I ordered you to Fort Donelson the last time I saw you," Johnston said, raising an eyebrow. "How is it that you are now bringing me dispatches from Island No. 10? Shouldn't you have come from Nashville with Colonel Forrest's men?"

Kyle felt a cold chill run down his spine as the Department Commander of the Western Theater and his generals held him under their scrutiny. "Umm…I did go to Fort Donelson…sir…just as you ordered. I got separated during the escape. I managed to get back to New Madrid after being chased by Federal cavalry, sir."

Johnston held him in his gaze for a moment and then let out a sharp snort, "Stand over there with the orderlies until I decide what to do with you. Until then I don't want you out of my sight."

"Yes, sir," Kyle said meekly as he found a place among the other junior officers who were waiting to carry off orders at a moment's notice.

"Gentlemen," Johnston returned his attention to his generals, "the troops coming from New Madrid are the last we can hope to add to our numbers. We cannot wait for Van Dorn's army to arrive from Arkansas. We must make our move and destroy Grant's forces at Pittsburg Landing before Buell's army arrives from Nashville to reinforce him. It's our only chance." Johnston eyed the nervous generals, looking for any dissension among them. "Pierre!"

General Beauregard sat up clutching his throat as he cleared it, "Yes, sir."

"Are the battle orders ready?"

"They are, sir," Beauregard croaked. He was still suffering from a sore throat that had been haunting him for months, "My chief of staff has them written up and ready for distribution, sir."

"Good," Johnston said, "let's get them into the hands of our field commanders. I want everyone ready to move at six in the morning."

Of course, nothing went as planned. Some of the corps didn't manage to leave until well into the afternoon. Rains, muddy roads, and confusing orders stymied the Rebel advance. The attack was supposed to happen the next day on Friday, but it had to be delayed and then delayed again. Kyle stayed close to General Johnston and his staff. The general grew more and more irritated as the delays and problems compounded. Kyle knew to stay quiet but tried to be as helpful as possible. He ran messages back and forth to the corps commanders. Several times he even lent his horse and his own shoulder to help pull a stuck cannon out of the mud.

By the time the Rebel army had finished most of the twenty-three-mile march, they were wet, muddy, hungry, and exhausted. Worse still, the sounds from the on-and-off skirmishes with Union patrols most assuredly had ruined any hope for surprise.

"Now they will be entrenched to the eyes," Beauregard said gloomily looking at the map before them. He, Johnston, as well as Generals Hardee and Bragg conferred Sunday morning over coffee and hardtack biscuits. The occasional sounds of distant musketry mixed with the crackle of their campfire. "Gentlemen, we must withdraw now while we still have the chance to save our army."

"Damn it, Pierre! This was your plan!" Johnston roared, causing Kyle to flinch. He stood behind him with the rest of his staff. They were waiting to carry off his orders on command. "You were the one that convinced me that this was our opportunity to attack!"

"Yes, but sadly that opportunity expired two days ago. Now, there is no way the Federals don't know that we're here. They'll be too well-prepared," Beauregard said, then flinched and held his throat after taking a sip from his coffee. "We are outnumbered and outgunned."

"I'd fight them if they were a million! Here," Johnston declared, taping a spot on the map. Beneath his finger was a marker for a small church called Shiloh. "This is where the great battle of the Southwest will be fought. They can present no greater front between these two creeks than we can." He pointed to the natural 'V' that Owl and Snake Creeks created. It was where most of the Federals were encamped. "They have placed themselves in a trap. My scouts say the arrogant fools haven't even bothered to build fortifications. All we need to do is cut them off from their gunboats and transports on the Tennessee River and trap them here where the two creeks meet."

Johnston's clear gray eyes glared at his subordinates looking for any argument. The increasing crackle of muskets filled the uncomfortable silence until the first boom of a cannon caused his eyes to widen and then narrow with satisfaction. "The battle has opened, gentlemen," he said standing up. "It is too late to change our dispositions." He mounted his large thoroughbred horse, Fire-Eater, and turned the beast to face his generals, "Tonight we will water our horses in the Tennessee River!" he pronounced as men around him cheered. He then turned and dashed off towards the sounds of battle. Kyle and the rest of his staff scrambled to their horses to follow him.

Governor Isham Harris was among them. Having been supplanted by the Federally appointed military governor, Andrew Johnson, Harris found the best use for himself was as an aide to the Confederate Western Departmental Commander. "General, please excuse my impertinence, but wouldn't it be wiser to command your army from the rear and out of harm's way?" he asked, as he caught up with the commander.

"Nonsense," Johnston said, "I can't see what's happening from the rear. We must win this day, Governor. I'm here to make that happen. Lieutenant Bethune!"

"Um, yes, sir," Kyle rode up alongside the general and the governor.

"Ride up there to Bragg's corps and get those men to dress that line! There can be no gaps!"

"Yes, sir!" Kyle rode off towards the long line of men advancing through the morning twilight into the sounds of battle. The ground with its woods, thickets, and ravines was difficult to cross and maintain battle formations. Johnston and his staff spent the morning riding up and down the advancing Rebel line, tightening the gaps and encouraging the men onward. Hardee and Bragg's corps spread out into two-rank battle lines that stretched across a three-mile front. Beauregard orchestrated from the rear. By 7:30 he sent in Breckinridge and Polk's corps to fill the gaps and extend the line. This turned the assault into a forty-thousand-man, full-frontal attack.

The effect was devastating and immediate. The Federals seemed to be caught completely by surprise. Soon the Rebels were tramping over the dead and dying Union soldiers.

"Doctor Yandell!" Johnston called his personal physician forward.

"Yes, sir," Yandell said, spurring his horse up to Johnston's

"Tend to those wounded men there, if you would," Johnston said, pointing to the injured soldiers in blue that laid before them.

"Sir, they're the enemy!" an aide blurted.

"Not anymore," Johnston was quick to correct his underling. "They're out of the fight now."

The Yankees could only offer an occasional, poorly organized line to return fire before falling back. The first thing to significantly slow the Rebel onslaught down was the urge to loot. Many of the Yankees, caught unaware by the attack, left their breakfasts still frying in the pan. The smell of bacon was simply too much for the hungry Rebels. Many had run out of rations days before on the march. Soon, they were snatching up food, clothing, supplies, and whatever they could get their hands on. The fleeing Yankees had left a bounty of comforts in the rows of abandoned tents. Some of the Confederate soldiers even sat down to read love letters dropped by the Yankees as they ran.

Johnston was furious. Kyle and the rest of his followers knew to keep quiet as they rode into the camp. Most of the soldiers were too busy ransacking to take notice of their commander. "Where the hell are the officers?" Johnston fumed. It was then that a lieutenant came out of a Yankee officer's tent, beaming at his armful of loot. He stopped only when he realized an enormous horse was blocking his path. The blood ran from his face as he looked up to see his commander glaring down at him.

"Uh…umm…I've secured these…uh…items for you, sir," the man stammered.

"I'll have none of that, sir," Johnston said coldly. "We are not here for plunder." The young man dropped his eyes to the ground as his face went from white to red. Johnston looked down at the embarrassed man and let out a sigh. "Very well, then," he said pulling out his saber. He used it to snag a tin cup from the man's pile. "Let this be my share of the spoils today." A few of his staff let out a low chuckle. "Now, young man. If you are quite finished with your shopping spree, do you think you could rally these men into some semblance of a fighting force for me today?"

The man looked up at Johnston and then threw his bounty to the ground, "Yes, sir!"

"Good. Get them back into the fight, Lieutenant. I expect great things from you today."

"I won't let you down, sir," the man said and then turned toward the mob of soldiers. "To me! Sergeants, get the men in line! We are moving out!"

Johnston smiled as the return of discipline swept back through the men. Kyle felt a wave of relief roll through the staff as well. Just then, a messenger rode in hard from the right. His horse turned and reared as he came to an abrupt stop before the general. "Sir! General Breckinridge sends his regards. His troops are pinned down by strong Yankee resistance on our right."

"Let's see what we can do to remedy that," Johnston said as he spurred Fire-Eater towards the sounds of raging battle before much of his staff could follow.

They came upon hundreds of men cramped down in a gully. Union soldiers poured volley after volley of musketry over their heads. The Federals had taken up strong positions behind the trees of a peach orchard that lay beyond a cotton field that separated the two forces. Johnston rode Fire-Eater into the huddled troops with his head held high.

"Are you going to let these Yankees see you cower like this?!" he shouted to them.

One man stood up and saluted his commander, "Hell, no, sir!"

"I didn't think so!" Johnston beamed at his boys as they began to stand. "Fix bayonets!" Hundreds of men stood up and clicked their bayonets into place. Johnston rode along their line, touching their blades with his newly acquired tin cup. Each man's chest filled with pride as the cup clanged against his bayonet.

"These must do the work!" he shouted. "Men, they are stubborn! We must use the bayonet!" The men whooped and cheered. Johnston turned Fire-Eater towards the withering musket fire and pulled out his saber. " I will lead you!" The cheers turned into a deafening, high-pitched yell as hundreds of men poured out of the gully into the cotton field. Johnston rode before them with his saber pointed forward.

The Federals replied with sheets of lead. Men dropped all around, some screaming, others were dead before they hit the ground. Still, the assault pushed forward. The sight and sounds of the screaming gray line with their bayonets gleaming in the sun proved too much for the men hiding behind the trees. Soon the Yankee line was in retreat. A cheer broke out along the advancing regiments. Johnston pulled Fire-Eater aside and watched his boys move forward with pride.

The general was quite a sight to see once Kyle and some of the staff finally caught up. A bullet had almost completely shot off the sole of Johnston's left boot. He took his foot out of the stirrup to show them the piece of leather which was barely hanging onto the toe of his boot. "They didn't trip me up that time!" he laughed.

"Did it hit you?" Governor Harris asked in bewilderment.

"No," the general chuckled. Kyle grimaced at the blood dripping from his exposed foot.

Just then, an explosion of fire and smoke from the left brought them back into the battle. "How the hell did they get their artillery up so quickly?" Johnston gasped at the cloud of smoke, which now was rolling across the field from the left. "Lieutenant!"

"Yes, sir!" Kyle answered.

"Ride off and find our closest artillery. I want them to counter that battery," he ordered. Then he turned to Governor Harris, "Governor, if you'd be so kind, order Colonel Statham to wheel one of his regiments to the left to charge and take that battery."

"Absolutely, General!" Harris replied and rode off.

Kyle was happy to find that a Confederate battery was already moving into position to contest the Union guns. He rode back to tell that news to Johnston. Harris had returned too. "General, your order's been delivered and is being executed" Harris proclaimed proudly. Johnston regarded him blankly. His face had gone a deathly pale. He began to slump into his saddle. "General, are you wounded?!"

"Yes," Johnston said softly, "and I fear seriously so…"

With that, he started to fall from his saddle. Harris caught him by the collar. Captain Wickham grabbed him from the other side. Together they led him from the field to a ravine and laid him on the ground. It was then that Kyle noticed that Fire-Eater too was bleeding from multiple places. Harris tore open the general's shirt and started frantically looking for a wound. He couldn't find one. "Captain! Fetch Doctor Yandell, but send back any surgeon you can find along the way!" "Lieutenant!" he then yelled at Kyle. "Find the rest of the staff and bring them here! We are running out of time!"

A small crowd of men had gathered around General Johnston when Kyle returned with the rest of the staff. They were searching his bare torso, looking for a wound. Someone tried plying him with brandy. It ran out of his mouth and dribbled down his cheek. A colonel stormed in on his horse, leaped to the ground, and shouldered his way through the ring of men. "Johnston, do you know me?!" he cried, shaking the general's shoulders. Johnston's head bobbled loosely.

Kyle could see the general's exposed skin had turned an unearthly pale.

"He's stopped breathing, gentlemen," Governor Harris said, cradling the general's head.

One of the other officers felt for a pulse under the general's chin. He looked up at the rest of the men and shook his head.

"My God, is it so?!" the colonel cried out.

Silence consumed the ring of men as the noise from the battle raged on around them. A shell whistled overhead and exploded nearby snapping the men out of their trance. Governor Harris looked up at Kyle. "Lieutenant, ride back to General Beauregard. Inform him of what's happened. Tell him he's now in command."

Kyle scanned the grim faces of the men crouched around the fallen general for a moment. Then, he turned to his horse and rode off. He came upon a field of Federal tents that surrounded a little log church. Sentries stood outside the small building's entrance as couriers dashed out to deliver orders to various parts of the sprawling battlefield. The sentries briskly blocked Kyle's entry by crossing their bayoneted rifles with a clang. "That's alright, boys" a voice croaked from inside, "he's with Sidney. Let him in."

General P. T. G. Beauregard sat slouched in a chair set before a table cluttered with maps, dispatches, an inkwell, and a pen. The room was dark and musty, lit only by sunlight that spilled through the open windows and a single candle that lit the Cajun general's sickly face as he mopped the sweat from his forehead with a rag. He then coughed into it, causing him to wince in pain. He looked deathly pale.

"Bethune, isn't it?" Beauregard smiled weakly, "I believe I'm an acquaintance of your father. He does business in New Orleans from time to time. Is that right?"

"Um, yes, sir," Kyle replied, not knowing how to broach the matter that had brought him.

Beauregard did it for him. "Well, I suppose this is no time for niceties. Have you news from Sidney?"

Kyle paused for a moment looking into the general's expectant face. Beauregard blinked slowly, "Well…?"

"He's dead, sir…You're in command."

Beauregard stared at him as his face grew even paler. "Oh, dear heavens…" he said softly.

Chapter Seven: Waiting for the Federals

General Albert Sidney Johnston's body was wrapped in a blanket and quickly carried to the rear. General Beauregard didn't want it to be seen by his advancing troops. The man that had inspired the men forward by leading from the front was dead.

Beauregard continued to lead from the rear. Kyle became one of the many horseback messengers to carry orders to the front and news to the rear as the battle raged on. The Federal flanks had collapsed inward leaving only a stout resistance in the center. There the Yankees found good cover along a low-lying farm lane lined with heavy brush and thickets. From there, they sprayed volley after volley of lead at every attempt to overrun them.

The effect was sickening. Kyle watched as line after line was formed up and sent in a full-frontal assault on the Union's most forward position. Hundreds of men dropped at a time as blistering rifle fire crackled from behind the heavy brush. Men died without ever even seeing the guns they were walking into. Their bodies began to pile on top of each other as each new assault marched over the dead and the wounded of the last.

"It's like walking into a God damn hornets' nest!" Kyle heard a man exclaim as he dragged his unconscious friend to the rear.

"Are you enjoying the view, Lieutenant?" another voice came from behind, startling him. He turned in his saddle to see General Braxton Bragg glare at him from under his heavy eyebrows. With him was a handful of officers.

Kyle quickly offered a salute, "Sir!"

"I suppose it's quite entertaining watching your fellow countrymen die from the comfort and safety of your saddle," Bragg said flatly.

"Sir, I was just…" Kyle stammered.

"If it's not too much trouble, do you think you could possibly be of service to General Ruggles here?" Bragg interrupted, pointing to the long-bearded general next to him, who merely shrugged and rolled his eyes. "General Ruggles has an excellent plan, but needs the help from some horsemen, if it's not too much of an interruption of your afternoon dalliance."

Kyle blinked at the cantankerous corps commander, "…of course…sir, I was just…"

"Excellent!" Bragg snapped and then turned to the long-bearded general at his side. "He's all yours, Daniel. You'll have to round up whoever else you can find."

"Yes, sir," General Ruggles saluted. Bragg shot one more glare at Kyle before spurring off on his horse, his staff following him. Kyle watched the corps commander ride off with stunned frustration.

"Don't worry, son," Ruggles put a hand on his shoulder, "that guy's a dick."

Ruggles' plan was blunt and simple. After collecting up a handful of junior officers, they set out to get as many artillery crews that they could find. Soon horses pulling cannons and caissons were converging in front of the thicket-shrouded road. The men were beginning to call it the "Hornets' Nest." The cannoneers jogged alongside and quickly unlimbered the guns and began to load them. Kyle had never seen anything quite like it. By his count, there seemed to be over sixty cannons pointed at the heavy brush that concealed, what they thought to be, two Federal divisions. The cannoneers loaded the guns with solid shot, shells that would explode once over their target, and grapeshot, which was basically a canister of metal balls that turned the cannons into giant shotguns.

General Ruggles grinned at the sight, "I've always wanted to try this."

Kyle couldn't help but notice his thick New England accent.

"Please excuse me for asking, sir, but are you a Northerner?" Kyle let out before stopping himself from asking the impertinent question.

"…and an abolitionist," Ruggles winked at him.

"Why are you fighting for the Confederacy?"

"Hmmmm…? I don't know…it's crazy… Hey, but watch this!" Ruggles took off his hat and held it high, exposing his bald head. Men watched along the line in anticipation. He dropped his hat. They pulled their lanyards. The entire line exploded in smoke and fire as the guns kicked backward with sudden violence. Kyle's horse reared in reaction. The cannoneers quickly reloaded their guns and rolled them back into position. They started firing at will. The sound was deafening. Kyle did his best to plug his ears as he watched the devastating effect the cannonade had on the thickets that hid the Yankees. Shot and shell tore tree limbs apart, reducing them to sawdust. Grapeshot peppered the brush, killing any man foolish enough to hide in it.

The Federals tried to reply, but the Rebel guns were overwhelming. Soon the remaining flanks crumbled away allowing Rebel infantry to encircle the remaining Union forces left in their overextended center. As the smoke cleared, Kyle could see a white flag. The Hornets' Nest had been exterminated.

Kyle rode along the Yankee prisoners as they marched toward the Confederate rear. There were more than two thousand of them. He scanned their tired, gunpowder-blackened faces to see if Carl was among them. He shook his head at himself, knowing he was being foolish.

Beauregard was quite satisfied with the capture of the Union General, Benjamin Prentiss, and the remnants of his forces. Other than the death of Albert Sidney Johnston, and several thousands of his own men, the day seemed to Beauregard to be a smashing success. The Federals were now pinned down with their backs to the river. With nightfall quickly approaching, Beauregard called off the attack. His plan was to finish them off in the morning. From the comfort of his captured Union headquarters at Shiloh Church, he sent a telegraph to the Confederate capital in Richmond. It read:

After a severe battle of ten hours, thanks be to the Almighty, we've gained a complete victory, driving the enemy from every position.

It didn't feel like victory to Kyle. He sat on his horse watching his fellow soldiers revel in their newfound booty. The Federals had left behind tents, clothes, food, even whiskey. Somewhere, someone started sawing off on a fiddle. Whoops and hollers joined in. But the jubilant noise couldn't mask the groans and cries for help that came from the hundreds of wounded still stuck out in the no-man's land between the two armies. Volleys of shells began to fall on those men, Rebel and Yankee alike. The Federal gunboats were bombarding the ground between them at regular intervals.

He couldn't shake the vision of the hundreds and hundreds of men falling to the ground in waves as volleys poured out from the Hornets' Nest, men twisting on the ground in agony, or instantly dropping dead. He couldn't shake the sight of General Johnston's dead eyes as he slipped from his horse. Kyle let out a sob and buried his face into his hands.

"Well, look who showed up to the party! I do believe it's Daddy's Boy, back in the action…!Oh, no, are we crying?"

The sound of Nathan Bedford Forrest's voice, the man who had taunted him at Fort Donelson, the man he was supposed to follow to Nashville, sent a shiver up his spine. Kyle turned to see the ferocious cavalry colonel on horseback behind him. Forrest was looking at him with a contemptuous sneer, but then his eyes softened as he peered into Kyle's bleary, tear-stained eyes.

"You were with him when he died," Forrest said softly.

"Yes, sir," Kyle sniffed, trying to regain his composure.

Forrest paused for a moment. "He was a good man…a fighting man," Forrest said looking up at the darkening sky.

"Yes, sir, it was an honor to serve with him, even so briefly," Kyle said.

"They say he bled to death," Forrest went on. "The tough son-of-a-bitch didn't even know he was shot…Right behind his knee, I'm told." Forrest returned his gaze to Kyle. "I'm sure he thought highly of you…Say, is that a new horse?" Forrest said smiling as he edged his own horse closer.

"Yes, sir. I took him from a Yankee," Kyle said. Forrest's eyes popped up from looking at the horse back and to Kyle.

"Did you kill the son-of-a-bitch?" Forrest gleamed with pleasure.

"I did."

"Ha," Forrest threw his head back, "I knew you were a cold-blooded killer, just like me!"

Kyle smiled softly and then looked to the ground.

"Say," Forrest said, "how about coming with me to kill some more tonight?"

"Tonight?"

"Sure, unless you're too busy crying. But first you'll have to put on one of these," Forrest grinned as he held up a bundle of Union uniforms that he had draped over his horse. Lightning crackled across the sky followed by the rumble of thunder. The sudden flash lit up Forrest's manic face. Kyle blinked at him silently. He was quite sure he was looking at the devil himself.

The rain began to patter on the ground as Forrest led him to a small wooded patch where several of his men were waiting in the darkness. Kyle could see the glow of their cigars before he made out the shapes of men on horseback.

"Well, I'll be damned if you ain't done dug up ol' Daddy's Boy! Good to be ridin' with you again, Kyle!" Forrest's brother, Jeff, clapped him on the shoulder.

"It's good to see you too, Captain Forrest," Kyle smiled.

"Alright, now that you two love birds are done kissing, we'll get on to business," Forrest said which was followed by a rumble of chuckles. "My damn son, off doing what he ought not to, saw Yankee ships unloading men."

"Are you sure they weren't loading them? I heard they're skedaddling 'cross the river, nursin' their whupped behinds," Forrest's other brother asked.

"That's what we're gonna find out, Bill," Forrest said.

"I'm going with ya, Pa!" one of the horsemen yelped out.

"You disobey my orders one more time and I will whip your bare behind in front of the entire regiment, do you understand me, Lieutenant!" Forrest hissed.

"Yes, sir…" the teenage rider dropped his head in defeat.

Forrest let out a sigh, "Y'done good today, son, capturing them bluebellies and spying on the Yankee ships and all, but I can't have you running off with your friends without my permission. Now, with me and your uncles doing some scouting, I need you here to make sure one of us is watching over men."

"Really?! Does that mean I'm in charge?" The boy brightened significantly at the prospect.

"Now don't get crazy, Willie. We'll be back shortly. Just keep alert and let me know if anything happens when we get back," Forrest said.

"Yes, sir!" Willie snapped a salute.

Forrest smiled at his son and then turned to Kyle and his brothers, "Come on."

The rain was coming down steadily as they made their way to the forward pickets. "Who goes there?" one of soldiers called out in the darkness as they approached.

"Colonel Forrest and company," Forrest called back. "We're going on a reconnaissance mission. Don't you go shooting us on our way back or by God I'll break your behind myself!"

"Yes, sir," the soldier said meekly in the darkness.

Once past the Confederate lines, they stopped to put on their captured Yankee overcoats before making their way across the no man's land between the resting armies. Lightning flashes and the fuses from the shells that sailed overhead gave them quick hints of what the battlefield looked like around them. Men lay in strange and distorted positions. Some were still alive and groaned as they squirmed on the ground. Some called out for help. Kyle fought the urge to go to them and offer some kind of assistance, regardless of their uniforms, but he knew the Forrest brothers would think him weak.

So he rode past and pitied the men scattered on the ground around them. He hoped their suffering would end soon. That's when he saw it. In the inky darkness made opaque from the searing lighting that flashed in the sky, Kyle saw some of the dead and wounded had a faint glow to them. A dull blue-green aurora seemed to emit from some of the bloody wounds the men clutched at.

"Come on, Kyle," Jeff whispered, "we'll save more men by completing our mission than stopping for these poor souls." Kyle wondered if he had gone mad or if the Forrest brothers saw the glow too. He decided it was best not to ask.

"Who goes there?" a voice hissed from the darkness as they approached the Yankee line.

"Cavalry patrol, soldier. Stand down," Forrest said with authority. Kyle's guts were tied in a knot. *They are going to shoot us right now,* he thought.

"Yes, sir," the man called back.

"Come on." Forrest looked back at Kyle and his brothers with a wink. They made their way to the river, tied up their horses, and crawled to the top of a mound to peer down at the water below. "That's Pittsburg Landing for sure…" Forrest whispered.

"They're sure moving around quite a bit," Jeff added. Below them, they could see several transport ships moving back and forth across the river.

"But are they coming or going?" Bill added. The four of them lay on the wet ground watching the ships steaming back and forth. A flash of lightning revealed the scene: Hundreds of blue-coated men were marching down the gangplanks onto the landing. There, they were forming up with the thousands that had already disembarked. Some of the regiments started moving into position along the Union line.

"I've seen enough. Come on," Forrest whispered as he slid back down the hill.

They rode back to their own Confederate lines, barely taking the time to see whether either the Union or the Confederate pickets believed that they were not the enemy horsemen as they blew past the bewildered soldiers who were set out to guard their forward positions. "We've got to find someone in charge," Forrest said to his brothers and Kyle. "We either attack them now or fall back to Corinth. Otherwise, we'll be whipped like hell by ten o'clock tomorrow."

It was a frantic and disorienting romp through the dark woods as Forrest tried to find someone in command. The initial battle plan of the day before had called for the individual corps to attack in waves. This meant all of them ended up thoroughly entangled along the front with no one sure of who was in charge of whom. Adding to the confusion, men slept anywhere they could. This made navigating their horses in the darkness difficult without stepping on sleeping men. A few howled out in the darkness as the Forrest brothers' and Kyle's horses clomped through the woods. "Sorry!" Kyle cringed with regret.

The four of them went from one officer's tent to another. The answer was the same each time, "Go back to your regiment and be ready for tomorrow." Kyle felt his exhaustion increase with every officer who turned them away.

Finally, Forrest relented, "Go find yourself a place to sleep, Daddy's Boy. You're gonna need it tomorrow." Kyle felt guilty for feeling relieved, but he reckoned that even his horse needed time to rest. He tied him to a tree, then lay down next to it. He tried to use his bedroll as a shield against the rain droplets that trickled through the branches. He thought the rain, thunder, and the steady shelling of the no man's land would keep him awake. But then darkness overtook him as he felt himself falling deeper and deeper into a black hole.

    RAT-TA-TA TAT TAT TAT TA-TAT
    RAT-TA-TA TAT TAT TAT TA-TAT…

It took Kyle a moment to recognize the distant sound of snare drums calling the advance. Far off, fifes joined in with a jaunty tune. *Are those ours?* He wondered, opening and rubbing his eyes. The sun had already risen. Men ran in all directions, some were still buttoning their trousers. "For Christ's sake, Lieutenant, get up!" General Bragg shouted as he rode by, "We are under attack!"

Kyle got to his feet and dusted off his clothes. Utter chaos and panic swirled around him. His horse, which he hadn't bothered naming since he took it from a dead Yankee, munched on the brush around him with quiet disinterest.

"Lieutenant Bethune!"

Kyle turned and was stunned to see General Beauregard with his staff behind him. They had several regimental flags among them that they had collected as they tried to bring order to the multiple units that had overlapped each other from the previous day of fighting.

"Get these men in a line and prepare to receive an attack. You must buy us time so we can get our corps in order."

"Yes, sir!" Kyle shouted as the Cajun General and his staff repeated the same order to other junior officers along the way. Kyle saw a boy who looked far too young to be on the battlefield. The boy stared blankly into the woods from where the Yankees were sure to come. His drum hanged limply in front of him. "Hey!" Kyle shook him out of his stupor. "Sound the assembly!"

"Huh?" the kid responded, still lost in shock.

"Sound the assembly or we die!" Kyle shouted. The boy's eyes focused as if he suddenly had woken. He started playing. Men paused in their panic to listen to the drum. "Sergeants! Form the men on this line and prepare to fire!" Kyle called. Sergeants started cuffing fleeing men, knocking the loot from the Federal camps out of their hands, and shoved them into line. Soon a ragged line of men formed. The sergeants yelled at them to prepare their muskets. The line thickened as men found their resolve and added themselves to the fight.

Kyle was beginning to see the blue shapes moving against the sunlight that broke through the woods. "Ready!" he called, drawing his saber. "Hold!" For a moment all he could hear were the competing drums of the two forces. The forward skirmishers of the Federal line broke through the woods. "Hold!" Kyle shouted. He could see the men in mixed and ragged uniforms of his own line. They stood shoulder to shoulder, aiming their muskets with grim determination.

The full Yankee line broke through woods, marching shoulder to shoulder, their muskets held out before them.

"Fire!" Kyle screamed, slicing downward with his sword. The crackle of fire rolled along his line. Several of Yankee soldiers fell. He could hear their leaders call a halt and to ready arms. His own men were frantically reloading. "Fire at will!" Kyle shouted pulling his pistol and firing into the mass of blue men. With great satisfaction, he watched one drop as the man was lifting his own rifle to his shoulder.

The Yankees fired back. The air was hot and full of what sounded like angry bees whizzing past them. Several of the Rebels fell. Something grabbed Kyle's upper left arm and jerked it back. His jacket was torn and blood trickled down from where a bullet had scraped him. He patted himself for more wounds, found none. "Fall back! Fifty yards and prepare to fire again."

The Federals kept coming. The Confederates continued to form, fire, and fall back, but the numbers were overwhelming. By mid-afternoon, Beauregard called for a full retreat. The Federals, having had enough themselves, let them go. The rains started

107

again as what was left of the Rebel forces crawled back to Corinth, leaving a wake of discarded guns and wagons stuck in the mud.

Corinth was flooded with the sick and the wounded. Many men, who were not injured in the fight, still fell ill. The town reeked of vomit and dysentery. The water was bad. Men deserted in droves, but some trickled in as well. Many were survivors from the Battle of Island No. 10.

It unnerved Kyle when he first saw him: the tall, lanky, green-eyed, ex-slave-catcher turned cavalry lieutenant, Lathan Woods. He rode into town with two of his men in tow. Kyle cursed himself when Lathan caught him watching. His instinct was to look away, but Lathan's cold eyes held him still. A smile slowly spread across his clean-shaven face as he tipped his hat, winked, and rode by.

Kyle's uneasiness abated over the next several days as Lathan made himself busy with organizing cavalry patrols and vedettes. Still, Kyle couldn't help but to feel threatened every time he was near. Worse yet, Lathan seemed to have an uncanny ability of catching him watching, to which he always replied with a smile, a nod, or a wink that caused the hair on the back of Kyle's neck to stand on end.

The arrival of General Earl Van Dorn's army from Arkansas brought some confidence back to the troops. The Confederates began to build up the town's defenses as the Federals cautiously inched their way towards them. Still, General Beauregard knew they couldn't stay long. He summoned Kyle to his headquarters. "Sir!" Kyle snapped to attention.

"At ease, son," Beauregard said softly, still nursing his throat. "You performed admirably during our harrowing fight and subsequent retreat."

"I wish I could have done more, sir," Kyle said.

"Don't we all…don't we all…" Beauregard said wistfully, staring out the window at the activity outside. He returned his eyes to Kyle. "Colonel Forrest speaks highly of you as well."

Kyle was caught by surprise, "I haven't seen him since we've gotten back. I was worried he didn't make it." Kyle worried that he sounded like he was trying too hard to appear sincere.

Beauregard chuckled, "He nearly didn't. He took a bullet while charging headlong into a brigade of Yankee pursuers during our retreat. Apparently, he found himself alone and surrounded by the enemy. He had to shoot his way out. The audacity of that man never ceases to amaze me."

"Is he alright?" Kyle asked, this time with real concern.

"He's recovering from surgery. They had to cut it out of him without any anesthesia. The man wouldn't even accept whiskey. Apparently, he doesn't drink. Anyway," Beauregard continued, "we lost a lot of good leaders in those two days at Shiloh church, and we are in need of replacements. I'm promoting you to brevet captain effective immediately. I'm wiring the war department to make it official."

Kyle stood stunned at the news. Beauregard smirked at the shocked look on his face. He continued,

"I don't know how long that'll take. In the meantime, once you've affixed your two new gold bars to your uniform, you will assist in reorganizing the men into companies. We will soon have trains arriving, many of them, often throughout the days to come. You will gather as many men as you can, as well as musicians, and greet each train with as much pomp as you can muster. Am I clear?"

"Um…yes, sir," Kyle said bewildered.

Kyle stood at the train platform with several companies of men formed up behind him. He read his sister's brief, encrypted, and alarming letter once more as the train approached.

Beware of the Woods. They know everything.

Love,
K

Kyle looked around to see if the tall cavalry officer was near. *No, he must be on patrol, thank God!* he thought to himself.

The train slowly inched to a halt before them. The band played "The Bonny Blue Flag" as some of the men sang along. Others stood in sullen silence. Kyle knew all of this must seem ridiculous to them. Still, he couldn't let them in on the ploy, not yet. So they played along, some better than others.

The train came to a stop, blowing out a billow of steam. Sergeants opened the car doors and everyone let out a cheer. The ones that didn't right away were shoved and prodded by their sergeants until everyone was cheering. They were cheering train cars that were completely empty.

Chapter Eight: A Familiar Face

The smell was horrific. It came on slowly as the transports carrying the 2nd Michigan Cavalry chugged their way to Pittsburg Landing. At first, Carl thought it was just from the hundreds of men and horses spending days together on a boat. But as they moved south along the Tennessee River, the smell got stronger. The boasting and cheerfulness from the men died away as they got closer to the source. Appetites dulled. Men threw up over the rails. Even the horses became unnerved.

"Jesus Christ, it smells like something died!" Private Max Bates exclaimed.

"Thousands did," Sergeant Barth said, as he joined the men milling around the guardrail. "At least that's what the papers say. They're probably still burying them."

The men fell silent as the large troop transports chugged along. Chucky broke the silence, "Wow, look at the cloud!" He exclaimed, pointing to the dark mass that roiled low in the sky. "It looks like it's moving!"

"That's no cloud, son," Barth said grimly. "Those are crows."

They passed Pittsburg Landing by a few miles and then disembarked at Hamburg Landing instead. There, along with the 2nd Iowa, they once again returned to patrol and vedette duties as the armies of the Union converged in preparation for the march on Corinth. To Carl, there seemed to be a difference between the men that had fought the great battle there and those who had just arrived. The new troops still carried a youthful excitement about the opportunity to see some action and to escape the boredom of camp life. The men who had already fought there were quiet and reserved.

One man was particularly haunting. Carl's patrol came to headquarters to report about their brush up with the Rebels at a small hamlet called Pine Hill. Captain Newman went into one of the officer tents. Carl waited outside with the rest. There, from a respectful distance, he saw a man sitting alone in a chair among the hustle and bustle of staff officers that swirled around him. The man seemed important, yet no one spoke to him or even seemed to notice him sitting there. He sat in his chair, nursing a cigar, staring at nothing. His blue eyes were the only bright spot between his dark slouch hat and his grisly beard.

Carl was taken by the tragedy in the man's eyes. It wasn't until those eyes found his own that Carl realized he had been staring at the man. It startled him. It was like he could see the horrors of war deep inside those blue eyes. He wanted to look away, but then the man's eyes changed from sorrow to surprise, and then to what seemed to be recognition.

"Take a good look, boys" Captain Newman's voice broke the trance. "That's 'Unconditional Surrender' Grant himself," he said tipping his hat to the general. Grant didn't take notice. He eyed Carl with stunned scrutiny. "Looks like he's trying to figure out why you're so ugly, Carl," Newman quipped and gained a round of chuckles from the men. "Come on, boys,"

Newman put his arm around Carl to lead him away, "we'll be back at it early tomorrow morning."

Carl looked back at the general one last time. Grant drew on his cigar, watching him walk away.

The rain fell steadily all night. Carl spent most of it trying to stay dry and thinking about the letter, the girl who sent it, and the friend in an enemy uniform just miles away. He thought about the cruel green-eyed Confederate lieutenant who had made short work out of him back at New Madrid. He wondered what he'd do if he saw him again. Could he fight him or would he cower?

"Get up, Smith," the hushed voice of Sergeant Barth came with a nudge, "we're moving out."

Elijah was handing off horses and helping troopers get into their saddles at the corral. He smiled as Carl approached. Carl rubbed his eyes and tried to reply with his own smile. "Have you heard from your sister at all?" he asked as the big man helped him into the saddle.

Elijah shook his head with sweet nostalgia. "No, not yet, but I'm sure she and Ms. Kathryn are alright." Elijah's eyes crinkled with impish delight as he mentioned Kathryn.

Carl let out a sigh, "Sometimes I wish you couldn't read me as well as you do." Elijah let out a deep chuckle that seemed to reverberate in Carl's own chest. Carl smiled at the big man.

"Take good care of my Bessie," Elijah said, patting Carl's brown Morgan horse on the rump, "and try not to shoot Master Kyle if you see him."

"I'll do what I can," Carl smiled, giving Bess a light spur that sent her into a trot towards where Company H was forming.

"The Rebels are like a wounded dog backed into a corner, fellas," Captain Newman was lecturing the men as Carl rode up, "which makes them as dangerous as ever. They have retreated to Corinth, just over the state line. They're protecting a rail hub there that's vital to their supply line. Scout reports tell us that trains are arriving every day, most likely with reinforcements. Not to worry though, boys, we are part of the largest force this continent has ever seen. Our combined three armies will crush whatever they got for us, but first, it's our job to push back their forward positions. We need to compress all they've got into one spot, which is Corinth. Then, it'll be just like reaping wheat. They'll fall with one fell swoop of our one-hundred-thousand-man sickle."

That got a round of confident murmurs and nods from the men. "Today, we're taking the road to Corinth. Along the way is a little village called Monterey that the Rebels have seen fit for an outpost. We're gonna show them the error of their ways. Fall in, boys! We're moving out!"

The rain petered out as the sun rose on the two regiments of cavalry. The 2nd Michigan and their twin regiment, the 2nd Iowa, moved cautiously towards Monterey. The long-absent sunlight appeared, warming their damp jackets. For a moment, Carl felt at peace listening to the sound of over a thousand horses stepping on the damp ground.

He found himself drifting off as Bess ambled along when suddenly a halt was called. With hand signals, several companies formed into battle lines. The rest were held in reserve. Word of enemy pickets a half a mile ahead was whispered along the line. Captain Newman pulled out his saber and held it high in the air as did the other officers whose companies were part of the first charge. Carl swallowed hard. He drew his pistol like the men around him while holding the reins with his left hand. Along the line, officers dropped their sabers from straight into the air to straight forward. The line lurched into a trot. Bess flinched her head several times fighting the bit in anticipation.

"Easy, girl…" Carl said softly as their pace began to quicken. Hundreds of horses made soft thumping sounds as they rode across the damp ground. Carl could see nothing ahead but trees. He was wondering if there was even an enemy in front of them at all. Then he heard the 'pop' of a pistol, then came another with a wisp of smoke. Soon men along the line were firing their pistols at what seemed to be an invisible enemy ahead.

Then he saw them. The Rebels had placed pickets forward of their camp to watch for such an attack. A few puffs of smoke appeared ahead as some of them fired back, but then quickly turned and ran. Carl could see the backs of men in gray and butternut uniforms clinging to their hats as they ran headlong into the woods. He fired his pistol towards them, not taking any particular aim.

"We got them on the run!" Private Bates shouted in glee. Soon they were through the trees. They came upon a freshly abandoned campground. Campfires were still burning. Guns, belts, bayonets, and other equipment were left scattered on the ground. The Rebels formed in a line and fired from across the way.

"Keep pushing," shouted Captain Alger from A Company. He had been put in command of the first charge.

The Rebels fell back, firing wild when they could as the Union horsemen pushed them through the tiny village. Carl rode up on a man desperately trying to flee while holding his pants up with one hand. The man stopped, crouched over panting for breath, then turned around with his free hand in the air. Carl held him at gunpoint, not sure if he would shoot if the man turned to run again. The man panted looking up at Carl. Sweat ran down his face as he squinted one eye in the sunlight, watching to see what Carl would do. Carl wasn't sure.

"Keep moving! Keep pushing! We've got them on the run!" Alger shouted as he galloped by.

Carl looked back at his prisoner, "…Um…stay here, I guess. We'll be right back." The man just blinked at him as Carl rode off to rejoin the advance. They pushed through the town and then across a wooded ravine, which slowed their pursuit.

Once reformed on the other side, Captain Alger pushed them on. They rode hard trying to find where the Rebels had fled. Carl caught a glimpse just before they fired. Rebel cannons crowned a small hill in front of them. Dug in below were Rebel infantry in support. The hill burst into smoke and flames, sending a hot hail of musketry and cannonballs towards the rushing horsemen.

With a dull thud, a cannonball thumped into the ground in front of him causing Bess to rear onto her hind legs, throwing Carl to the ground. He lay there breathless as more cannonballs bounded past him.

"It's a trap!" he heard Captain Newman holler. "Fall back to the ravine!" Carl closed his eyes. He thought he'd just lay there and die when something pressed against him. He opened his eyes to see Bess nudging him with her muzzle. He sighed.

"Alright, then…" Carl got to his feet, still short of breath. Newman pulled up alongside him, putting himself and his horse between Carl and the enemy line. He whacked Carl on the back with the flat of his sword.

"Get on your damn horse, son! Ain't no time for lyin' around!"

Carl jumped onto Bess and followed the captain along with the rest of their company back to the ravine. Captain Alger and his lieutenants were trying to reorganize the fleeing companies into some kind of order. "Jesus, Russ! Are you trying to get us all killed!" Newman shouted at him.

Captain Alger glared back and then slumped his shoulders with a sigh, "I suppose I got a little too excited, Chester. Help me get the men back in order."

From there they rode back to the village where the two cavalry regiments were reforming. Carl sat on his horse waiting for orders. To his surprise, a Rebel soldier came out of his hiding place and walked up to him. He was holding his trousers up with one hand. Carl flinched, reaching for his gun, but then rested his hand on the handle once he recognized the man from before.

"Um," the man said, "what am I supposed to do?"

Carl blinked at the man for a moment, "I guess follow us," he said.

"Y'all got any food?" the man asked

"Um...," Carl stammered for a moment and then dug into his haversack. "Here you go," he said as he handed the man a piece of hardtack.

"Much obliged, sir," the Rebel soldier said and then gnawed on the hard tasteless cracker.

"Here, wash it down with this," Carl said, handing him his canteen.

The column marched back to camp at Pittsburg Landing with their prisoners and captured supplies. Some were disappointed they didn't try to take the battery of artillery, but their orders were clear: no major engagements until General Halleck's full force sat on the Rebels' doorstep at Corinth, some twenty miles away.

Halleck, who commanded all Federal operations in the West, assumed control of Grant's Army of the Tennessee, making Grant his second in command. He combined that army with Buell's Army of the Ohio and Pope's Army of the Mississippi to create an unstoppable force that was 100,000-man strong.

That unstoppable force crept southward from Pittsburg Landing toward Corinth. Rain, floods, and obstacles hampered their movement. They had to fell trees to corduroy the roads in order to move the cannons and supply wagons over the muddy and swampy ground.

Halleck's own caution compounded the Federal's slow pace. Not wanting a repeat of the surprise and near defeat at Shiloh, Halleck ordered the men to dig new fortifications at the end of each day of marching. All of these factors led to the enormous force advancing less than a mile a day.

Pope's army was the exception. High on his nearly bloodless victory at Island No. 10, Pope pushed his army forward on the left, outpacing Buell's army that occupied the Union center. This left Pope's flanks exposed, creating a target too enticing for the Confederates who were looking for any chance of breaking up Halleck's unstoppable force before it arrived in its entirety.

Lieutenant Lathan Woods was furious. *Captain?! They made that privileged good-for-nothing a captain?!* He spat on the ground. It was hardly fair. Here he was out doing a man's work while the now "Captain" Kyle Bethune cozied up with General Beauregard at headquarters. Apparently, the general and Kyle's father were friends and that's all it took.

But Lathan had more important things to deal with that morning. Even though he was still merely a lieutenant, he had been doing the work of a captain or more by leading reconnaissance patrols and raids on the Yankees as they crept their way to Corinth.

Most of them were cowards, cautiously tiptoeing their way south and then immediately digging in and hiding each night, but whoever was commanding the Federal left was an arrogant, bold, and foolish son-of-a-bitch. He had out-paced the other two wings and set up camp in the village of Farmington, immediately east of Corinth. From there he sent his cavalry and field artillery to feel out the Confederate defenses. Lathan had been doing the same, riding around the Union army, pushing back their pickets, and looking for weaknesses. There were plenty. The Yankee fools were too far in advance of their support lines. General Beauregard knew this, but apparently, the Yankee general didn't. So Beauregard sent General Bragg and General Van Dorn's divisions forward to teach him a lesson. Lathan and his men rode around the enemy's left flank and began to probe along Seven Mile Creek.

Carl watched the ongoing posturing from Big Tree Signal Station which sat on a hill. From there he could see the enemy building defense works around Corinth. He could also hear the trains arriving daily and the cheers of the Rebels each time they pulled into the station. It was frustrating.

"They're reinforcing every day as we sit here twiddling our thumbs!" Bates lamented.

The big Federal siege guns lay silent in the field below. Pope's Army of the Mississippi had gotten to their position at Farmington first. Now they had to wait for the rest of the Federal forces to get in their places before the attack on Corinth could begin. With orders to not bring on a major engagement until that happened, the 2nd Michigan and 2nd Iowa Cavalries passed their time patrolling and observing.

"What the hell are they doing?" Captain Newman's voice interrupted Carl's thoughts.

"That's a line of Rebel infantry marching on us!" Sergeant Barth said, describing what everybody on the hilltop was watching.

"Look alive, boys. We might be thrown into this soon," Newman said.

A man scurried out of the telegraph hut and began to hoist signal flags onto the 12-foot poles set outside. A trumpet sounded below followed by the rolling of snare drums. Soon the 2nd Iowa Cavalry were forming into battle lines. Carl looked back across the field. The Federal pickets were falling back to the line of siege guns for cover. Musket cracks followed by puffs of smoke began to appear on the field.

The 2nd Iowa surged forward, their officers pointing their sabers straight ahead. A startling boom exploded from the left where Rebel field artillery had been carried forward to support their infantry advance. The newly arrived field pieces poured enfilading fire into the advancing Iowans, sending several men and their horses to the ground where they floundered in agony.

"Good God..." Carl gasped at the horror unfolding below. As the first charge fell back, a second line of Iowans rode forward to meet the new challenge. Soon the Rebels were upon the Federal siege guns. A brisk melee of swords and bayonets broke out before the Federal gunners and pickets began to fall back leaving the big guns behind.

Carl's attention was snatched away from the unfolding violence as a rider crested their lookout post on his sweat-lathered steed. He held the reins with a brass claw that had replaced his left hand. With his right, he returned Captain Newman's salute.

"Yes, Captain," Newman said to the newly arrived officer.

Captain?! Klaus is a captain now? Carl felt his situation getting worse by the minute. He was the reason, the now Captain, Klaus Schmidt was missing a hand. It was all over a misunderstanding with Klaus's love-sick sister back in Detroit that ended in a duel. This was certainly still fresh in the German immigrant's mind. Carl looked down at the ground hoping the short brim of his kepi hat would hide him from the furious German's eyes.

"Captain Newman," Klaus spoke, "you are to take your company back to the camp below. There you'll rejoin your regiment."

Oh, God, they're sending us into that mess! Carl thought.

"The Rebels are making a strong demonstration on our left along Seven Mile Creek," Klaus continued, "it's not clear which of these two assaults is a feint and which is the main attack."

"Got it!" Newman said, and then to the rest, "Alright, boys. On your horses! It's time to dance!"

Carl looked up to sneak one more glance at Klaus before he rode off. He flinched when he realized that the German was already glaring at him. "Be careful," Klaus said to Newman, not taking his eyes off of Carl, "it could be a trap."

Carl's cavalry patrol spread out along Seven Mile Creek. They were looking for signs of further

Confederate attacks south of the main Federal line where the fighting was fierce.

"Let's tie our horses here and move forward on foot," Newman instructed his men. "No need getting our horses shot while walking into a trap."

"What about us?" Bates quipped.

"You're replaceable."

The men let out a muffled laugh as they pulled their Colt revolving carbines from their saddle holsters. Carl couldn't remember the last time he loaded his. He made a quick check to see that he had indeed placed primers on each of the firing pins. It was an odd weapon. It was pretty much like his pistol, but in short rifle form, complete with a shoulder stock but no forestock. It had six cylinders that he had to load separately with black powder and a ball.

They tied their horses to the trees near the creek and then climbed down the ravine, waded across, and then climbed up the other side. They spread out in a line and moved forward, crouching low as they went through the marshy woods.

CRACK!

"Get down!" Newman shouted.

More muskets sounded. The air began to smell of gun powder. Carl dropped to the ground and shouldered his carbine. Having no forestock, he had been trained to cradle his trigger hand with his left. He couldn't see the enemy, but he could see the puffs off smoke coming from the trees ahead. The men around him started firing their Colts indiscriminately at the unseen threat, quickly emptying all six chambers of their carbines before switching to their pistols. Carl shrugged and took aim at one of the puffs of smoke. He pulled the trigger.

BAM!

The flash from the overloaded cylinder spread, igniting all six at once. The gun exploded as all the cylinders fired, blowing the barrel clean off. The blast singed Carl's face with a flash of hot metal particles.

"Fuck!" he screamed in agony, clutching his face and rolling onto his back. The gunshots tapered off as both sides had fired off all the rounds they had loaded. Carl was in a daze. Everything sounded like he was underwater. His eyes were bleary with tears.

"Fall back!" Carl could hear Newman shout.

"Wait…wait…" Carl gasped with little more than a croak. His head was spinning in the silence that followed. *I have to get up!* He thought. Then he heard it. *Is that some kind of animal?* It sounded like a high-pitched yelp. Several voices added to the horrifying sound. Carl could hear the footfalls of men running towards him. *Fuck, I've got to get up!*

He sat up and then stumbled to his feet. He could see dark blurry figures rushing towards him. They had long shiny things in their hands that glistened in the sunlight that broke through the woods. Carl shook his head to clear it. He tried to focus his eyes as he pulled out his saber.

A pistol shot from behind, knocking one of the figures to the ground. The rest slowed to a stop just in front of where Carl thought he stood alone. He blinked hard, trying to make out the faces of the men that pointed their sabers at him. He was finally able to focus his eyes on the man directly in front of him. The man's green eyes widened in shock as he stood half crouched with his saber out before him. Carl recognized the tall, slim, clean-shaven man that had been in his nightmares since New Madrid. The two stood in stunned amazement staring at each other.

"You!" Lathan gasped, his eyes nearly popping out of his head.

BAM!

Another pistol shot came from behind Carl, dropping one of Lathan's men to the ground. A rough hand snatched Carl from behind and pulled him back.

"Come on!" Newman growled, as he dragged him backward with one hand while holding his pistol on the Rebels with the other.

Lathan stood up straight, laughing as Captain Newman pulled Carl back. Soon more shots rang out as Carl's company had reloaded and were now firing from the safety of the ravine. The Rebels started falling back. Carl looked one more time at Lathan. The menacing Confederate lieutenant was standing upright, laughing as his men retreated. Newman shoved Carl into the ravine where the rest of the men were taking cover and then climbed down himself.

"Carl! Cousin Carl!" Lathan called out. "Haha! I knew it was you! I know who you are!"

"Friend of yours?" Newman lifted an eyebrow at Carl.

"Hardly," Carl said, sitting up and placing his back against the ravine wall. Lathan's voiced poured into the ravine.

"I knew you were a blue-belly son-of-a-negro Yankee!"

"I'm French, you bastard!" Carl shouted back.

"Oh," Lathan shouted with feigned surprise, "is that what they call them up north?!" A light chuckle broke out among the men in the ravine.

Lathan cupped his ear, listening for a response. Then he returned his cupped hand to his mouth, "I'm coming for you, Carl! I'm going to see your treasonous friend hanged as well! But I'm coming for you, Carl!"

"He sounds like he's in love with you," Captain Newman said quietly, causing the men around him to laugh.

Carl scoffed.

"And that little redheaded whore that helped you!" Lathan called out.

That was enough for Carl. He went to stand up but Newman put a hand on his shoulder, holding him down with his eyes. That's when another voice broke through from their own side.

"Why don't you go fuck one of your own toothless yokels, you pansy! Carl's ours!" Carl and Captain Newman broke their staring contest and slowly turned their heads toward Private Max Bates who was still cupping his hands around his mouth.

"Well, that was interesting, Bates…" Newman said raising an eyebrow.

127

"Fuck that guy," Bates spat.

"You heard him, boys," Newman said to the rest of the men, "if we ever get our hands on that man, we'll all take turns." The men of H Company broke into a laugh.

Lathan spat on the ground, listening to the Yankee laughter that rolled out of the ravine.

"I'll teach you to laugh…" he said to no one that could hear him before turning and walking away.

Chapter Nine: The Siege of Corinth

Braxton Bragg's corps succeeded in pushing the Federals back, but when Earl Van Dorn's troops failed to arrive in time to attack Pope's other flank, Bragg was forced to withdraw, giving back the ground he had taken. Upon hearing about the heavy skirmishing, General Halleck ordered Pope to withdraw his troops as well, until the full brunt of the Federal forces could be brought to bear upon the Rebels hiding behind the earthen walls of Corinth.

Carl lay in a hospital cot with his face wrapped in bandages. He stared at the roof of the large tent listening to the moans and cries of the other men. Some were sick with fever, some in agony over their wounds, others lamented their missing limbs. Carl felt the sooner he could get out of there, the better. His experience from being in a hospital at St. Louis taught him that the longer you stay, the more likely you'll die, and more likely from disease which killed more men than the Confederates could ever hope to.

He closed his eyes and tried not to think of the invisible death that crept around him. He tried not to think of what the exploding gun had done to his face. The doctor said he had some superficial burns and cuts. They had to remove some of the metal fragments from his face with tweezers. Carl remembered clutching the sides of the cot while the doctor cooed, "There, there, almost done…" It was an experience he didn't want to ever have to go through again, although he had to admit, it was far better than the fellows he saw having their limbs sawed off. *Good God!* He thought, *They can just kill me!*

"How is he?" a familiar voice snapped Carl's eyes open.

What in the world is he doing here! Carl thought in panic. He suddenly felt exposed and unable to defend himself.

"He's going to be fine, Captain," the doctor said. "We'll take the bandages off in a few days and see how much of a face is left." The doctor chuckled, "Don't be alarmed, Captain. He'll be fine…maybe a few scars to impress the ladies back home."

"That is the least of my worries, Doctor," the officious captain said sharply. Then he started stomping towards Carl with his large cavalry boots and jangling spurs.

Oh, God, here he comes!

Carl peered through the bandages that gave a tunnel-visioned view of the world. Klaus Schmidt walked into his narrow field of vision.

"They tell me you will be fine," Klaus said flatly.

"Yes, but perhaps not my face," Carl replied.

"Good! Maybe that'll discourage my sister's childish affections," Klaus said with a huff.

"God, I hope so," Carl said too quickly. Klaus's face flushed red as his eyes burned into Carl's.

"You are not worthy of my sister's love," Klaus hissed, "it is not yours to take lightly!"

"I'm sorry…Klaus…I didn't…"

"My sister is of pure and noble German blood that will perhaps be called for again in the motherland!

Until then, I'll be damned if I see it tainted by the blood of a mongrel dog as yourself!"

"I'm French, Klaus, I…"

"That's bad enough!" Klaus glared at him, his brilliant blue eyes seemingly on the verge of popping out of his head. His veins pulsed in his temples with fury. "One day, the German people will rise to their place as rulers of this world. You'd do well to learn your place now."

"Okay…" Carl said meekly, sinking into his pillow.

Klaus's face flattened as if all the fury suddenly left with the flick of a switch. "In the meantime, I will report to my sister that you are fine." Klaus turned to walk away.

"Klaus," Carl said, stopping the German in his tracks, "I'm sorry about your hand."

Klaus looked down at the brass claw that had replaced his left hand. He let out a breath and turned back to Carl. He held up his claw, examining it with what seemed like pride.

"It was a duel," he said and then looked back at Carl. "Perhaps once my sister's affections have moved on to a man worthy of her blood, I'll be free to once again pursue my satisfaction. I will take great pleasure in killing you." With that, he turned and walked away.

"Okay, let's take a look at what's left of your face," the doctor said with a bit of the humor that Carl was beginning to get used to from him. The doctor sat down and started cutting the bandages away from Carl's head. He handed them to a young woman who held a small bucket to collect them. Carl caught himself holding his breath, and then chided himself for being so apprehensive. *It'll be okay*, he thought. They had to stitch up part of his face and pull small fragments from others. The ordeal had been agonizing since his face was still tender from the burns. The doctor said the wounds were superficial, still, Carl's vanity kept him worried. Would the girls back home still like him? Would Kathryn still think he was handsome?

Carl hissed in pain as the doctor peeled away some of the cloth that was stuck to his face with dried blood.

"Good God!" the doctor gasped as the last piece came off. "That's a face only a mother could love!"

Carl immediately felt sick.

"Stop it!" the nurse laughed slapping the doctor's arm.

"Naturally ugly I'd say, but not from any exploding guns," the doctor continued with a chuckle.

"Don't listen to him," the nurse said, sitting down on the bed. She started dabbing Carl's face with a wet sponge to clean up the dried blood. She was pretty with brown hair tied up in a bun. Loose strands fell in front of her deep brown eyes. Carl felt the embarrassment of arousal from her tender touch. He quickly gathered up the bedsheets in his lap to hide his excitement.

"There, you're looking better already," she said, focusing on her work and not seeing Carl's eyes as he admired her.

"Do I have any marks?"

"None that I think will last, except most likely here, where the stitches are," she said, gently touching the left part of his chin.

"Can I see?" Carl asked.

She stopped and sighed, now looking into Carl's eyes. "You boys are so concerned with your looks!" she chided him playfully. "Alright," she said, seeing Carl's embarrassment and apprehension. She got up and came back moments later with a shaving mirror, "Here you go, Romeo."

Carl's swollen face was a shock to him.

"Don't worry," the nurse said, reading him easily, "the swelling will go down eventually."

Carl examined his chin, lightly touching the line of stitches that started from the corner of his mouth and then arced downward to his jaw. It gave the illusion of a frown.

"The doctor says we'll take those out in a few more days. We don't want your face splitting apart on us," she said, walking away leaving Carl with the mirror and his battered face.

Carl was happy to leave the hospital tent once the doctor took out his stitches. That was almost as unpleasant as when he sewed them in. Carl cringed and hissed as the doctor snipped the threads and then pulled them out of his face. Still, it was worth the agony to get out that den of sick and dying men.

The 2nd Michigan and its twin, the 2nd Iowa, moved out during his stay in the hospital. Both regiments had been depleted through sickness, which seemed to kill more men than bullets. Together, they formed a little more than an average regiment with fewer than twelve hundred men between them. They moved in a wide-arcing path to some forty miles south of Corinth in hope of rounding up fleeing Rebels once the general assault would begin.

This left Carl temporarily without a regiment. Instead, he was attached to General Halleck's headquarters as an orderly until he could be reunited with his unit. This meant he and his horse, Bess, would be on hand to deliver messages between Halleck and his army commanders. But mostly, he sat around bored. He spent a lot of time cleaning his uniform and grooming himself. He did so with sullen resentment at first. Officers constantly chided him for his "unmilitary-like appearance" during the first few days of his headquarters duty. He thought these fancy peacocks only looked sharp because they didn't have to actually fight in the field like him. But soon, he felt a bit of pride in his uniform and appearance. He wondered how the girls back home would receive him if they saw him wearing it.

He wanted to find a reason to go back to the hospital to show himself to Emma, the nurse who had cleaned his face, but he knew he was being foolish. She had told him she was married to an officer and had followed him to war out of a sense of duty. She found working in the hospital was a good way to make herself useful. Carl showed her his picture of Anna that he carried in a locket. It was his clumsy way of pretending like he wasn't trying to proposition her.

He looked at it now as he lay in his tent. Her high and full cheeks and subtle chin shaped her face like a heart. She had golden locks that hung alongside her face and big blue eyes that held a puppy-like sadness. She was pretty. Carl snapped the locket shut and let out a sigh. He tried to pull up an image of Kathryn in his mind, Kathryn with her long rich red hair and almost cruel green eyes. He lay in bed trying to recall what it was like to hold her.

Lathan was laughing at him as he cowered. Why he forgot to put on his pants before the battle, he didn't know. But here he was, naked, as the man he feared the most mocked him. Lathan pulled out his sword and walked towards him. Carl tried to pull his, but it was stuck in the scabbard. Why couldn't he get it out? Lathan was getting nearer, his green eyes glaring, burning with malicious intent. Carl turned to run. He was stuck in the mud. He couldn't get his feet to move. He wanted to scream, to cry, to beg. Then his fear turned to rage. He screamed like a frightened child as he ran headlong into his attacker, swinging his fists wildly. Nothing seemed to hurt the laughing man.

"Carl!" a voice shouted, startling him from his sleep. He sat up, damp with sweat. It was the same dream again and again. He put his pants on and stepped out into the cool night air. He didn't know what time it was but a slight glow from the east told him that morning was coming. The ground was damp and soft under his feet. He started walking. He felt fresh with an energy that he hadn't felt since before he had been forced into the army and made to fight this war. The walk turned into a trot and then an all-out run. His feet sloshed on the wet ground as he sprinted along the tents.

"What in the hell is that fool up to?" he heard a man say as he crawled out of his tent.

Carl was sweating freely now. He was winded, too. It felt good. A bugle called the reveille. Men started coming out of their tents and tending to their breakfast fires. He made it back to his tent and began to do pushups.

"Take it easy, buddy, you're making the rest of us feel bad," a man quipped to a round of laughter.

"Sorry!" Carl smiled. He grabbed his bar of soap and sprinted off to the creek.

The inspiration stayed with him all day. In his time waiting for orders, he practiced his fencing footwork, parrying phantom blows and thrusting at imaginary foes. This was quite amusing to several of the officers. While carrying dispatches between the Union armies, he galloped hard, drawing his sword and whacking saplings in half as he passed. If he ever had to face Lathan again, he was determined to be ready.

The three Federal armies inched their way towards Corinth, finally digging in within shouting distance of the Rebel fortifications. From there they could see the big black cannons poking out from behind the earthworks and abattis. They could easily hear the trains arriving and the cheers of the men behind the fortifications. Word spread through the camp that a Rebel attack was imminent.

Federal troops manned their own fortifications in the pre-dawn darkness and watched for the Rebels to come screaming over the ramparts. Gun crews stood by their cannons ready to pour shot, shell, and canister on the mass attack to come. The silence was maddening. Every man was quiet, listening as hard as he could for signs of the enemy.

Carl could hear the crackling of a large fire coming from somewhere. In the early morning darkness, he could make out a flickering glow coming from behind the earthworks that surrounded the town. With the first light, men could see a cloud of smoke hovering over the town. An uneasy rest crept through the ranks. Men uncocked their rifles. Cannoneers rested on their ramrods. Carl took a seat on one of the wooden boxes outside General Halleck's headquarters. Horsemen came and went carrying updates to and from the scouts and forward pickets.

Carl started feeling drowsy as the humidity began to build in the early afternoon. A courier riding hard all the way up to Halleck's tent shook him from his slumber. The man tossed Carl his reins and marched hurriedly into the tent.

"What?!" Carl could hear Halleck exclaim. "Ready my horse, I want to see for myself!"

Carl fell in behind General Halleck and his staff with the rest of the orderlies. It made him nervous riding towards the big guns and the men he could make out next to them along the Rebel fortifications. Halleck stopped momentarily to examine one of the guns and its "crew" before spurring his horse forward. Carl was stunned by the lack of concern until he got closer to the large black cylinder pointing outward towards the Union lines.

"Quaker guns," the man next to him scoffed. Up close, Carl could see what he thought was a cannon was nothing more than a tree trunk painted black. Around it stood straw dummies wearing gray uniforms.

The town was completely empty: no people, nothing of worth, just a smoldering pile of supplies the Rebels had burned. In the town square, a man in a blue uniform hanged from a tree. Halleck rode his horse to the dangling man. He saw that it, too, was a straw dummy stuffed into a Federal uniform. Next to it was a sign that read:

"Halleck outwitted — what will old Abe say?"

Halleck bristled at the insult and then quickly turned away, feigning as if he hadn't taken notice. His horse then stumbled as its legs got entangled in some telegraph wire that had been cut and left on the ground. He fought for control, nearly falling off before calming the animal. He turned around sharply to see whether any of his staff dared to laugh at him. He saw nothing but quiet and shocked faces.

"I want this wire remounted immediately! We must inform Washington that Corinth is ours. I want a detachment of cavalry and horse artillery to find where the hell they went!"

Carl stared at the empty train tracks that crossed in the middle of town. The Rebels were gone.

Part II: Perryville

Chapter Ten: The Battle of Memphis

The news kept getting worse. Kathryn read the *Memphis Daily Appeal* as she walked past what was left of the River Defense Fleet. It lay tied up in the river below as men loaded the ships with whatever coal that could be found for their engines, as well as shot and shells for their small cannons.

Kathryn shook her head at the small, thrown-together naval force that was supposed to defend her then returned her eyes to the newspaper. She tried her best to keep up with any news about the Union advance as well as Beauregard's Army of Mississippi. She scanned the papers daily looking for any news about her brother. It was frustrating. She didn't even know if he was still alive. Did he fall at Shiloh? Was he one of the hundreds that succumbed to disease at Corinth? Had he been denounced by Lathan and hanged as a traitor? It was all very disconcerting.

Then came the mystery which only led to more frustration, Beauregard's General Order No. 54, as printed in the *Daily Appeal*: All news correspondents were ordered out of Corinth. *Why?* It was bad enough that all officers and enlisted men were forbidden to write about the army's movement. Now no news would come at all from Corinth. There was no way of knowing if her brother, if he was even alive, was receiving her letters, or if he understood her encrypted warnings. She had to be careful in case her letters were intercepted and read by the censors. After all, she didn't want to be the one to reveal her brother's interaction at New Madrid with a man most would consider a Yankee spy: Carl.

The mystery was finally solved, first through rumor, but now in the paper. General Beauregard sneaked the entire Army of Mississippi out from under the noses of the Yankees. While the Northern hordes inched their way to Corinth, Beauregard slipped south to Tupelo, Mississippi. He made a complete fool out of the Yankee Commanding General, Halleck.

So if her brother was still alive, she at least knew where he might be. But there were more immediate concerns mounting in Memphis. The lost of Corinth meant the rail connection Memphis had to the rest of the Confederacy was gone. Instead of trying to save the city, the Confederate command stripped her of most of her defenses. They abandoned the nearby forts and sent most of the troops south to Vicksburg, Mississippi, where they would make their last stand to hold the river.

Memphis lay wide open to the Yankee invasion. All that was left to defend her was a small fleet of eight civilian riverboats. They had been armored with sheets of iron with cotton stuffed between the iron plates and the wooden hulls. The cotton was supposed to absorb the impact of Yankee cannonballs. People jokingly called them "cotton-clads," a mockery compared to the big Federal ironclad gunboats. But nobody was laughing now that a Union attack was imminent. The ships were armed with only one or two small caliber guns, each with small crews lent by the army to man them. Their main weapons were their iron-reinforced prows. The plan was to use them as rams to smash the attacking Federal gunboats and send them to the bottom of the river.

It was a foolhardy plan but the boisterous riverboat captains seemed to believe it would work. Kathryn tried to ignore their bravado as they tried to impress her. They made predictions of their own impending glory. Kathryn was one of the only pretty young and unmarried ladies left in town, so she had to endure much of their boasting and advances.

Most of the sensible ladies had left for Vicksburg or elsewhere, leaving Memphis to its doom. But Kathryn stayed. Her family owned a townhouse there where she, Liza, and Enon could live comfortably until the madness was over and her parents returned. Furthermore, Liza was now in no condition to travel anymore. So they decided to stay in Memphis and ride out the storm.

"I don't know if he's still alive," Kathryn heard Enon speaking to Liza as she approached the door. "We spread the rumor that he done died, but that was just to keep them from looking."

Both of them looked up as Kathryn opened the door. Their expressions seemed as if they had just been caught in some terrible crime.

"Oh, for heaven's sake!" Kathryn exclaimed. "What do you think I'm going to do? You're free and my parents are gone! Please, don't stop because of me!"

Liza smiled, rubbing her swelling tummy, "Enon was telling me about my daddy. There's just so much I want to know."

Kathryn smiled warmly. She crossed the room and hugged her friend. Enon looked out the window as if something else had taken his notice. "I want to know, too, for you and for the baby," she said.

"Any news about Kyle in the paper?" Liza asked.

"Only that Beauregard retreated to Tupelo. He's probably there with him now. I will write to him immediately, but I don't know if any of my letters will get through," Kathryn said.

"Please, like I said…don't tell him about the baby. I don't want him to be concerned and I don't want to hurt him if it gets read by the wrong people. I don't know what his reaction would be…" Liza cut off the last bit with a sob that she quickly fought to control. Kathryn smiled with warm kindness. She drew Liza into another hug.

"My brother loves you, Liza, as do I. He may be a fool, but he's a good man with a good heart. I know he'll be happy. Nothing matters anymore. The rules are all gone."

Liza sniffed, "Thank you."

"Come on. I was able to get some bacon and a loaf of bread for our supper. There's okra, too. It'll fry up nicely in the grease."

Warm food and a little wine loosened Enon's normally reserved tongue. The girls took full advantage, prying whatever they could from the old man. "Your father, James, was like no other," he told them. "He talked funny. He could read, too. Said he was born free, somewhere far away."

"Where?" Liza asked.

"I don't recall. It's been so long," Enon answered. "He said he was a sailor but got captured and sold off as regular ol' slave. Never could accept it. They tried to beat it out of him, but he just wouldn't accept it." Enon shook his head as he looked off into the distance. The three sat in silence for a moment, then Enon continued, "He came back for you, you know."

"What?!" Liza's eyes widened.

"He run off when your momma was pregnant with Elijah, but he came back. He wanted to take you, her, and the baby away somewhere, but she died. Your brother was too big for her. She died giving birth. Ol' James was in a rage. He wanted to go into the house to do terrible things. We had to hold him back. He wanted to take you, but you children were too young to go with him, not without your momma. I told him I'd look after you. I did the best I could." A single tear rolled down the old man's face.

"Oh, Grandpa!" Liza got up and walked around the table to hug him. "You did and I thank you. I love you."

"Well, I love you too, I suppose," he said.

A single cannon shot split the silence of the night. It startled Kathryn from her bed.

"They're coming! The Yankees are coming! To arms!" Shouts from the street began to come through her bedroom window.

"Good Lord, they're here," Kathryn gasped, clutching her bedclothes to herself as she peered out from the upstairs window. She could see torches and lanterns swirling around in the early morning fog like fireflies below. Men were running frantically up and down the street.

"Get to your stations! They're coming down the river!" she heard someone shout.

Kathryn turned to see Liza standing at her bedroom door. The large whites of Liza's eyes contrasted with the candlelit gloom. Enon appeared behind her. He had the shotgun in his hands.

"Stay here with Liza," she told him. "Don't let anyone in. I'm going down to the river to see what I can see."

"You be careful, Ms. Kathryn. I'm supposed to look after you too," Enon said.

Kathryn smiled at the old man, "I'm grateful for it, Enon."

A crowd of people was gathering on the bluffs to watch the imminent naval battle. *What fools these people are!* she thought, until it dawned on her that she was one of them. Still, there was a cheerful atmosphere among the crowd that she didn't share. It was as if they were there to watch a horse race.

"There they are!" a woman called out.

"Ooh!" an eager voice called in response as the crowd hushed and concentrated on peering through the mist of the early morning gloom to catch a glimpse of the invaders coming from the right. Kathryn could see nothing in the darkness, but she could hear the hum of the great steam engines and the churning of the water passing through the paddle wheels now that the crowd had hushed.

BOOM!

A deafening roar startled the crowd, causing some of the women to faint. Some of the men tumbled backward, landing hard on their rear ends in the mud, others flinched into a crouch. The opening cannonade split the darkness with flashes of fire and smoke. Kathryn was rendered breathless from the percussion.

The flashes revealed the enormous, hideous monsters that formed a line across the river north of the city: the Federal ironclads. The cannons ripped through the darkness again, causing more gasps and screams from the crowd. The ships looked like giant metal turtles that had crawled out of hell to belch their fire and brimstone upon the living. Kathryn was overtaken by the sour smell of sulfur that rolled off the water in billowing clouds of smoke. She fought for breath. *Hell has truly arrived,* she thought.

"Here come our boys!" a man shouted. A cheer broke out among the crowd. Kathryn covered her mouth and coughed as she looked to her left. The converted Confederate riverboats were steaming to meet the Yankee challenge in two columns with the city's riverfront behind them.

"My God, they'll shell the city!" a woman gasped.

Kathryn let out a scream as the Federal ships unleashed another furious round of fire. The shells exploded in and around the defenders. The Rebel ships looked so inadequate to her compared to the Yankee leviathans.

A shell screamed over the smokestacks of the ragged Rebel flotilla and landed in the city with a flash of an explosion.

"They'll flatten the city if those fools don't give up now!" a man cried.

The Confederates fired back with their small-bore cannons as they steamed toward the Federal line. Some of the rounds hit their mark but glanced off the iron plates with not much more than a loud clank. The sun rose up from behind the spectators and burned off what was left of the mist. The river was now filled with smoke instead as the two fleets hammered away at each other.

"Look! More of 'em are coming through!" a man shouted. Kathryn looked back at the line of Federal ironclads. They were holding their positions in the river, firing their rear guns at the advancing Rebel fleet. Two Yankee ships burst forward through the gaps between their gunboats. These were smaller, leaner ships that belched a fury of sparks and black smoke from their twin smokestacks.

"Those are rams! They're coming at our boys full-steam!" someone shouted. Kathryn held her breath as the lead boat bore down on one of the Rebel ships. She could see a man standing between the smokestacks on the top deck rallying the other ship to follow by twirling his hat in the air. Cannon fire whizzed past him as he did. *What a madman!* she thought. The Rebel ship suddenly lost its nerve and turned hard to avoid a head-on collision. This caused it to expose its full flank to the speeding ram.

The impact was devastating. An ear-piercing clang rang across the river. The smokestacks from the Confederate ship crashed across the Federal deck as the boat rolled over onto its side and started to sink. Rebel sailors leaped overboard, some scrambled on to the Federal deck where a brawl broke out. A pistol fired. The madman riding between the smokestacks clutched his leg and tumbled into the fray. The fight was suddenly interrupted when another Confederate ram slammed into the Federal ship, knocking everyone on deck to the floor. With one of her side wheels wrecked, the Yankee ship drifted out of the fight and beached itself on the Arkansas side of the river

The crowd cheered at seeing the Yankee ship disabled. Kathryn felt the elation of hope for a moment, but there were more Federal sharks in the water. The second of the Federal boats was bearing down on another Rebel ship. The Rebel ship that had just knocked out the first Yankee ship, turned to join this new fight, but lost control and ended up sideswiping the ally it meant to help. The crowd cringed and hissed as the Rebel ship tore off the side wheel of the other, knocking its own partner out of the fight. The Union ship then turned hard and rammed the remaining Rebel boat, sending it to the Arkansas side to slowly sink. The Federal gunboats continued to blast away at it. Smoke and steam billowed out of the dying ship as it slipped under the water.

An all-out smash and dash contest broke out among the remaining ships. The big Federal gunboats continued to pound away at the Rebel ships with shot and shell. The faster and more nimble Yankee rams continued to out-maneuver their Rebel counterparts. The contest became hard to follow as clouds of smoke hung on the water. Still, the crowd lingered to follow the action blow by blow. Slowly their cheers turned to moans as the faster Federal ships destroyed the Confederates one by one. Some were shoved aground, others were sent to the bottom of the river. Within two hours the contest was over. The River Defense Fleet lay in ruins. Only one Confederate ship managed to escape the slaughter, slipping downstream towards Vicksburg.

The crowd started to break apart as people saw the naval defeat as a cue to flee the city. The remaining military personnel was among the first to scurry out of town. None of them wanted to end up in a Federal prison camp. Kathryn saw the white flag go up on the shorefront.

The big Federal guns quieted and soon a detachment of Yankees was rowing ashore to accept the city's surrender. Within an hour, the Confederate flag went down at the post office. The US flag rose in its place. This caused a chorus of angry shouts from the mob that formed around the building, trapping the small Union detachment inside. The mayor and his aides came to plea with the murderous crowd. They begged them to let the Union men return to their ships in peace. Hurting or detaining them could cause the Federal gunboats to shell the city into a pile of dust.

The wild threat of violence breaking out in the street was enough to send Kathryn back home to her family's townhouse. People shouting and running up and down the street made her flinch as she knocked on the door. A window curtain moved in her periphery as someone inside was checking to see who was at the door. It opened. Enon stuck his head out, looked both ways, then beaconed her in. He cradled his shotgun in his arms as he shut the door and fastened the lock. He then returned to watching the chaos outside the window.

"Good heavens, what's going on out there?" Liza hurried to her.

"The Yankees have destroyed our fleet. The city is lost. It's only a matter of time before they come marching in," Kathryn told them.

"We should run now," Liza said. Enon turned from the window to hear Kathryn's response. Liza's eyes were wide with fear as the noise from the street filled Kathryn's pause.

"Where would we go?" she smiled bitterly. "My parents are gone, the house is lost, the Yankees are everywhere."

Liza blinked for a moment, "We need to get to Kyle! We now know they're in Tupelo. We need to warn him he's in danger! We could follow the army. I could cook and clean for them. They'd protect us!"

Kathryn looked at her friend, the pretty young black girl cradling the ever-growing bump in her belly. "That's no place for you to be carrying a child, Liza. We don't even know if he's there with them." She stopped herself from saying they didn't know if he was still alive. "Right now, we have a roof and a little food in the cupboard. Perhaps we can appeal to the Yankee commanders for protection from their brutes."

"Those soldiers could very well have their way with us and leave us for dead!" Liza said, her eyes hardening. Enon wrung the shotgun with his hands. "We in a war, there are no rules!"

Kathryn paused for a moment. There was no telling what would happen once the Yankees arrived, but how would they fare in the war-torn countryside? How would they get around the marauding Yankee armies to get to her brother? What would they do when they got there? How could they save him from Lathan's accusations? Was it too late?

A loud knock at the door startled her from her thoughts. Liza let out a gasp. "They're here," Enon said flatly, wringing his shotgun.

"They're here? Who's here?" Kathryn gasped.

"The Yankees," Enon said, lifting his shotgun to his shoulder.

The knocking came again. This time harder.

"How many?" Kathryn asked.

Enon peered out the window, "Five or six. They armed."

Kathryn sucked in a breath through her nose and then let it out slowly. "Open the door," she said as she straightened herself.

Liza swung the door open as a man in a blue captain's uniform was swinging his knuckles down to strike it. His fist found only empty air causing him to stumble forward into the house. Enon immediately stepped forward training his shotgun on the stunned man. The soldiers behind him quickly brought their muskets to their shoulders with a rattle of hammers being cocked.

"Whoa…! Whoa…" the officer said, putting his hands up in the air. "Everybody, just calm down!" Enon sighted him with his shotgun which caused another rattling from the muskets outside as the men tightened their grips and stepped forward.

"Guys! Guys!" the captain motioned to his men with his arms, "Lower your guns." The blue-clad soldiers looked at each and then brought their rifles down from their shoulders. "Alright, old man," the captain said with his hands still up, "you ain't gonna shoot me, now? We mean you no harm."

"It's okay, Enon," Kathryn said, not taking her eyes off the captain. "You can put it down." Enon lowered the barrel and uncocked its two hammers.

The captain let out a breath. "Okay, now that we've taken care of that…" he doffed his kepi hat and took a deep bow. "I am Captain O'Connor of the 43rd Indiana," he said and then pulled out a piece of paper and handed it to Kathryn. "I am here to inform you that your residence has been requisitioned by the US War Department. You may remain on the premises for the time being so long as you are cooperative." Kathryn gasped and looked to Liza. "Your slaves, of course, are now free as they are behind our lines and considered contraband of war."

"We already free, fool!" Liza let out.

The captain's eyes widened and then looked back at Kathryn. "Do you always let her speak like this?"

"She's free," Kathryn said, crossing her arms, "remember?"

Chapter Eleven: The Return

The evacuation of Corinth had been somewhat of a victory, although few outside of Beauregard's command thought so. True, the Confederates gave up an important rail hub that connected Memphis to Chattanooga, and Mobile to Louisville, but Beauregard had saved his battered army to fight another day. "I can't believe the Yankees are so dumb!" Kyle heard many fellow officers say. Surely, if the enormous Federal force knew that the Rebels were fleeing the safety of their fortifications at Corinth, they would have pounced, easily destroying the sick, tired, and under-equipped Army of Mississippi. But Beauregard had fooled them by leaking false reports of reinforcements and pretending that empty trains were full of men and supplies.

    Instead, the Confederates tumbled southward, looking for clean water and a place that was defendable. They arrived at Baldwin and then turned their weary eyes back toward a possible Yankee pursuit. When it didn't appear, they slipped further south to Tupelo, Mississippi, and settled in. Kyle worked hard during the retreat to prove he was worthy of his newly acquired captain's rank. He organized the marches and supply trains, riding up and down the lines making sure the men and materials arrived safely and intact. Surely Beauregard would see his worth, but then he was gone.

"Gone?" Kyle stammered outside of headquarters. Kyle had a handful of status reposts from corps commanders to deliver.

"Yup, gone yesterday!" the sentry answered cheerfully. "Went to a spa on the gulf coast to recover his health. Must be nice! We could all use a day at the spa!"

"What the hell is all that racket?!" General Braxton Bragg's voice erupted from inside. All the joy in the sentry's eyes evaporated and was replaced by fear and panic. He stiffened as the general stormed out of the building, glaring under his heavy brow. "Do you think you're here to chatter, Private?" he glared at the trembling soldier.

"No, sir," the man said weakly while staring forward at nothing.

"What is your name, Private?"

"Um, Roberts, sir, Eli Roberts, 1st Tennessee, sir," the terrified soldier replied.

"When you are relieved from your post, you are to tell your sergeant that you were gabbing like a woman instead of tending to your duties. He's to report to my staff what your punishment will be or I'll have both of you strung up for dereliction of duty. Do I make myself perfectly clear?"

The trembling soldier swallowed hard. "Yes, sir…"

"What is it, Lieutenant?" Bragg's dark eyes turned to Kyle, "Why are you here distracting my sentries from their duty? Do we need to find something useful for you to do?"

"Um… it's Captain now, sir. I have status reports from…" Kyle tried to answer.

"Captain?! Good God! By whose authority?" Bragg exclaimed, snatching the dispatches from Kyle's hand.

"General Beauregard. It's a brevet rank, sir. We are waiting for confirmation from Richmond."

General Bragg's already connected eyebrows scrunched further together as he examined Kyle closely. Kyle held his breath. "We shall see…" Bragg mumbled before turning and going back inside.

Kyle looked at the sentry with exasperation, trying to understand what just happened. The poor man just looked to the ground, unable to meet his eyes.

Braxton Bragg turned out to be a brilliant organizer, but a strict disciplinarian. The ragtag mob of men that scurried like rats from the sinking ship at Corinth started adopting a more military air under his command. Food and supplies starting coming in too, but so were the punishments. Men were whipped, branded, and even shot for everything from petty theft to desertion. Kyle turned his eyes in disgust at scenes of men stripped completely naked, howling and crying under the lash as they dangled from their wrists with their feet barely touching the ground. Even farmers were given the authority to shoot any man they caught stealing from their crops. Under the hot June sun, Tupelo had become a place of intense heat and fear. It didn't take long before Kyle had to choose between being fearful or feared.

"Me?" Kyle blinked at the major giving him his orders.

"The general says if you are to be a captain, you'll have to start proving your worth," the major said, and then smiled softly. "Sorry, son, his words not mine." Kyle blinked at the man in bewilderment and then looked around like a frightened squirrel.

"But with who? I don't have a command," he stammered.

"You have captain's bars," the major said patiently, pointing to Kyle's newly sewn-in rank. "Find a sergeant on duty and have him put together a squad for you. It shouldn't take long, really." The major initiated the salute that Kyle was supposed to give to end the conversation. Kyle reluctantly lifted is hand to brow, still in shock.

"Yes, sir," he said softly.

The major smiled, "Good day, sir," and walked back towards headquarters. Kyle looked around the street. Men were passing back and forth, carrying out their duties or milling around idly. The mid-morning heat was just beginning to build, and Kyle could feel the cold sweat dripping down his temples.

"Sergeant!" he called to a heavily mustached man walking by with a particularly military air.

"Yes, sir!" the sergeant barked with a crisp halt and salute. He was a short man but with his straight back and protruding chest, he still managed to be intimidating.

"Are you…busy?" Kyle asked, not quite sure how to speak to the man.

"I am at your disposal, Captain."

"I need a firing squad of ten men."

"I have just the men, sir," the sergeant's eyes gleamed with enthusiasm.

"Very good…" Kyle said, "…um fetch them, please, and accompany me to the stockade."

"Sir!" the barrel-chested man barked with a crisp salute and strode off. Kyle stood in the street for a moment, not knowing what to do with his hands, so he looked back down at his orders and read them again, mostly to avoid making eye contact with passersby.

It was a relief to see the sergeant return with his detail of men after Kyle had been trying to look engaged in something important while he waited. The men marched in step alongside the officious sergeant, his own tight martial gait was almost absurd. "Halt!" he called, and then with a salute, "Ready, sir!"

"Uh…thank you, Sergeant…" Kyle returned the salute.

"Daniels, sir! Sergeant Daniels, 7th Arkansas"

"Okay, Sergeant Daniels. Let's go."

They marched to the city jail that was now being used as a military stockade. Kyle kept his head down, avoiding eye contact with the people who stopped to watch their procession go by. He sent Sergeant Daniels and two of his men inside with the paperwork. A small crowd of people started to gather as they began to recognize the ritual unfolding before them. Kyle wiped the sweat that trickled down the back of his neck and then swatted at a fly that seemed to take interest in him. Its buzz seemed like the only sound he could hear on the hot, windless day.

Then, Sergeant Daniels emerged into the hard sunlight again. Behind him, his men held a man by his arms between them. The first thing the prisoner did was lift his shackled arms to block the sunlight from his face. He squinted in agony from the light, "Jesus!" he mumbled. He was unshaven with wild, greasy dark hair that tumbled over his eyes in curls. He wore a dirty blouse with no uniform vest or jacket. His trousers ended in tatters above the ankles of his bare feet. Kyle didn't realize he was staring at him until the man, blinking rapidly in the sunlight, shrugged his shoulders with an expression that seemed to say, "…Well?"

"Let's go," Kyle said to Sergeant Daniels.

"Firing detail! Forward! March!" Daniels bellowed.

Kyle began to hear the drums as they approached the killing ground. A crowd of people had gathered there. Some of the soldiers were formed up in an open square to witness the punishment, others, as well as several citizens, milled around casually, waiting to watch the spectacle. The detail came to a halt. Sergeant Daniels unshackled the man's hands and led him to the stake while his men formed a line in front of it. Daniels tied the man's hands behind his back and then walked back smartly to his squad of men. He executed a sharp military about-face to turn himself towards the condemned man. The drumming stopped. The man spat on the ground. Heads started to turn towards Kyle in anticipation.

Kyle cleared his throat as he unfolded his orders. He looked back up at the crowd as he did. Among the people standing by to watch the morning's entertainment were the cold green eyes that had haunted him since New Madrid. Lieutenant Lathan Woods' clean-shaven face was drawn up in a bemused smile as he watched Kyle carry out his orders.

Kyle quickly dropped his eyes to his papers and cleared his throat again. It was so painfully quiet. "Private Hiram Nielsen, you have been found guilty of treason, espionage, desertion, and fraternizing with the enemy by a military tribunal conducted by the Army of Mississippi of the Confederate States of America, commanded by General Braxton Bragg. You are sentenced to die. Any last words?"

"For the last time, I was trading for coffee and trying to send a letter home - my home which is now behind enemy lines because we can't defend anything!" the man said and spat on the ground. "I'm tired of this God-forsaken place and this fool's army, anyhow."

Silence followed. Sergeant Daniels turned his head to Kyle…waiting. Kyle pulled out his saber and held it high. The drums began to roll again.

"Ready!" Daniels barked. His men pulled their rifles to their shoulders. "Aim!" The drums continued to roll.

Kyle's eyes found Lathan's again in the crowd. Lathan raised his eyebrows as if to say, "…Well?"

Kyle looked back at the blindfolded man at the stake. The man's lips were drawn tight as he tried to control his trembling. It was the first time he seemed to show any fear. Kyle couldn't bear to look at him. He closed his eyes and dropped his sword.

"Fire!"

The crackle of muskets punctuated the end of the drum roll. Silence had returned. Kyle opened his eyes. The man hung slumped forward as his dirty shirt began to soak with blood.

Kyle sat in the shade staring at the field before him. Men were out there at all times of the day, marching and drilling, so much more so now that Bragg was in command. "It's not easy killing one of your own, is it?" The voice sent a chill through Kyle. He turned to see Lathan smiling at him. "…Captain," he added with a slow salute. Kyle clumsily returned the salute as he made to get up. "Oh, don't get up on my account…Captain." Lathan towered over him.

"I did my duty," Kyle said flatly as he returned his eyes to the men drilling before him.

"Of course!" Lathan said with cool delight. "The man was a criminal! A traitor! Spying and sharing our secrets, fraternizing with the enemy, that's a shooting offense to me! Don't you think?"

Kyle stared ahead, lost for words. Everything inside him screamed to get away from this man. "I did my duty…" he said absently.

Leaving Tupelo and the graves they had dug there was a relief to Confederate soldiers who suffered there. General Halleck had declined to pursue and crush what was left of diminished Confederate forces at Tupelo. Most agreed he certainly could have done so with his enormous combined Union army. But instead, he divided it, sending a division to Arkansas and Buell's Army of the Ohio east towards Chattanooga.

The rest he dispersed across the region to guard rail lines and garrison the towns that were now under Union control.

General Bragg pondered for weeks over what he should do with his army, now that it had been spared by Halleck's timidity. Taking back Corinth was tempting now that the Union force there was smaller. But Bragg's Army of Mississippi was still outnumbered. Furthermore, he had overseen the defenses built there himself. It would take a much larger force than he had to dislodge the Northern invaders. Even if they couldn't, he couldn't hope to hold it for long without major reinforcements and supplies.

Reinforcing the forces at Vicksburg on the Mississippi was tempting too. It was the last Confederate stronghold on the river. But how long could they resist the Federal ironclad gunboats that had so easily taken Memphis and New Orleans?

The answer and remedy to his indecision came with a plea and an offer from General Kirby Smith, Commander of the Confederate Department of East Tennessee: bring his Army of Mississippi to Chattanooga, combine it with Smith's force, and assume total command. Together they could beat Buell's Army of the Ohio and then take back Middle Tennessee and possibly liberate Kentucky from the Federals. Kentucky: a state teeming with Confederate sympathizers who would fill their ranks once freed from the Northern yoke.

But they'd have to beat Buell to Chattanooga first, so they'd take the train. Kyle spent the days to come organizing the move. He helped oversee the loading of supplies and some 30,000 men onto trains. It was tedious work, but it gave him something to do and kept his mind off of the horrors he had seen and participated in. It also kept him away from Lathan, who had left with the cavalry to patrol the rails and safeguard the army's move to Chattanooga.

Kyle worried greatly about Lathan. His sister's letters had begun to reach him. The messages were encrypted enough to fool the censors, but clear to Kyle. Lathan knew that Kyle's Yankee friend, Carl, had helped them smuggle their ex-slave, Elijah, out of New Madrid. It wouldn't take much to conclude that Carl was then able to give a detailed account of their defenses there to the Federals, enabling them to take the town and Island No. 10. Even though Kyle's only intention was to save the brother of his beloved Liza, he could easily be deemed a traitor.

But did Lathan have enough evidence to accuse him openly? Kyle pondered that as he boarded a train himself to make the journey. Did he have anyone who could corroborate his claims? Surely Lathan would have called him out by now if he did. Still, Lathan seemed awfully confident every time Kyle encountered him. Lathan just grinned at him as if to say he knew everything and was merely biding his time.

It took a week to move the Army of Mississippi to Chattanooga and even more time to organize them into camps and officers' quarters. General Smith had moved his force north to Knoxville out of fear that Buell's army would get to Chattanooga before Bragg.

But Buell was taking his time, repairing rail lines as he went.

Kyle kept busy helping with the organization of the troops pouring into the city, day after day. Stragglers, reinforcements, new recruits, and even prisoners of war that had been freshly exchanged for Yankee prisoners needed to be sorted, assigned to units, and housed. It was a lot of work that required hundreds of staff officers to sort out. In the daily hustle of reorganizing an army consisting of tens of thousands of men, it was easy not to notice one.

The man had come by train all the way from Vicksburg where several Confederate officers had been exchanged for Yankee counterparts. This young man, although handsome, was terribly thin from spending months in a Northern prison camp. He wore a shabby, torn uniform that marked him as an artilleryman. He once had a nicer uniform that he kept for special occasions, but it had been stolen. Stolen possibly by a woman he once had feelings for.

Who was he kidding? He still couldn't get her out of his mind. The image of Kathryn Bethune's beautiful face was what he dreamed of, what he clung onto during his darkest days at Fort Warren, out there on an island in Boston's harbor. He had been such a fool! He showed her and to her "cousin" nothing but kindness. Who was that man? Was he really a Yankee spy? Did Kathryn know? Did her brother know? They had already fought an unsatisfactory duel. One that he had to concede because the Yankee attack on New Madrid interrupted it.

The humiliation was too much to bear. He and his battery had been overwhelmed without a fight. The glory he had dreamed of at the beginning of the war became nothing more than a soggy surrender. There was no point in sacrificing his men's lives, but it still made him feel like a coward, a pitiful coward sitting in a prison camp waiting until the Yankees decided he could leave in a prisoner exchange. The shame and defeat he felt ate away at his stomach, his nerves, his soul.

"Lieutenant Michael Davis, I thought I'd never see you again," the voice behind him sent chills through his body. Davis turned around to see the man it came from.

"Lieutenant Woods, you startled me," Davis said.

Lathan smiled, holding Davis in an uncomfortable gaze for a moment. "I seem to have that effect on people," he said at last.

Davis paused for a moment, not sure what to say to the grinning green-eyed cavalry officer. "I didn't expect to see you here," he finally managed.

"I got away before the blue-bellies could get me. Joined the rest at Corinth and then came here. I got to kill a few Yankees along the way."

"I'm sure you did," Davis said, wondering how to break away from this conversation he didn't want to have. "Well…here we are…" was all he could he come up with.

"Yeah, here we are," Lathan replied, scanning Davis over. "There's a lot of us here now, actually. Many of your friends, I'm sure."

"Well," Davis said, feigning a laugh, "that's good to hear."

"Yeah, your friend Kyle is here. He's quite busy though," Lathan said, smiling at the change of color in Davis's face.

"Um…you mean Lieutenant Bethune?" he stammered.

"Captain now!" Lathan grinned. "Seems like he made a lot of progress while you were sitting in prison. It's amazing what a man can accomplish when most of his competitors have been hauled off to Yankee prisons."

Davis blinked at him aghast, "…Captain?"

Lathan smiled because he knew he had him now, "Of course, it's not his fault you and thousands of our brothers were captured during those dark days at Island No. 10. It's not like he was *helping* the Yankees or anything…"

"…Um… of course not," Davis stammered.

Lathan smiled at him for what seemed to be an excruciatingly long time. Finally, he put his hand on Davis's shoulder. Davis flinched, looking up into Lathan's green eyes. Lathan spoke again, "Might I have a word with you in private, Lieutenant?"

Chapter Twelve: Back in the Saddle

The 2nd Michigan Cavalry came galloping back into Farmington. Their new commander, Colonel Phillip Sheridan, rode stone-faced at the head of the column. Behind him, the men rode dry, dusty, and weary, but flush full of victory.

Carl watched the column ride back into camp with a tinge of regret and embarrassment. He had been happy to miss duty while recuperating, but now, seeing his regiment ride into camp with such grim purpose and hard-earned pride, he suddenly felt inadequate. He sheathed his sword and fetched his jacket, which hung over the fence that ran along the field. Suddenly, practicing his fencing lessons all by himself felt childish.

"Oh, you should have been there!" Chucky beamed as he dismounted.

"I kinda wished I had," Carl said, helping him remove the saddle from his exhausted horse.

"'Fightin' Phil' is a heck of commander, he ain't afraid of nothin'! Cool as a cucumber!" Chucky crowed.

"He probably wouldn't have been so cocksure if he knew we were poking at Old Beauregard's entire army," Bates chimed in.

"Wow!" Carl exclaimed. "They were completely gone from Corinth when we rode in."

"Well, apparently, they were all passing by Booneville the same time we were burning their supplies," Bates said, carrying his saddle off.

"Yeah, we got in a scuffle with some of them. Some of their cavalry tried to run us off, but we dismounted and gave them a hell of a volley! They couldn't match our revolving carbines. We ran them off good!" Chucky continued, "You should have seen the stuff we burned, though! Car after car of food, guns, everything! I heard we even got our hands on some of Old General Polk's personal effects. We tore them tracks up, too. They won't be gettin' any supplies from that train line anytime soon!"

"Sounds like a grand ol' time," Carl said passively.

"Alright, listen up, girls!" Captain Newman strode into the stables. "Get some chow and some rest tonight. We'll be headin' back out in the morning." Newman stopped at Chucky and Carl, his heavy mustache hiding his grin, "Well, Smith, just when I thought you couldn't get any uglier!" Carl grinned, looking sheepishly to the ground. "How's your face, son?"

"It's fine, sir," Carl looked up and saluted.

"Good to hear. It looks a lot like the damn train we burned back in Booneville," Newman said to a round of chuckles from the men. "Make sure you're geared up and ready to go with us in the morning. No more playing sick for the pretty nurses for you."

"Um…sir…my rifle, it was destroyed in the misfire…" Carl said.

Newman paused for a moment to think and then said, "Go find Sergeant Barth. Tell him to give you Keller's old gun."

"Isn't he going need it?" Carl stammered.

"Not anymore, son, He's dead." Carl stared agape as the handsome captain turned on his heel and strode off, his high boots and spurs clanking on the ground.

It turned out that Private Keller had died in the hospital, succumbing to the fever and dysentery that seemed to kill more men than Rebel bullets. Carl accepted Keller's Colt revolving carbine with trepidation, imagining the dead man's weapon was dripping with disease. He barely wanted to touch it as he slid it into his saddle holster. Worse yet, he was afraid of firing another rifle so close to his head after the last one exploded and nearly blew his face off. He pulled out his Allen & Wheelock revolver, holding it straight-arm as he looked down the sights at the lantern that lit the stable in the early morning gloom. Maybe, he thought, it would be safer to fire this one instead the next time he was in the heat of things.

"Don't shoot my light out, Carl! I gotta see what I'm doin'!" the big bass voice interrupted his thoughts.

Carl holstered his pistol and turned to face his friend, "Oh, I'm just checking the sights, Elijah. It's been a while since I've shot it."

The big man smiled warmly at his friend. His soft brown eyes always seemed to read right through Carl. "You be fine out there. Lemme help you up." Elijah took the reins and held Bess in place as Carl hopped into the saddle, adjusting his saber as he settled in.

"I got a letter from my sister," Elijah said, and then laughed at the surprise and anticipation that washed over Carl. "I think Miss Kathryn is teaching her to write." Carl blinked at him with dumb surprise,

"That's…um…great! How are they…um…I mean, how is she?" Carl flushed with embarrassment, knowing he had easily revealed his longing to hear any news about Kathryn.

Elijah mercifully just smiled back at his friend's discomfort, "Do you think you could help me read it when you get back? I'm not much for readin', but I'm trying to learn."

"Of course!" Carl said with great anticipation.

"Alright, then," Elijah said, patting Bess on the rump, "you take good care of my girl."

"Sure thing," Carl smiled, and spurred her out into the yard to join the rest of the regiment.

It was still mostly dark as the column moved out of Farmington. It was eerie riding through the once Rebel stronghold of Corinth. The men kept a reverent silence as they passed the abattis and earthworks that had been built and manned by their enemy. Carl wondered if Kyle had walked these streets, if he had looked out from the battlements and had seen Carl and his fellow soldiers inching their way closer and closer.

They passed a work crew who seemed to be digging up a large gravesite. *Is Kyle buried there?* he thought. He was shocked at what seemed to be such a sacrilegious act. Relief spread through him, however, as passing by revealed that the men were actually uncarthing large siege guns that the Rebels tried to hide underground instead of leaving them outright for the Union army as they fled.

From there, they headed south toward Booneville. Having spent weeks north of the Rebel line at Corinth, it felt odd to be so deep into enemy territory. The men were quiet, scanning the surroundings, waiting for the puff of smoke, the crack of a musket, or the boom of a cannon that would announce the trap they were most surely riding into.

Booneville still smoldered from the regiment's last visit. Carl looked in awe at the line of burned-out train cars. The ground was covered in cannonballs and unexploded shells that were hurled from the cars when they exploded.

"The Rebs must have thought we were attacking in force when those cars went off," Bates said.

"It did sound like a huge battery of artillery," Chucky said, scanning the destruction in awe.

"Good thing," Bates replied. "If Beauregard knew how little our force was, he would have crushed us."

"Alright, boys" Sergeant Barth interrupted, "Captain says we're camping here tonight. Let's set up a perimeter. Smith, Scott, you're on first vedette duty. I want you on the Blackland Road a few hundred yards out. We'll send relief around supper time. Hop to it, boys!"

The column moved west towards Blackland the next morning. Carl tried his best to get a glimpse of the stoic new colonel who was now leading the 2nd Michigan Cavalry. Colonel Sheridan put up a hand as they approached a creek that was more mud than water. The hot July sun had burned away most of the surrounding water sources. The company commanders, lieutenants, and sergeants repeated the Colonel's hand signal along the line until the whole column came to a halt. The sun beat down on Carl's wool cap making him feel hot and stuffy. He swatted at a fly buzzing around his ear before reaching for his canteen.

A crackle of muskets stopped him short of bringing it to his mouth. A small cloud of smoke drifted across the creek. He caught a glimpse of butternut jackets turning and running into the woods on the other side. Sheridan unsheathed his saber, shouted something, and the entire column lurched forward. Carl fumbled to re-cork his canteen as Bess jolted ahead with the rest of the horses.

"Fuck!" he gasped as he tried to regain his balance. Bess thundered across the wooden bridge beside Chucky's mount. The river of horsemen emerged on the other side of the bridge and spread out into a battle line. Carl found himself close to the Colonel as they pushed through the woods. They overwhelmed several Rebel pickets and stragglers along the way. The Rebel soldiers quickly dropped their guns and threw their hands in the air as blue-clad men rode them down with sabers and pistols

"To the rear!" Captain Newman shouted at the newly captured prisoners. The men were quick to comply. Carl marveled at how ragged and thin they looked.

The cavalrymen pushed through the woods. Carl used his saber to chop the branches in his way. As he cleared his way through, he began to see them: large iron tubes with butternut men scurrying around them carrying swabs and ramrods. Rebel artillery was set up on the hill just outside the trees. A division of infantry was formed below in support. A few of the Rebel pickets that had escaped the Federal charge were scurrying to the well-fortified line.

"Oh, shit!" a Union officer exclaimed. The cannons erupted with smoke and fire. The branches overhead snapped and disintegrated into sawdust as shells exploded. Colonel Sheridan's hat flew straight off his head and landed a few paces behind him. His impassive face turned to see where it landed. An orderly jumped off his horse and handed it to him.

"A rather close call, Stephenson," he said softly with just a hint humor. Then raising and twirling his saber in the air he shouted, "To the bridge!"

"Fall back to the bridge!" the command was repeated down the line. The Rebel infantry unleashed a volley of musketry and buckshot as the Federal horsemen turned and dashed away. Cannon fire erupted again, smashing trees around them with solid shot and exploding shells.

"Dismount and form a line here!" Captain Campbell shouted at the companies under his command.

"Come on, boys," Captain Newman said to H Company, "bring your rifles."

Their horses were led back by the companies that were still mounted. Carl grimaced at having to draw his newly acquired Colt carbine from the saddle holster. He hoped he wouldn't have to fire it. The dismounted men watched for the enemy to emerge from the woods as the rest of the column retreated across the bridge. Satisfied that no Rebel pursuit was coming, they remounted and fell back to Booneville to make their report.

Carl loaded his plate with as much food as he could fit and stuffed his pockets full of biscuits. He left his comrades to their campfires and headed for the stables. He was relieved to find Elijah alone, sweeping the floors in the dim lamplight. The other stablehands had already gone to their camps. The big man smiled and put his broom down, "You're here to read the letter."

"Well…I brought food too!" Carl laughed, knowing his friend could see right through him.

"Alright, come on then," he laughed, "got something too," Elijah said, reaching behind the bales of hay. He pulled out a bottle of golden brown liquid.

"Wow! Where'd you get that?" Carl's eyes brightened at the thought of whiskey with his dinner.

"These officers think they have to give me something to take good care of they horses. Shoot, I do it anyway," he said with a shrug as he poured a little whiskey into two tin cups.

"I swear, you have to be the most popular man in camp," Carl said, accepting his cup.

"I try to be nice to everybody," Elijah said, clinking his cup to Carl's. The whiskey was like flaming silk running down Carl's throat. He shuddered at the effect and then let out a sigh as his face flushed with warmth.

"They sure do make this stuff well down here," he said.

" I guess I wouldn't know any different," Elijah answered.

They divided up the food and then sat comfortably in the hay. Carl marveled at the envelope as Elijah handed him the letter. "It's from Memphis!" he said with wonder.

"Yeah, the family got a house there," Elijah said looking at the rafters.

Carl pulled the letter out and started reading.

Memphis, Tennessee, June 11, 1862

My dear baby brother,

Do not fear for me or Miss. Kathryn. We fine. We had an adventure. More than I can write. But I need to tell you so much. The house is gone. Lathan burned it down trying to get Miss. Kathryn and me, but Enon got us away safe. We are here now in Memphis at the townhouse. The Yankees have taken the city. Some of the officers are now living in the house with us, but they treat us real fine. Honestly, I think they all try to outdo each other for Kathryn's affection. She's got them all under her control as you might think. The good news is we can send you letters now that we behind enemy lines.

I worry about Kyle. Lathan said he knows everything and is going to get him hanged. We fear for him every day. He's too kind and trusting for his own good.

There is more, Elijah. We got family! You and I were not bought like they told us. We was born on the plantation. Our momma was a woman called Abigail and our daddy was called James. Our momma died, but our daddy ran away. He might be still alive! There's more. You already met your granddaddy, can you guess? It's Enon! He's our momma's daddy! He's with us now. He told me to tell you be a good boy and be safe. Please be safe! Come back to Memphis when you can. There's more that I cannot say in this letter. But remember, you got family and we love you very much. I know you don't write, but please find a way to let me know you're okay.

Love, your big sister,

Liza

Carl wallowed in his own disappointment: not one mention of him. Wasn't Kathryn even curious? Worse yet, he wondered just how friendly Kathryn was getting with those officers. The thought of it made him burn and then despair. What chance did he, a mere private, have in winning her over? Then, he realized that Elijah had gone silent. The big man just looked at the rafters. A single tear rolled down his cheek. "Are you okay?" Carl asked.

Elijah turned to him and smiled with teary eyes, "Yes, of course…I got a family."

"Hey, congratulations, big guy," Carl reached over and gripped his shoulder, giving him a soft shake.

Elijah let his enormous body move freely with Carl's hand. He looked back up at the rafters and said, "I think I always knew."

Carl was happy to pen Elijah's letter to Liza and vowed to do so as long as they corresponded. Of course, he made sure to write, "Penned by Carl Smith," in hopes of piquing some interest in himself from the girls. Writing and reading letters was one of the few escapes in the weeks that followed that were otherwise filled with the doldrums of camp life, vedette duty, and patrols. The enemy had withdrawn further south to Tupelo. The only real threat seemed to come from disease. Carl watched their numbers dwindle as men succumbed to the heat and bad water. Some managed to come back to duty after a stay in the field hospitals, some got to go home after their fevers broke, others died.

The first day of July brought a break in the boredom. Carl woke to bugles calling the regiment to arms. "What in the world...?" Chucky sat up in their tent. The drums began to join in.

"I think we're under attack," Carl said, buttoning his shirt while peering out from the flaps at the men rolling out of their tents and running to the stables.

Captain Newman addressed them moments later as the now mounted H Company found their place in the formation. "Boys, the Rebs have pushed in our pickets about three and a half miles southwest of here. These are the same cousin-fuckers that have been harassing that position all week. This time it looks like they mean business. We are to form as part of Captain Campbell's battalion and support Lieutenant Scranton's position. He is being pressed hard as we speak. The rest of our boys, along with our sweethearts from the 2nd Iowa, will ride in on the enemy flanks. Let's go get 'em!"

The crackle of musketry got louder as they followed the Booneville Road to where it split with the Blackland Road. Campbell's three companies dismounted and crept forward, leaving their mounts with a small guard detail. Scranton's men were spread out across the road, taking cover wherever they could. Campbell's men filled in with them. Scranton saluted Campbell, "You're in good time, sir. We've repelled two advances so far, but we've lost ground. I think those were just skirmishers. I expect a full assault soon."

At first, just the heads of the men at the front of the Rebel column could be seen as they crested the hill in the road ahead. A rattle of clicks trickled along the Union line as men cocked their hammers back. "Steady now, boys. Hold your fire," sergeants tried to settle their nerves. The Rebel column halted and started to spread out on either side of the road, revealing their numbers.

"That looks like two regiments to me," Captain Campbell muttered to the officers around him, then to an orderly, "Ride back to Colonel Sheridan. Tell him the enemy is in force. We need support."

"Jesus, here they come," Bates let out.

"Hold your fire," Sergeant Barth reminded them.

Carl sighted at the rumble of Confederate cavalry as it came thundering across the field.

"Pick your targets, boys, make 'em count," Captain Newman passed behind his men, his saber in one hand and a pistol in the other.

The line got ever closer. Carl could hear their terrible high pitched yell mixed in the rumble of hooves. He found a target: a rider in gray crouching low in his stirrups with his reins in one hand and a pistol extended forward in the other. They were nearly upon the Federals when the command came all along the line.

"Fire!"

Carl pulled the trigger half expecting his own face to be blown off. The carbine kicked hard, punching the Rebel rider clean off his horse. *Wow! Did I do that?* he thought.

"Keep firing!" sergeants screamed. The riderless horse veered to the left following the other beasts as the sustained firing from the Union revolving rifles proved to be too much for the charging Rebels.

"They're forming on the flank! Fall back!" the shout came along the line. Carl pulled the hammer back causing the cylinder to rotate on his Colt and fired again into the mass of Rebels still charging at their front. He hissed in regret at the tumble of fallen horses and men that created a mound of dead and dying flesh before them. He pulled back from his tree and stumbled back towards the new line of Federals forming in the rear. Rebel bullets whizzed through the air like angry bees as he found cover next to Chucky.

"Jesus, Carl, I almost shot you!"

"Glad you didn't," Carl said, cocking his rifle and firing again.

"There's too many of them!" Bates called out in the din.

"Shut up and keep firing!" was the answer that came from somewhere.

"Here they come again, boys," Sergeant Barth called out.

Across the field two ranks of Rebel infantry marched shoulder to shoulder, their fixed bayonets gleamed in the sun.

"Jesus, are they going to stab us with those things?" Chucky gaped at the new threat.

"Not if we shoot them first." Captain Newman came up from behind with his pistol and fired into the approaching line.

The Rebels marched stoically, some of them falling to Federal bullets as they approached. They stopped just short of the trees, shouldered their muskets, and let loose a volley that tore through the woods that hid the Union line. Carl turned away hearing the buckshot and bullets thump into the trees they were using as cover. Then the terrible blood-curdling yell erupted from the Rebels.

"Fuck, they're coming for us!" someone yelled.

Cold panic poured through Carl as he cowered behind his tree.

"Shoot! For God's sake, shoot, you idiots!" Captain Newman shouted as he fired his pistol into the rush of approaching men.

Like jumping off a cliff, Carl pushed himself from the tree, turned, and fired the rest of his cylinders into the rush of men with little effect. A heavily bearded man tore after him with his bayonet. Without thinking, Carl deflected the blade with the barrel of his carbine, but the man's forward motion barreled him over and soon, Carl found himself on his back with the man on top, squeezing the air out of his neck. He grabbed at the man's wrists and struggled to get free. Then he remembered his pistol. He patted his side frantically until he found it. The bearded man, sensing the new danger, turned to grab the gun. Carl fired as the man pushed his arm away causing the bullet to strike him in the shoulder.

"Aaagh! Damn it!" the man screamed as he fell off and rolled on the ground in agony clutching his shoulder. "You shot me, you son of a bitch!"

Carl scurried to his feet, holding his pistol on the man who was now reeling in pain. He looked up and saw he was surrounded by scenes of hand-to-hand fighting. Then several of the Rebels started shouting, "Fall back! Fall back!"

All around Confederate soldiers started to look up from their individual fights only to have their faces turn from fury to fear. They quickly disengaged and joined the retreat. The ground began to shake as a heavy rumble took over the sounds of fighting. Carl looked back at his opponent who had gotten to his knees. Still holding his shoulder, the man's face went white with horror. Carl turned to see the nightmare scene unfolding. Hordes of blue-clad horsemen came thundering through the woods. At the head of the column rode a man with furious blue eyes. He held the reins with his brass claw as he hacked his way through the crowd of fleeing Rebels with his saber.

"Good God…" Carl murmured at the terrifying scene.

"Hey, if you ain't gonna kill me, I'm gettin' the hell out of here," the man behind him spoke. Carl turned to see his opponent scramble off with his hand still clutching his shoulder. For a moment, the murderous sight of Klaus reaping men down like wheat gave him the urge to run too.

The small detachment of dismounted men with their repeating Colt rifles had held off the Rebel advance just long enough for Colonel Sheridan's two columns of Iowa and Michigan cavalry to ride around and smash into the enemy's flanks. The effect put the

Rebels on the run. Sheridan's men gave chase but called it off once the Rebels slipped back into the marshland and disappeared in the evening twilight.

Comparatively, the weeks that followed were calm with only small skirmishes between opposing patrols. The 2nd Michigan Cavalry moved camp several times in search of good water. A drought was wringing the Upper Middle South dry. The rumor was that the Rebels had moved to consolidate their forces at Chattanooga and the 2nd Michigan, now part of Buell's army, was soon to follow.

The chatter around the evening fires at their camp at Rienzi, Mississippi was about the heavy skirmishing on Ripley Road that day. The Rebels showed up in force to push in the Federal pickets but were soundly repelled once the combined Kansas and Michigan Cavalry appeared. Their colonel barely escaped, losing his hat in the effort. It was quite a trophy. Carl listened to the stories everyone had to tell about his part in the day as he scooped his plate of beans and salt pork into his mouth with his finger.

"All right, boys," Captain Newman abruptly broke up the chatter as he approached their campfire. "Get a good night's sleep. We breaking camp tomorrow."

"Are we going to Chattanooga then?" Bates asked.

"Nope, Bragg is moving towards Kentucky to threaten our supply line. We've got to get there first."

Chapter Thirteen: Munfordville

Like a big, fat juicy plum hanging low in a tree sat the Federal detachment left to guard the train bridge at Munfordville. General Chalmers was determined to pick it before anyone else could. General Kirby Smith's Army of East Tennessee had gotten the jump on grabbing all the glory to be gotten in Kentucky. His army had lurched into the Blue Grass State from Knoxville and already defeated the unprepared Federals at Richmond taking over 4,300 prisoners. Then, they marched unopposed into the state's capital city of Frankfort and planted the Confederate flag to wild cheers of the civilians there. Kentucky, it seemed, would soon be part of the Confederacy.

Braxton Bragg's Army of Mississippi crept into Kentucky late to the game. Their goal was to cut off Don Carlos Buell's Army of the Ohio before it could resupply at Louisville. Chalmers's Brigade led the advance and was within striking distance of the forsaken Federals at Munfordville. This was his chance to snatch up an easy win before the rest of Bragg's army caught up.

The 1,800-foot train bridge towered 115 feet over the Green River, smack dab in the center of the state. It was a midpoint along the rail line that connected the invading Yankee armies in Tennessee to their supply depot in Louisville. Cavalry reports suggested there were only a few cannons and not more than 1,800 poorly trained Federal troops manning the earthworks and unfinished rifle-pits south of the river. Chalmers figured a bold dash with his brigade of Mississippians would be more than enough to overwhelm their defenses.

Chalmers got to Munfordville at 10 o'clock at night and immediately put his game pieces in place. He placed his four cannons on Lewis Hill overlooking the Federal position. He then sent one regiment around to the west to attack the Federals' right flank. He placed three regiments on the left, and a battalion of sharpshooters in the center, leaving one regiment in reserve. The trap was set.

The Federal commander there had already refused a Confederate cavalry patrol's demand for surrender during a brief skirmish. Now that Chalmers's full brigade was set to pounce, he decided to give him one more chance. Not wanting to risk any of his own officers, he sent the young upstart of a captain to demand the surrender. The young man had arrived earlier with dispatches from Bragg. Chalmers didn't want the young man to ride back and inform Bragg of his intentions of taking the fort until he already had it in hand. Otherwise, the overly cautious Bragg might order him to wait until the full force of the Army of Mississippi arrived. Chalmers wasn't going to give up this opportunity for glory that easily, so he sent the young captain to the fort under a flag of truce.

Kyle rode into the dark streets of Munfordville carrying a white flag. He couldn't see the Yankee pickets but he could hear the clicks of cocking rifles as he approached. A man holding a lantern stepped into his path and saluted him stiffly. "That's far enough, sir," he said with an Irish brogue. "We'll have to blindfold you before taking you to the colonel, sir, lest ye be spying on our defenses."

"Of course, Sergeant," Kyle returned the salute and dismounted.

"Y'can leave your weapons with the horse, sir. Our boys will keep a good eye on them for ya."

It was a strange feeling walking blindfolded into the fort with only enemy soldiers to guide him. It was odd that he should put so much trust in the men he could very well be shooting at the next day.

They came to a stop. A nervous chuckle broke the silence. "They're sending them younger and younger, aren't they?"

"That they are, sir," the sergeant answered.

"Go ahead a remove your blindfold, Captain, you're among friends here," the nervous voice said with a chuckle.

Kyle took off his blindfold to see the Union officer sitting at a small desk in his tent. By the flickering lantern, he could see the Colonel wasn't much more than 30 years old himself. He had wide, deep-set eyes filled with nervous energy, short-cut brown hair parted on the side, and a dark beard with a clean-shaven upper lip. Kyle snapped a salute, "I have a message from General Chalmers, sir."

"Of course," the colonel said, getting off his stool and returning the salute. Then turning to the sergeant, "That'll be all for now, Sergeant. I'll call you if this Rebel gets out of hand," he said with chuckle and wink towards Kyle.

"Sir!" the sergeant barked with a salute and then turned crisply on his heel before marching out of the tent.

"John Wilder, Indiana," the colonel extended his hand.

"Kyle Bethune, Tennessee, sir"

"Ah, beautiful place, Tennessee! Won't you have a seat?" Wilder beckoned to the empty stool across from his desk. "Do you drink, Kyle?"

"Um, occasionally, sir."

"I hope the occasion suits you," Wilder said as he produced a bottle of brown liquid and two tin cups. Kyle felt the tension burn away as the first sip of whiskey slipped down his throat. "Ah…" Wilder emitted after taking a sip. "So what's your strength out there, Kyle?"

"I'm not at liberty to say, sir, only that it's more than enough to overwhelm your works, sir," Kyle replied before taking another sip.

Wilder blinked at him for a moment and then broke into a chuckle. "Ah, I knew you weren't a fool, Kyle. Please forgive me for testing you."

"It's quite alright, sir," Kyle assured him. "Are you expecting reinforcements?"

"Ha!" Wilder exclaimed with a laugh. "Now it is I who is taken for the fool!" he said with a laugh.

"I meant no offense, sir…"

"None taken, my friend," Wilder smiled as he uncorked the bottle and refreshed their cups. "Come, let's have a look at what your General Chalmers has to say."

The colonel's brow furled as he opened the envelope and read the letter. "Hmm…he seems awfully sure of himself," Wilder's smile returned. Kyle shrugged his shoulders. He wasn't quite comfortable talking about a superior officer with the enemy. Wilder broke the silence with a nervous laugh. "I think we'll fight for a while! Come, I'll write a reply for you to take back." Then lifting his gaze to the open tent flap, "Sergeant!"

"Yes, sir!" the sergeant's voice snapped from outside.

"See Captain Bethune safely to his lines. Of course, we'll have to blindfold him again."

"Of course, sir," the sergeant said, stepping into the tent.

Colonel Wilder offered his hand as they stood up, "You're a good man, Captain Bethune. Do keep your head down tomorrow. I'd hate to see it shot off."

"Might I suggest the same, sir," Kyle replied.

"Ha!" the Colonel let out a laugh. "Of course, my friend!"

Kyle didn't realize he had dozed off until a crackle of musketry woke him. It was still dark. He was quite sure the attack wasn't supposed to happen until dawn. He threw off his blanket and pulled himself from the ground which was now damp with the early morning dew. General Chalmers's headquarters camp was already abuzz with activity. Ahead, the town began to glow as several of the buildings were burning.

"Sir, our skirmishers have made contact with the forward Federal pickets" an orderly was briefing

Chalmers. "They're falling back to the fort. Major Richards says they've set several of the town's buildings afire."

"Ah, that's to keep us from using them for cover," Chalmers mused. "Is our right wing in place to start their assault?"

"Not yet, sir."

"Damn it!" Chalmers hissed as the skirmishing intensified. "They started too soon."

At that moment, a line of Confederates marched into the fray from the west, stopping to offer volley at the entrenched Federals. The Yankees began to return fire from behind their works, dropping several of the Confederate men from their line.

"Damn it!" Chalmers hissed. "What the hell are they doing?!"

"That's Colonel Smith's 10th Mississippians; they must have thought the fires were the signal to start the assault."

"I know who the hell they are!" Chalmers yelled at his orderly. "They must have support while our right wing gets into position. Signal the battery to commence firing. We've got to give our boys a fighting chance!"

The guns set on Lewis Hill opened fire, but their shells fell short of the Federal entrenchment. "Get those guns down from there, God damn it! They're not doing a damn thing from that range!" Chalmers yelled.

After a series of signals, the four artillery crews limbered their guns and ran them down the hill only to place them within the range of the Federal cannons.

The Yankee gunners took full advantage and proceeded to pound them before they could even unlimber and set up to return fire.

The Federal guns had also pinned down the 10th Mississippi in front of the fort. Chalmers sent wave after wave to support them only to lose more men in the attempt. By mid-morning it was quite clear, Chalmers had neither the men nor the guns to wrest the small earthen fort from its Federal defenders. Not wanting to admit defeat, he sent another demand for an unconditional surrender.

"Tell General Chalmers, I shall defend myself until overpowered," Colonel Wilder said with wide-eye blinking incredulity at the new demand for surrender.

"Look at your men, Kyle," Wilder motioned to the field of dead and dying men that lay before the fort's earthen walls. "They lay there by the hundreds! What a terrible waste!" Wilder let out a nervous chuckle while shaking his head, "No, I don't think I shall surrender. But I shall allow a truce so you can collect your dead and tend to your wounded, God rest their souls."

Kyle was relieved to be sent away from the gruesome task of collecting the dead and dying men in front of Fort Craig. But he dreaded having to deliver the news of the defeat to the cantankerous Braxton Bragg.

"Who in God's name gave him the order to attack?!" General Bragg slammed his hands on his desk as he sprung from his chair. Kyle flinched at the outburst but none of the other officers seemed to be affected. They appeared to have become accustomed to Bragg's fits of rage.

"Perhaps General Chalmers wanted to take the fort before the Federals could send reinforcements," General Simon Bolivar Buckner spoke up. "I grew up in Munfordville. I know the importance of that bridge well. Surely they wouldn't leave such an important train crossing poorly defended now that we've entered the state." Kyle marveled at seeing the Kentuckian General again. It was the first time since the fall of Fort Donelson. The General was thinner from his months of captivity, but his face still held an air of stoic duty with a deep sense of compassion in his eyes.

Bragg slumped back into his chair, clutching his hair with both hands. "This foray into Kentucky is not going as promised," he groaned. "Where are the tens of thousands of volunteers we were promised? I have 15,000 new rifles to hand out and I can't even unload the arms of our dead! Your damn Kentuckians sure love waving our flag but they won't rally to it!"

"The Federals have threatened to confiscate the property of any man who takes up arms for our cause, sir," an aide offered. "Kentucky is still part of the Union."

"We hold the God damn capital!" Bragg slammed his fists on the desk. "Once I install our own Confederate governor, the state will be ours and every man in it will be subject to our conscription law! By God, we will make them fight! In the meantime, I can't have our first action in Kentucky be a loss. Inform our division commanders to ready their troops. We march on Munfordville!"

With the arrival of the 50th Indiana and a stream of new recruits, the Federals were able to increase their number to 4,000 men. Their pickets quickly fell back into the fort after brief skirmishes once Bragg's Army of the Mississippi began to arrive and take positions the following morning. Soon, the small earthen fort was surrounded by 25,000 Confederates. The Federals refused the first demand to surrender, asking for proof of the Rebels' superior numbers.

"Proof?! They want proof?!" Bragg blurted. "I'll blow them to kingdom come from all four directions! How's that for proof?!" Still, Bragg waited out the agreed truce for the foolish Federal commander to come to his senses. At the end of the day, Kyle was once again handed a letter to carry into the fort demanding its unconditional surrender.

"Might I have a word with you, Kyle," a voice from behind startled him just as he went to mount his horse.

"General Buckner!" he blurted in surprise. "I'm happy to see you returned to us."

"I'm happy to see you made it out of Fort Donelson in one piece as well, and now you're a captain! Good work, son. I'm proud of you!"

"Thank you, sir," Kyle said sheepishly. "It's only a brevet rank. We're still waiting on approval from Richmond."

"I see," Buckner said thoughtfully. "This Colonel Wilder, is he a good man?"

"I believe so, sir."

"So do I, but foolish and perhaps way in over his head. Kyle, we can save hundreds, maybe thousands of lives if we can convince Wilder to do the right thing. I know what he's feeling. I've been there. Surrendering Fort Donelson was one of the hardest things I've had to do. I spent months in that Federal prison thinking about it."

"I'm sorry, sir," Kyle offered, not sure what else to say.

"I want you to carry this letter along with General Bragg's demand for surrender," Buckner said, pulling an envelope from his jacket. "I may be a fool myself, but I hope I can change that young man's mind. Will you take it to him for me?"

Kyle blinked at the general for a moment and then gulped, "Of course sir."

Colonel Wilder looked up from his desk as Kyle was escorted into his tent. He gave out a nervous chuckle. "Well, Kyle, I've seen so much of you over the last few days I almost forgot you're not one of my own!"

Kyle handed him Bragg's letter. "Sir, I'm here to inform you that if you don't surrender the fort, General Bragg will commence his attack at dawn."

"I see…" Wilder said, as he opened the letter and scanned its contents. "May God help the right," he said with a smile as he dropped the letter onto his desk.

"Sir, I also have a letter from General Simon Bolivar Buckner," Kyle said pulling the second letter from his jacket.

"Ah, a hero from the Mexican war, for sure. Won't you sit down?" Wilder offered.

"Yes, sir," Kyle answered. "General Buckner has recently rejoined us after being exchanged since his surrender at Fort Donelson."

"I see…" Wilder murmured as he opened the letter and read its contents. His nervous smile dropped as he read. His eyes began to soften. Upon finishing, he pulled out his bottle of whiskey, poured some into two tin cups, and offered one to Kyle. "This Buckner is a good man, wouldn't you say?"

"One of the best, sir" Kyle answered.

"Hmmm…I need to ask a favor of you, Kyle," his now more serious eyes felt piercing.

"I am at your service, sir."

"I appreciate that, my friend," Wilder's smile returned. "To start with, I may need to borrow your blindfold."

It seemed to General Buckner that he had just managed to fall asleep when an orderly roused him. "Sir, Captain Bethune is here to see you with…um…a most unusual guest."

"Of course," Buckner said, sitting up. "Send them in." He struck a match and lit the lantern on the table next to his cot. The young captain from Tennessee entered. With him was a 30-something-year-old Union officer wearing a blindfold.

"You can take his blindfold off, Kyle," Buckner said, standing up. Wilder blinked as the blindfold fell from his eyes. Buckner held out his hand, "Colonel Wilder, I presume."

"Yes, sir, and you are General Buckner. It's a pleasure and honor to meet you, sir."

"Thank you," Buckner said as they shook hands, "I have to say, this is most unusual."

"I suppose it is," Wilder said with a nervous chuckle. "I read your letter. I found it to be honest and sincere. I've come to find out what I ought to do."

Buckner blinked at him for a moment and then spoke, "You are in command of your troops and you must decide for yourself what you ought to do. However, I think you should know what you're facing before you do. Colonel, would you accompany me on a walk?"

"Of course," Wilder agreed. The three left Buckner's tent and walked among the thousands of Rebel soldiers slumbering before the assault was to begin in the morning. Buckner then showed Wilder the batteries of cannon set up on all sides of the fort ready to rain shot and shell upon the heads of the Federals at dawn.

"How long do you think your command would live under that fire?" Buckner asked him.

Colonel Wilder was pensive for a moment, and then, "Sir, I think I should surrender."

"No, Colonel," Buckner told him. "If you have information that would induce you to think that the sacrificing of every man at this place would gain your army an advantage elsewhere, it is your duty to do it."

Wilder let out a nervous chuckle while looking down at his own feet. He kicked at the dirt for a moment then looked back at General Buckner, "I believe I will surrender, sir."

"Very well," Buckner placed his hand on the Colonel's shoulder. "Let's go talk to General Bragg."

The sound of drums broke the morning silence instead of cannons. The Rebels formed up and stood at attention as 4,000 Federal soldiers marched out of the fort and stacked their arms in front the Rebels. The thin, barefoot, and ragged Confederate soldiers looked greedily upon the Yankee prisoners in their new uniforms, still fat from just previously leaving civilian life. Colonel Wilder marched out, saluted General Bragg, and handed him his sword. A wave of relief spread through the ranks of both armies.

Within a few days, the Yankee soldiers were paroled and sent marching northward to their own lines minus their arms and much of their equipment. Only the high ranking officers were kept. They would be exchanged for Confederate officers held as prisoners of war. Many of the Rebel soldiers were overjoyed at the boon of new shoes and equipment captured with the fort, but for the commanding officers, reality soon set in.

"Gentlemen, our position here at Munfordville is untenable," General Bragg addressed his officers. Kyle sat nervously in the back, wondering why he had been summoned to attend such a high-level meeting. Bragg continued, "Our quartermaster says if we stay here, we will run out of food in a matter of days. The Federals have already stripped the surrounding area of resources. For that reason, I've decided to pull back to Bardstown and consolidate our forces there."

"But, sir," an officer protested, "if we leave now we will forfeit all that we've gained and open the door for Buell's army to pass through to Louisville uncontested."

Bragg let out a sigh, "It hurts me to do so, but the truth is, without General Kirby Smith's army, we cannot beat the Yankee hordes. We will fall back to Bardstown until Smith arrives." A murmur spread through the room. Bragg cleared his throat, "There's one more matter I need to address. Mr. Bethune…"

"Um, yes, sir," Kyle said, standing up. He awkwardly walked passed the seated officers before standing at attention before Bragg's desk.

"I have here your promotion to captain approved by Richmond. I just need to sign it to make it official."

"Uh…thank you, sir," Kyle said.

Bragg stared at him for a moment, dangling the paper in his hand. "I understand it was you who led Colonel Wilder behind our lines without prior permission."

"Sir, I was just trying to help bring about the surrender."

"By bringing an enemy into our lines?! How we force a surrender is not up for you to decide!"

"Yes, sir," Kyle gulped feeling the blood drain from his face.

"It appears that's not the first time you sneaked an enemy soldier into our lines," Bragg said coldly. Kyle felt his blood turn to ice. "Bring them in!" Bragg shouted, not taking his eyes off of Kyle. Kyle was stunned to see Lathan Woods enter the room. Lathan smiled at him with malicious delight, behind came a gaunt and disturbed looking Lieutenant Davis.

"Michael…!" Kyle gasped. Davis looked at him briefly and then quickly looked away.

"You know, Lieutenant Davis?" Bragg cocked an eyebrow at Kyle.

"Yes, sir. We are childhood frie…acquaintances," Kyle answered.

"Would you say Lieutenant Davis is a good and honest man?" Bragg asked.

"Of course, sir," Kyle said, straightening himself.

"Interesting…" Bragg mused. "Lieutenant Davis, is this the man you mentioned in your report?" Bragg asked.

"Yes, sir," Davis said softly.

"And you say he stole your uniform and gave it to a Yankee soldier whom he brought into our camps at New Madrid?" Bragg prodded.

"Yes, sir."

"Lieutenant Woods, you say this Yankee spy attacked you and stole away with vital information about our defenses at New Madrid which the Federal forces used to easily overwhelm our works?"

"Yes, sir," Lathan smiled slyly.

"Why did you not report this sooner?" Bragg prodded him.

Lathan hesitated for a moment and then answered, "I had to be sure before leveling such accusations against such a prestigious gentleman as Mr. Bethune. It wasn't until Lieutenant Davis's return that I could collaborate my suspicions."

"Hmph…" Bragg pondered whether to pry more at Lathan's story.

"Sir, I…" Kyle grasped for words.

"Save it for your court-martial," Bragg cut him short. "Sergeant, arrest this man. As for this…" Bragg held up the paper bearing his promotion, "I don't think I'll be signing it just yet."

The sergeant walked up to Kyle and motioned for him to follow. They walked past the gloating Lathan Woods and the sick looking Lieutenant Davis. Kyle paused to gaze upon him, "Oh, Michael…" he said with sorrow. Lieutenant Davis looked away.

"Come on, sir," the sergeant urged him on.

Kyle sat stunned in the jail cell at Munfordville. The sounds of the army preparing to march to Bardstown poured in through the window. A door opened and soon General Buckner stood before his cell.

"Is it true, son?" the General asked.

"I guess so, in a way, but there's more to it…I'm not a traitor, sir," Kyle looked up at him with tears forming in his eyes.

"I see…what can I do to help you?" Buckner asked.

Kyle dropped his head into his hands, sniffed hard, and then collected himself. "Please get this message to my sister, Kathryn Bethune, in Memphis. Tell her what I'm accused of. Tell her that I don't think I can fight it. Tell her not to leave Memphis. She and Liza are safe there. Tell her I love her, as well as Ma, Pa…and Liza."

Chapter Fourteen: Forgiveness

Carl sat back and enjoyed his afternoon buzz. His comrades around him chatted and sipped the whiskey that flowed freely among the boys in blue. After weeks of suffering half-rations and severe drought conditions in Northern Mississippi, the men were loaded onto train cars, and then riverboats, and shipped up to Louisville where food, new uniforms, and back pay awaited them.

New recruits poured into town, and now a general lawlessness turned the city into a circus as idle soldiers with money to burn were met by whiskey merchants and enterprising women. Many of the men from Indiana slipped across the river for unauthorized trips home, many others went along with them for the adventure. Carl, not wanting to get in any more trouble, stayed and loitered with the men that lounged along the busy street, killing time with bottles of Kentucky bourbon and camp gossip.

"Wait, Bull Nelson was shot by Jefferson Davis? I thought he was in Virginia!" Chucky just couldn't believe the news.

"Not President Jefferson Davis, you idiot! General Davis of Indiana! One of our guys," Bates chided. "Apparently, Old Bull blamed the Indiana men for his loss at Richmond."

"Virginia?" Chucky broke in again.

"No, moron, Kentucky!" Bates sighed, "There's more than one Richmond and there's more than one Jeff Davis," Bates blinked at him for a moment with annoyance before continuing. "So anyway, this Davis calls him out, right in the lobby of that fancy hotel, the Galt House, or whatever. Get this, Davis crumples up a piece of paper and throws it right into Old Bull's face! Well, Bull ain't havin' none of it, calls the man a puppy and slaps him across the face, right in front of everybody and then just walks off."

"Wow!" Chucky gasped. "That's grounds for a duel!"

"Apparently Davis thought so! He borrows a pistol from one of his pals and follows Bull into his room and bam! Shoots him dead, right through the heart!" Bates said with the satisfaction of delivering such a story to his friends.

"That General Nelson's a big man," Chucky pondered.

"Was, Chucky…was," Bates corrected him.

Carl was only half-listening to the banter. His thoughts turned to the pretty girls he saw walking past them on the busy street. He wondered if he'd get the nerve to talk to any of them. One particularly caught his eye as she made her way down the street. Her sculpted face, accented with freckles, seemed full of apprehension as she stopped along the way to ask an officer something. The red wisps of hair that spilled out of her bonnet reminded him so much of Kathryn.

He began to feel the embarrassment of arousal growing in his pants. He tried to adjust them before his friends noticed and teased him. He looked back up at her, hoping to drink in as much of the image before she disappeared into the street. The officer speaking to her nodded and then pointed in the direction of Carl and his friends. She nodded her thanks to the man and started walking towards Carl and his little group. Her eyes met his and then the realization hit him like a cannonball, "My God…it's her…" He mumbled.

"Carl?!" Kathryn gasped. Her worried eyes softened with the beginning of tears as she dashed into his arms, nearly bowling him over. Carl was both exhilarated and embarrassed that she might feel the arousal he was trying to hide. "I just knew I'd find you!" she gasped into his ear. He could taste the saltiness of her tears against his cheek.

"Well, well, well…" Bates broke the moment. "Now, who is this?"

"None of your damn business," Carl snapped back.

"I'm his cousin, and we need to talk about a family matter," Kathryn said, quickly getting control of herself and the situation. She then turned to Carl, "Is there somewhere we can go?"

"Um, yeah…follow me," he said clumsily. The two walked off, leaving a group of stunned cavalrymen in their wake.

"I didn't know he had a cousin…" Chucky gaped.

"Kyle's been arrested for treason. I don't know if they've tried him yet but he's certain he'll be found guilty. Oh, Carl, they'll hang him!" She let out a sob and then looked out to the boats churning their way along the Ohio River.

"My God! Whatever for?" Carl just couldn't believe what he was hearing.

"I suppose all that business we did in New Madrid. We did sneak you in and put you in a Confederate uniform," she said softly. "I suppose what you saw there was a great aid to your army…"

Those last words stung. He wanted to say that he had only gone along with their crazy plan to help them rescue their runaway slave, that it wasn't his fault that he saw things. Heck, he almost faced a court-martial himself after he returned to his army. But it was his inside knowledge of the defenses at New Madrid that saved him from the firing squad.

Now his own mind was accusing him. Even though he knew it didn't make any sense, he couldn't help but think: he had avoided an execution by passing it on to his best friend. "Where is he now?" Carl asked with new determination.

"Last I knew, he was being held in Bardstown. I believe that's where we are consolidating our forces before we push the Yankees out of Kentucky."

Carl sighed. He looked into her beautiful green eyes and knew there was no getting around this: he was a fool and he'd go to the gates of hell for her and his best friend. "Alright, then," he sighed again and rolled his eyes to the heavens. "We'll slip out tonight and find a way into Bardstown."

"Oh, Carl!" Kathryn threw her arms around him. "I knew I could depend on you!"

"I'm sure you did," Carl sighed, allowing himself to enjoy the embrace. "I'm sure you did…"

Sneaking out of town was relatively easy. Getting away from his friends and comrades was a bit more difficult. He told Chucky he was stealing off to the Indiana side of the river for a few days to visit some family with his cousin. He asked him to cover for him the best he could. Chucky seemed to buy it since many of the troops had slipped away for short sojourns while they waited as Buell reorganized and prepared his army for the pending push into Central Kentucky. The 2nd Michigan Cavalry was also going through a leadership change. Phil Sheridan was promoted to brigadier general and given an infantry division to command. The chaos of reorganization left plenty of time and space for mischief among the idle men.

Carl was most worried about Elijah. He feared the big man would insist on coming along once he found out they were planning on rescuing Kyle. Of course, the big man would be a great help in a fight, but it was hard enough to imagine how Carl and Kathryn would get into a town full of Confederates even without bringing an enormous black man with them.

Mercifully, Elijah was away when Carl came to the stables to get Bess. He felt guilty not telling his friend about what was happening, but resolved that it was for Elijah's own protection to keep him out of it.

Carl rode through town after nightfall, waiting to be called to a halt by a provost and challenged at any minute. Surely, he was going to be caught. He buried his eyes in his visor and feigned confidence. The soldiers manning the defensive works on the outskirts of town merely looked up from their cards for a moment before returning to their game. He was out! He wondered if getting back in would be as easy.

Kathryn was waiting for him as planned. The sight of her was shocking. Gone were her big hooped dress and bonnet. Instead, she wore brown pants, riding boots, a man's blouse, jacket, and a wide-brimmed hat that held back most of her hair. At first glance, she looked like a wisp of a boy, but as she lifted her face from beneath the brim of her hat, she was still undeniably a beautiful woman.

"Good heavens, Carl!" she chided. "You're going to get us shot riding into town wearing a Yankee uniform like that!"

"It's all I got!" he said, taking her arm as she swung herself onto his horse. A thrill raced through him as her legs molded themselves around his hips and her arms laced around his waist. He still couldn't believe it was her. He still couldn't believe how stupid he was being either. But in this moment, he was happier than he ever imagined he could be.

"We'll have to find you something else to wear before we get there," she said as he gave Bess a nudge, sending her ambling along the way.

"I guess we'll figure it out as we go," he said, feeling foolishly inept. It occurred to him that they had no plan. He was AWOL, or absent without leave, he was riding into the enemy army wearing his US uniform, and he was carrying the woman he loved. He was sure he was an idiot, but a happy one.

They rode quietly in the darkness for a few hours before encountering other travelers. Not knowing if the approaching horses belonged to civilians, guerrillas, or cavalry patrols of either army, they decide to move off the road and take shelter in the woods.

"Maybe we should sleep a bit before dawn. We can't tell who we're facing in the dark," Kathryn whispered.

"Good idea," he agreed. He tied Bess to a tree and pulled out his bedroll. "I only have one blanket. You can have it."

"Don't be silly. We can keep each other warm," she smiled softly at him. Carl tried to hide his delight. Kathryn snuggled up to him as he wrapped his arm around her and held her tight. *This is what heaven is like*, he thought as he drifted into darkness.

It was light when he woke. A wave of panic swept over him when he realized that Kathryn wasn't next to him, but then he smelled the smoke and coffee. Kathryn sat next to a small fire stoking it with a stick.

"How'd you learn to make a fire?" he asked sitting up and rubbing his eyes.

She let out a short laugh, "I grew up on a farm, Carl. I'm not completely useless."

"No, you are not," Carl said happily, as she handed him his tin mug full of hot coffee.

"Careful, the grounds are still in it. Without a kettle, I had to make it the old-fashioned way."

"It works for me!" he said sipping the hot coffee carefully.

"What happened to your face?" she asked with concern.

205

"Oh, that," he said, self-consciously rubbing his scar, "I had a gun blow up on me. I guess I'll never look the same."

"Well," she said with a smile, "I think it makes you more handsome."

Carl smiled and dropped his eyes to the ground. They shared the cup, dipping a few pieces of hardtack in it for breakfast before continuing their journey.

It was still exceptionally hot for early fall. Soon they packed away their jackets and rode in open blouses. The less he was in uniform the better, he thought. He was thankful that both of them brought canteens. Finding a creek that wasn't dry was becoming harder and harder. Carl felt bad for offering only muddy puddles to Bess.

"If we don't find clean water soon, all three of us are going to be in trouble," he said only to be answered by a rumble of thunder.

Kathryn looked up at the darkening skies and smirked, "Careful what you wish for, city boy." The first drops were a relief but then the skies opened up and soon they were drenched by pelting rain. Kathryn buried her face in Carl's back as he urged Bess on. In the blurry haze of rain, he saw salvation. An old wooden barn sat amid a seemingly unkempt field. He hoped it was abandoned but if it were still in use, he hoped no farmer would be out in this rain.

Bess was more than happy to get inside. They pushed the barn doors closed just as the hail began to beat upon them. The smell of fresh rain mixed with the smoked tobacco stalks that hung from the ceiling and the fresh apples that lay in bushels on the floor.

Bess was quick to help herself. "Wow, what a boon!" Kathryn marveled, as she handed one to Carl. He immediately took a bite. The juice instantly soothed his thirst. "We must get out of these wet clothes or we'll catch a cold," Kathryn said, shimmying off her riding boots and unfastening her pants.

Carl blinked dumbly at her for a moment and then started disrobing quickly until they stood before each other in nothing more than soaking wet blouses. Her blouse clung to her petite frame revealing her small delicate breasts. Carl stood dumbstruck before her. Kathryn let out a small laugh. "Well, I guess there's no getting around this," she said, and then pulled her blouse up over her head. Carl instinctively turned away and took off his blouse, embarrassed that his arousal was plain to see. Soft hands lay on his shoulder and his hip. He turned and there she was. Her beautiful wild red hair was undone, laying in wet tangles on her delicate but firm white and freckled shoulders.

He embraced her, leaned into a kiss, feeling his arousal pressing against the softness of her belly. They fell into the hay, rolling, kissing, feeling each other as the rain beat against the roof, the thunder rumbled, and Bess gorged herself with apples. Kathryn ended up on top of Carl, gently kissing the olive skin of his shoulder. He groaned, trying to control himself from being overcome with ecstasy. "You don't have to do this to save your brother…" he whispered softly.

Kathryn stopped cold, glared at him, and then slapped him across the face. "How dare you?!" she scolded. Carl blinked at her, stunned. "Do you think this is some kind of transaction? Do you think so poorly of me and my affection? You men think this is all about you, your war, and your suffering! Don't you think for a moment that others are suffering too? You think you've seen some hard things, felt pain, loss? Why can't I just want to feel good for a moment in all of this misery, for goodness sake?! Are men the only ones who need comfort?"

Carl blinked at her, completely bewildered, "Forgive me, I was just…"

"Oh, shut up and kiss me, you fool!"

Lieutenant Michael Davis returned to his tent full of bitterness. The trial had been mercifully quick. Kyle barely tried to defend himself. He didn't deny that he had not returned directly to duty after the fall of Fort Donelson but instead went home. He did not deny that he helped sneak a Yankee soldier into New Madrid and that the Yankee soldier stole Michael's uniform and secrets about the defenses built around the town. But Kyle claimed the Yankee was an old friend from school who was merely helping him recover a runaway slave. When asked the identity of the Yankee friend, Kyle merely dropped his eyes and said, "I would not betray a friend, for he would be in trouble with his own people if his identity got out…"

"Are we not your friends?!" The presiding officer chastised him, "What about betraying your own country?"

Kyle merely shook his head and said, "I am no traitor."

They found him guilty of treason and sentenced him to die by firing squad at first light. When Michael stole one last look, Kyle merely smiled at him and shrugged his shoulders as if to say, "Well, that's that…"

"How dare you forgive me!" Michael blurted out to the raindrops beginning to fall on his tent.

"Excuse me?" a voice came from behind. Michael turned to see the postmaster poking his head through the flaps.

"I'm sorry, sir, I thought I was alone," Michael said stiffly.

"Are you Lieutenant Michael Davis?" the postmaster asked.

"I am he."

"I have quite a bundle of letters for you. It seems they have piled up during your captivity. I'm glad to finally unload them."

"Thank you," he said, receiving the bundle. He untied the twine that held them together. Most of them seemed to be from his mother, who insisted on writing almost daily. He had corresponded with her since his release, so he was in no hurry to read her outdated letters. He shuffled through the rest. A few were from friends, some from other family. There were a couple of outdated military dispatches. But then the smell came through with the wind from the coming storm that fluttered his tent flaps.

Michael got up to secure them and then sat back down with his pile of letters, and in the mix, he found it: A simple envelope with a lady's handwriting that smelled of perfume. It was from Kathryn Bethune, postmarked from Memphis, April 14. His hands trembled as he opened it. The first line was devastating. Upon finishing it, he let the letter drop to the ground, dropped his face into his hands, and began to sob. The rain was coming down now in full torrents.

The rain had tapered off before Carl woke. Kathryn lay sleeping naked in his arms with a line of drool that ran from her lips, down his chest, and tickled his side. The post-rain, late-day sunlight broke through the spaces between wooden slats of the barn creating a golden glow on the tobacco stalks that hung from the rafters. "Hey," he nudged her softly, "we better go."

"Hmmm?" she murmured, and then, "Where are we?" Carl was about to answer when he realized she was just now coming to her senses after a deep sleep. "We're still probably a few hours ride from Bardstown as far as I can reckon," he said anyway.

His clothes were still damp and cool when he put them back on. There was no time to let them dry further. It felt like they were quickly running out of time. They ate apples as they rode in the twilight. Several times they had to scurry off the road and hide from patrols. It was fully dark when they realized they weren't far from the Confederate pickets that guarded the entrance into Bardstown.

"What do we do?" Kathryn whispered.

"I suppose we wait for a lone rider that we can overpower and steal his uniform," he answered, not quite sure how this would work. And so, they tied Bess up out of sight, hid by the road, and waited. Patrols came and went, but all of them were too big for the two of them to confront. Carl was beginning to worry about their plan as the night wore on.

Kyle sat in his cell and stared at the window, smiling. What could he do? He had always tried to do the right thing and this was where it got him: awaiting death in the morning. He decided it was no good crying about it. This is just where life brought him. He let out a sigh and thought of Liza, her smile, and how it felt to hold her in his arms. He hoped she would know that he truly loved her, that she wasn't merely something a foolish white boy played with as he grew into a man. She would have been the woman he wanted to spend his life with. *To hell with the rest of mankind.*

The rattle of keys and the opening door broke him from his reverie. "Michael!" he said, surprised to see the vengeful lieutenant appear before his cell.

"Shut up," Lieutenant Davis replied, and then to his companion, "Sergeant, put that man in irons."

"Isn't it a little early?" Kyle said as the sergeant opened the cell and secured shackles to Kyle's hands and feet.

"Shut up or I'll have you gagged," Davis said with a fury that silenced Kyle immediately. Kyle hobbled along to keep up with him and the sergeant. Davis spoke again once they were outside. "That'll be all, Sergeant. I am to deliver the prisoner in secret for further interrogation. There are still secrets to pull from this traitor before he dies. If you'll excuse us, please."

"Of course, sir!" the sergeant replied, handing Davis the key to the shackles.

Davis prodded Kyle with his pistol, "Move." Kyle hobbled along, trying to keep up. Davis let out a sigh. "Oh, for God's sake!" he hissed, as he squatted down to unlock the shackles from Kyle's feet. "Do try to be quiet, please," Davis said curtly. Kyle was surprised when he tossed the shackles into the bushes and then nudged him on.

The farther they walked, the stranger it all seemed. Davis gave a curt nod to the sentries on the edge of town who were mostly just trying to look like they were alert for the passing officer and his companion. It became clear to Kyle, once they entered the woods, just what was going on. *He's going to kill me himself*, Kyle thought. They came to a clearing where a horse had been tied to a tree.

"That's far enough," Davis said. "Turn around and show me your hands." Kyle complied, bewildered at the strange sequence of events. Davis put away his pistol and unlocked the shackles which fell between their feet. "Go," he said. Kyle blinked at him in confusion. "Get on the horse, go, and never come back."

Kyle blinked again, "Why, Michael...?"

Lieutenant Davis let out a bitter laugh. "Tell your sister I accept her apology. Tell her...I am the man she thought I was. I hope that someday I can be forgiven as well. Now, go before I shoot you."

"Someone's coming," Kathryn nudged Carl from his snooze. It was a miracle. Finally, a solitary rider came down the road in the gloom.

"Okay, just like we said, I'll stop him from the front. You step behind and point the pistol at him," Carl whispered as he readied himself. He checked his revolving rifle one last time.

He waited until the rider was nearly upon them and then lurched out onto the road, seizing the reins, and leveling his rifle at the rider. The horse reared and neighed in fright. The rider clung on tightly to keep from falling.

"Make a sound and I will shoot you dead right now," Carl hissed at the man.

The rider looked at him, let out a short laugh, and said, "Well, Carl, it looks like this time, I'm your prisoner."

Chapter Fifteen: The Offensive

Captain Lathan Woods pushed his horse and his men hard along the Bardstown Pike towards Louisville. He was sure this had to be the way the fugitive, Kyle Bethune, must have run: straight into the arms of his Yankee masters. Lathan knew he couldn't keep this pace for long. The exceptional October heat and lack of drinkable water would surely kill the horses of his recently awarded company of cavalry. It would not look good for the newly breveted captain, but he had to make up for lost time. Kyle already had a head start from the night before.

Lathan could not believe the weakness and betrayal of Lieutenant Michael Davis. Why in the world would he free the man after agreeing to denounce him and testifying at his trial? What a fool! Not only did he set Kyle free, but he waited until the execution detail discovered him missing before Davis turned himself in, fully confessing his crime. Now precious time was lost. At least he'd be able to take great pleasure in watching Davis's execution, even if he was denied watching Kyle's. But Lathan was not a man to be denied anything. Kyle was out there and Lathan was the best tracker around.

"I told you not to leave Memphis," Kyle chided his sister.

"Since when have you ever been able to tell me what to do?" Kathryn replied.

"Well, it's only out of my concern for your safety," Kyle said softly as the three made their way along the Bardstown Pike. They had debated staying off the road altogether but decided to take full advantage of their head start. By now the Confederates at Bardstown would be fully aware that Kyle was not present for his appointment with the firing squad. Once the confusion settled, they would most likely organize search teams, but by then, the three friends would be hours ahead.

Carl felt his eyes growing heavy as the heat grew. His shirt was damp with sweat from where Kathryn wrapped her arms around his waist. They had been so natural with each other before, but now it was odd that Kyle was there with them. Did he know? Should he tell his friend about his affection for his sister? It seemed like now was not the time. There was so much to say, so much to talk about, but the three weary friends had been mostly silent, listening hard for the pursuit that had to be coming for them.

Kyle broke the silence again. "We have to rest the horses or we'll kill them." Carl felt a sense of relief that he didn't have to be the one to suggest it.

"But they'll find us," Kathryn said. "Surely we can rest once we're safe." Carl kept quiet. He hoped his friend would win the argument. The two horses came to a halt in the morning sun. The road was full of dust from their ride that filled Carl's mouth with even more reasons to hold his tongue. He was hot, tired, and thirsty. Kyle squinted his eyes as he looked around for possible shade and perhaps water for their horses. Kathryn sighed as she fanned herself. They seemed to be in a bowl of dust as they stood in a low part of the road between two hills. Carl couldn't imagine Bess climbing another hill in this heat. He considered getting off and walking alongside while Kathryn rode. But even the effort to get off the horse seemed exhausting.

He looked ahead at the hill before them. Was that another cloud of dust on the other side? He wondered.

"Did you hear that?" Kyle broke his thoughts. Kyle turned back to the hill behind them. Kathryn stopped fanning herself and listened.

Carl could hear it crystal clear. "Riders," he said flatly.

Riders in gray began to crest the hill behind them.

"My God, they've found us," Kathryn gasped.

Lathan called his men to a halt at the top of the hill. He could see two riders and a passenger clearly in the valley below. The one with golden hair had to be Kyle, but the other two…*are those Yankee uniform pants?* "My God, it's Cousin Carl…" he mumbled. The passenger on Carl's horse turned to look back revealing long wisps of red hair. "Well, I'll be damned…" he grinned. Lathan signaled his column of men to fan out into a line and then forward down the hill at an even trot. The fugitives spurred their tired horses forward. There was no way they'd escape him now.

"Sir," his lieutenant called out, "I think they're surrendering!"

Carl and Kyle had clearly put their hands in the air but were still moving away from Lathan's men. Kathryn waved a white handkerchief frantically over Carl's shoulder, leaning as far forward as possible.

"Halt!" Lathan sudden threw up the hand signal, "For God's sake, halt!"

Lathan's battle line stumbled to a halt as his men quickly reined in their horses. A cloud of dust rose over the next hill before them, then hundreds of Federal horsemen spilled over the top. A horse artillery crew appeared and quickly started unlimbering their six-pound gun.

"That's no patrol…" Lathan said. He was cut off by the boom and flash from the cannon. The shot slammed into the ground near him causing his horse to rear. He fought to regain control and then called out to his men, "Fall back! Fall Back!" They rode hard back up the hill while being chased by artillery rounds. Once atop, Lathan stole another look at the river of blue-clad men spilling over the other hill. The Federals were on the move in force.

Carl didn't know if he was relieved or mortified by the huge Federal force that seemed to be led by his very own regiment, the 2nd Michigan Cavalry. Soon he and his friends were surrounded by the men in blue. *What are they doing here?* he wondered. He had so been sure that they would still be back in Louisville for weeks. All he knew now was that he was in big trouble.

Captain Campbell, who now appeared to be a lieutenant colonel, sent two companies to chase after the Rebel patrol. Carl and his friends sat on their horses as Captain Newman and his entourage rode up to them. Carl slowly lowered his hands and then his head.

"Son, at the bare minimum I'm going to skin your bare behind with my belt. That is if they don't hang or shoot you for desertion first," Newman glared at him.

"Sir, I am his prisoner, or rather it is I who's the deserter," Kyle tried to deflect some of Newman's rage from Carl.

Newman's eyes snapped to Kyle and then widened with the surprise of recognition before focusing again in anger, "Kyle Bethune from school. I should have known you two would find a way to get in trouble together in this damn war."

"Sir, perhaps I could help explain…" Kathryn attempted.

"Who the hell is this?" Newman exclaimed looking at the young woman in men's clothing, "That's no boy!"

"It's my sister, Deputy…I mean Captain Newman," Kyle tried to explain.

"You and your treasonous sister are now prisoners. Sergeant!" Newman turned to Sergeant Barth, "Have these two secessionists escorted to the rear and guarded. We question them later. Carl, fall back in for now, but consider yourself under arrest. We'll deal with you later as well. If you haven't noticed, we're currently in the midst of a major offensive."

"Freemen of Kentucky!" General Braxton Bragg shouted to the overcrowded State Chambers of the

Kentucky State Capitol in Frankfort. "I present to you, His Excellency, Governor Richard Hawes!" The room exploded with applause as Hawes made his way the podium. Bragg shook his hand before sitting down to hear the speech. He waved off a concerned-looking messenger. Now was not the time. He was well aware of the Federal movement into middle Kentucky. General Polk had already withdrawn from Bardstown and was headed east towards Perryville. Bragg would soon order him north so they could combine their forces and crush the Federals, but first things first.

Now that the capital was in their control, it was time to install their Confederate Governor. Richard Hawes had already been sworn in in exile, but Bragg insisted on the full pomp and ceremony of an inauguration at Frankfort to convince the Kentuckians that the Confederacy was in charge. The men of the Bluegrass State who had failed to volunteer for the *Cause* would now be compelled by the same conscription laws that the rest of the Confederacy had to obey. The time lost for preparing for the Federal attack would be well worth it once tens of thousands of Kentuckians swelled their ranks.

"…the fixed purpose of a dominant North," Hawes spoke to the hundreds that crowded the room, spilled into the hall, and on to the Capitol steps, "to abolish slavery in the District of Columbia, to monopolize the Territories by the exclusion of slave property; to nullify the Fugitive Slave Law; to abolish slavery in the states where it existed…"

Bragg half listened as he took inventory of the situation at hand in his mind. He was certain that the

Federal column that poured into Bardstown was merely a feint. The real prize was right under his chair: Frankfort, the Capital of Kentucky. Reports were already coming in that another Federal column was headed directly their way. General Smith and General Buckner had advised postponing the inauguration until the Federal threat had been dealt with, but doing so would show fear and that would damage the confidence they had worked so hard to build in a Confederate Kentucky.

"May a kind Providence incline your minds and hearts to conciliation and peace, and the establishment of your personal and political liberties on a solid basis," Hawes finished his speech to an uproar of applause and a standing ovation. Bragg stood and applauded, trying to ignore the persistent messenger who was now shouldering his way through the crowd to get to where Bragg stood with the rest of the dignitaries.

"Sir," the young officer tried to whisper above the din, "our pickets are falling back into the city. The Federals will soon be within artillery range."

"Now's not the time to show fear in our moment of triumph. Inform our commanders to hold a defensive posture, but do not provoke a major engagement. We'll deal with the invaders in good time, but first, we have a luncheon and an inaugural ball to attend."

The young man didn't seem convinced, but scurried off to carry the message nonetheless. The thousands of citizens that poured into the capital for the inauguration must not think for a moment that

Confederates didn't have a firm grip on the state of Kentucky. Trembling before the Yankees now would certainly send the wrong message.

The dignitaries retired to the dining room of the State Capitol for a luncheon after the ceremony. Well-groomed slaves in white jackets poured tea, lemonade, and served plates of roasted chicken, ham, vegetables, and biscuits. Guests made grandiose toasts. A call came for Bragg to make one as well. Guests clanged their forks against their glasses in anticipation. Bragg smiled putting up a hand as he gathered himself and rose from his seat. "My dear friends," he started, "our victorious armies have driven the invaders from your capital and have restored civil liberty to your land." Applause swept across the tables. "But soon it will be time to yield appropriate deference to the civil authorities and defend your power and your territory with the discipline and valor for which this army has been preeminently distinguished."

The applause abruptly stopped as the booming of cannons broke the tranquility of the afternoon. A shell whistled overhead and exploded somewhere in town. A woman let out a scream. A nervous chatter broke out among the guests. Bragg stood there still holding his glass, stunned by the sudden turn of events. More Federal guns fired in the distance as guests began to rise from their seats. "Please do not fret," Bragg tried to calm the crowd. "We will deal with the Federal threat in good order, but for the time being, it's best we skedaddle…"

Without sufficient forces to make a stand at Frankfort, Bragg withdrew his troops south towards Polk and Hardee's divisions. Once combined, the Confederates would make a stand in the Battle for Kentucky to come. By nightfall, Federal general Joshua Sill's 20,000 troops poured into Frankfort. The inaugural ball was canceled.

Farther to the south, General Gilbert's III Corps was pushing the Confederates hard in what was becoming a running battle between his vanguard and the Confederate rear. They had pushed the Rebels out of Bardstown east towards Perryville. General Crittenden's II Corps was circling around from the south and General McCook's I Corps was swinging in from the north. General Buell hoped to catch the Confederates between the three prongs of his main offensive and crush them.

Carl did his best to keep his head down and stay unnoticed. It was easy. At the vanguard of Gilbert's III Corps was the newly formed 3rd Cavalry Brigade commanded by Ebenezer Gay. The 2nd Michigan rode in the lead. They pushed the rear of the fleeing Rebel army seemingly nonstop through Bardstown and then into the parched Kentucky countryside towards Perryville along the Springfield Pike. They barely took time to sleep a few hours on the ground before continuing the pursuit. Water was even more sparse than slumber. Tired and dry-mouthed, few cared to talk or pry Carl about his absence, but he still felt the resentment coming from his fellow troopers. Even Chucky seemed distant.

Carl wondered about his friends too. Where were they keeping Kyle and Kathryn? The memory of her arms wrapped around his waist was his only comfort in the cool early morning.

An eruption of cannon fire followed by a crackle of musketry snapped him out of this fantasy. Their horses reared and whinnied as shells screamed overhead and cannonballs buried themselves in the ground around them.

"Fall back! Form a line!" the call was shouted and repeated by sergeants. Carl peered ahead at the hills that stood between them and the Chaplin River. The Rebels had placed a battery and a line of muskets along the heights that overlooked the road six miles west of Perryville.

"Looks like the enemy has found a good place to make a stand," Captain Thatcher said cheerfully as he rode forward from headquarters to relay orders. "Since this is Kentucky soil, it's proper that a Kentucky regiment have the first opportunity to crush the invaders," he told the captains commanding the lead Michigan companies. "The 7th Kentucky will charge the enemy on the heights. You will dismount your companies and be ready to support them."

The 7th Kentucky rode down into the valley, spread out into a battle line, and then charged up the hill towards Rebels. They looked resplendent in their crisp new uniforms riding in tight formation. Seeing a full regimental charge was an awesome sight. The men of the 2nd Michigan unknowingly held their breath as the horsemen charged the Rebel line.

The Rebels could wait no longer. They fired their cannons packed with grapeshot and canister, spraying the Kentuckians and their mounts with iron and lead. Several of the men and their mounts tumbled back down the hill. The rest turned their horses and dashed away, losing their hats as the galloped back to safety.

A laugh broke out among some of the Michigan men watching the debacle. Carl looked at Max Bates incredulously as Bates called out to the fleeing horsemen. "You greenhorns got a little more than you bargained for, didn't ya?!"

"That's enough, Bates!" Captain Newman snapped. "We're next!"

Carl could see a ripple of fear flash across Bate's face before returning to feigned confidence. "We'll show them how it's done," Bates mumbled, clutching his Colt carbine.

The signal was passed along the ranks and soon the four lead companies of the 2nd Michigan were up and moving. The remainder stayed mounted, ready to support them. Carl crept forward in a crouch, flinching at every puff of smoke that appeared on the hill before them. The air whistled with hot lead. Shells screamed above them. Cannonballs plunged and bounded around them. A man on his periphery tumbled to the ground.

"Get down!" the command echoed along the line. Men threw themselves down and found cover. Cannonballs threw up piles of dirt. A few men started firing back at the gray-clad men on the hill. Loud booming erupted from behind. The Federal artillery had caught up and started unlimbering their guns.

"Fall back! Fall back!" the command passed along the lines.

"Come on, boys," Captain Newman called. "It's time to let our gunners do their share of the work."

The two lines of artillery traded fire with each other from opposite hills. Carl watched as a crew pulled their guns into line with horse teams, unlimbered them, rammed in charges, then ducked and plugged their ears as one of them pulled the lanyard. The gun belched out fire and smoke as it kicked back several feet with a deafening roar. Men wheeled it back in position as another man stuck a rod with an iron corkscrew at its end into the barrel to fish out leftover debris. Another man rammed in a wet swab that sizzled as he slid it out. Then another charge was rammed in before they fired the gun once more. This all took a matter of seconds. All along the line, crews performed this well-choreographed routine with seemingly automated precision.

The artillery duel raged on for hours as more of Gilbert's III Corps began to arrive and fill in the line. By mid-afternoon, two divisions began to push the Rebels off their heights and back towards Perryville. The Federal advance came to a halt within three miles of town as Rebel sharpshooters found cover behind haystacks set along a ridge, and then found targets among advancing troops. Armed with their Colt revolving carbines, several dismounted companies of the 2nd Michigan were thrown out ahead to counter the new threat.

The Michigan boys made use of the cornfields that lined either side of the road. In them, they could crouch low enough to hide from sights of the Rebel marksmen, but for Carl, not being able to see what was ahead of him was equally as terrifying. Bullets whizzed passed and fluttered leaves around him. The dense cornfield not only obscured his vision but deadened the sound, leaving him feeling closed in and isolated. He could barely detect who, if any, of his comrades were close. He kept expecting every clearing of stalks and leaves in front of him to reveal the bringer of his death.

But it wasn't his eyes that detected the new impending danger. It was his ears. It was a rumble at first. Then the ground began to shake. Then someone called out, "Horsemen!"

Carl straightened up onto his tiptoes to see them coming: a mass of men in gray, hacking their way through the corn with their sabers. "Holy shit…" he murmured. Dread poured through him, paralyzing him to the spot.

"To me!" Captain Newman broke the spell. Carl stumbled through the corn to see his fellow troopers form a line behind the wooden fence that lined the road. He turned back to see the oncoming threat crashing through the corn. Their leader, upon a powerful gray stallion, held his saber forward, driving the charge.

"Steady…" Newman hissed. Carl's stomach crawled into his mouth as the Rebel cavalry came impossibly close.

"Fire!" Newman roared and the Colt revolving rifles echoed his call. The leader of the enemy squadron tumbled from his horse as the rest of the men broke and dashed away. Several of the Michigan boys fired their remaining cylinders at the fleeing horsemen. The gray stallion remained. In the chaos the horse merely stood near his rider, nudging him with his muzzle.

"Come on," Newman urged them forward. The Confederate captain lay there among the broken stalks of corn. Blood ran from his mouth as he tried to speak. "Take it easy, buddy," Newman said, crouching, uncorking his canteen to give the man a drink.

An explosion threw up dirt nearby causing everyone to flinch and duck. Rebel artillery had found their place among the sharpshooters and started dropping shells into the cornfields below. "Bates! Secure that horse!" Newman roared. "Smith, Scott! Make a litter with his horse blanket. We'll carry him back with us!"

The Michigan troopers fled back to their lines, chased by Rebel shot and shells. Once back, Carl and Chucky carried the injured Rebel officer to a farmhouse that had been commandeered and turned into a field hospital. In the meantime, a detachment of Federal infantry and horse artillery found their way around the left flank of Confederate sharpshooters and cannons placed along the ridge. Soon their enfilading fire drove the Rebels from their heights and back into the town of Perryville.

A peace spread over the hills as the guns quieted at dusk. Carl sat alone looking at the plump orange moon as it rose full over the hills before them. The men chattered around the fires as they ate dinner. Carl had enough of the chiding from his fellow troopers. "Oh, I thought you had run off again," Bates had called out at him as they returned from delivering the Confederate officer to the surgeons. Word was he was dead now.

Carl tried to talk to Chucky, but that didn't go well either. "You lied to me," Chucky told him. Carl tried to explain that he was only trying to protect his friend from being complicit in Carl's ill-advised adventure, but his words fell flat. The sense of betrayal in Chucky's eye stung him to the core. He simply gave up trying to explain.

"We are here for Private Smith," the German-accented voice cut through soft mumbling din of the evening. Carl's blood turned to ice.

"I'm sure you are, Klaus," Newman's voice followed. "He's right over there, pouting by himself."

"*Komm*!" Klaus snapped to his two corporals. Carl turned to greet the three Germans as they marched smartly towards him.

"Private Smith, you are to come with us," Klaus said coldly. "Take this man into custody!" he barked at his corporals.

Carl smiled weakly, "Hi, Hans, Hi, Deiter."

"We don't like you," Hans replied.

"I know," Carl said.

Chapter Sixteen: Punishment

"For the last time," Kyle sighed tiredly, "I'm a deserter, but I'm not a traitor."

"You're a traitor to the US and a Rebel spy!" acting Major General Charles Gilbert blurted at the siblings sitting before him. "The only thing that can save you from the noose is what you can tell us of your forces!"

The rest of the officers in the command tent shifted uncomfortably. Some looked to General Buell to intervene. Buell merely looked on with tacit interest. He was propped up on a litter after having taken a spill from his horse earlier that day.

Kathryn was the only one to speak up. "Sir, my brother is an officer and a gentleman who should be afforded his due respect according to the proper conduct of war. He is hardly a traitor for defending his homeland from such vulgar invaders."

Gilbert's eyes nearly popped out of his head, "Who is this harpy in men's clothing?!"

"Hmph!" Kathryn let out as she began to stand. Kyle squeezed her hand, reining her back into her chair.

"You're not helping…" he whispered sharply.

A sergeant interrupted the scene, "Sir! Captain Schmidt is here."

Gilbert let out a sigh, "Send him in."

Kyle was stunned to see his erstwhile classmate enter the room wearing a crisp captain's uniform. The son of German immigrants had always been officious, but now he commanded an intimidating military air. The brass claw that had replaced his left hand made him seem more machine than man. Klaus caught his gaze with a sneer of contempt before turning his eyes to Gilbert. He snapped to attention and gave a crisp salute.

"General!" Klaus barked.

"At ease, Captain. You're making the rest of my staff look bad," Gilbert said humorlessly as he scanned the room full of officers. Several glared back at him with open contempt. Gilbert sighed, "Well…bring him in."

Klaus motioned with his claw to his entourage outside, "*Komm!*"

Hans and Dieter entered holding Carl between them. The first thing Carl's eyes found was Kathryn's red hair. Her eyes widened at the sight of him and then softened with warmth. She gave him a soft, sad smile that washed over him like a warm summer breeze. For a split moment, he felt content.

"Move forward, please!" Hans hissed at him with a shove.

Carl stumbled forward catching his balance. His hands were bound with rope before him. He caught Kyle's bitter smile. Carl smirked and shrugged his shoulders as if to say, "Well, we tried…"

"Stand at attention and wipe that grin off your face, soldier!" Gilbert's voice brought him back. "I understand you're a deserter."

"No, sir. I did leave without permission, but I came back, as I had planned. I didn't know we were going to leave Louisville so soon. I thought I had time."

"Well, by that you have just admitted to absconding," Gilbert told him. "Explain yourself."

Carl did his best to explain his friendship and his sense of duty to save his friend from a Confederate firing squad. When he finished, the entire room of officers was staring at him in disbelief.

"Well, that has to be the dumbest story I've ever heard," Gilbert broke the silence. A light chuckle passed around the room. "What can you tell us of our enemy's disposition from your…um…adventure?"

"Not much, sir," Carl said. "We met Lieutenant Bethune as he was escaping outside of Bardstown."

"Captain…" Kyle interjected softly, "It's Captain Bethune now…"

"Captain?! What the hell?!"Carl blurted at his friend in protest.

"You didn't notice the bars?" Kyle answered.

"Enough!" Gilbert erupted as he stood, "I'll hang all three of you damn impetuous kids if you don't watch your mouths!"

Kyle and Carl dropped their heads mumbling, "Sorry, sir…" Kathryn just glared, pressing her hand to her chest.

"Sergeant!" Gilbert barked. "Take these two back to their quarters while we decide whether they're prisoners or defectors, and return this sorry excuse of a soldier back to his regiment. We are on the eve of the fight for Kentucky. We'll decide what to do with him later." Gilbert then turned his focus to Carl, "In the meantime, I suggest you die in battle tomorrow. It might be best for you."

"Sir!" Klaus interrupted.

"By God, what is it, man?!" Gilbert shouted.

Klaus was unfazed by Gilbert's irritation, "This man is an admitted absconder. That is enough for at least some kind of corporal punishment. He must be made an example before the men."

Gilbert sighed. "Fine, fine," he said dismissively. "Have him bucked and gagged overnight. We'll still need him in the morning to catch cannonballs."

Kyle hissed in anguish. Having witnessed the punishment administered to wayward soldiers in his camp himself, he knew what was in store for his friend.

"What does that mean?" Kathryn whispered.

"It's not good," Kyle replied.

"Sir!" Klaus barked.

"What is it, Captain?" Gilbert asked warily.

"I would like to invite our…guests to witness punishment," Klaus lingered.

Gilbert looked at the German with a cocked eyebrow. "Yeah, um, sure…"

Klaus clicked his heels and snapped a salute, "Sir!" Then he turned on his heel and marched out with his prisoners and corporals.

After watching the small party leave, Gilbert turned back to his officers. "I know he's on our side, but that guy gives me the creeps."

Carl was marched out to the forward position held by the 2nd Michigan Cavalry. Klaus had the men who were not engaged in picket duty called to formation to witness the punishment. He then informed them that Carl, by his own admission, was guilty of absconding and was to be immediately bucked and gagged before the regiment.

"What does that even mean…?" Carl mumbled.

"Sit!" Hans barked at him. Carl sat on the ground. The two corporals pushed his knees up to his chest and then looped his bound hands over them. Then they slid a rod under his knees but over his arms before tying his hands to his shins and binding his ankles together. The result left Carl tied in a ball in which he could not stand or rollover due to the long ends of the rod. He groaned in agony at the strain on his muscles. He was just about to cry out when Dieter placed a stick across his mouth and then bound it with rope tightly around the back his head. The gag stretched his mouth back and pressed his tongue making it impossible to speak or cry out. Carl could only manage a whimper.

Klaus squatted before him and offered a rare smile. He tapped the stick in Carl's mouth with his brass claw. "You see, I promised my sister I would protect your life, but she never said anything about protecting you from pain. Perhaps if she could see you now, she would see the coward and, please correct me if I'm pronouncing this wrong, the *cur* that you are." Carl could only answer with a moan as tears rolled down his cheek.

Klaus stood up. "Here's what happens to those who abandon their friends!" he spoke to the men. "Sergeant! You may dismiss them!"

"Oh, Carl…" Kathryn said softly as Hans placed a sign around his neck that read "absconder."

233

"You've gone too far, Klaus," Kyle growled at his ex-classmate.

Klaus stopped to regard him for a moment, then offered an ironic smile, "Perhaps it is you who has overextended himself. We shall see, shortly." Then he spoke to his corporals, "See these two back to their tent. It's yet to be determined if they are spies."

Carl watched as his friend and the woman he was in love with walked away. His humiliation rivaled his pain. "I guess you won't be running off this time!" Bates said, as he blocked Carl's last glimpse of Kathryn's red hair walking away. Carl didn't bother looking up. Bates walked off. Chucky came next. Carl looked up at him. Chucky just shook his head and walked away. Carl looked back at the ground in despair. A pair of riding boots stepped before him. Captain Newman squatted down and looked at him for a moment with his dark eyes set deep behind his heavy mustache.

"For a moment, I almost thought I had made a man out of you," he said, his eyes boring holes into Carl's heart. "I've failed."

Commanding General Don Carlos Buell and his staff had ridden along with the 22,000 men of Gilbert's III Corps from Louisville to the doorstep of Perryville. It was clear that the Rebel army was done running and was now ready to make a stand. He sent dispatches to McCook's I Corps circling in from the north, and Crittenden's II Corps circling around from the south, to place themselves on either side of III Corps by three in the morning. Then at ten, the combined 55,000-man force would commence an all-out assault on the Rebels from three directions.

But when it became clear later that evening that the two corps would not be in position in time, Buell decided to postpone the attack one more day. But the tens of thousands of men clutching their guns in the darkness would not be so patient. The soldiers in both armies had been pushed hard through the drought-plagued land for days. Now there was water to be had, and they were willing to fight for it.

The boys from the 10th Indiana came down from their hilltop to fill their canteens in the pools of water that remained in the mostly dry Doctor's Creek. There they crossed paths with the boys from the 7th Arkansas who had also come down from their hill that lay on the other side of the precious water source. Soon the sound of musketry rang out in the darkness. It was two o'clock in the morning and the Battle of Perryville was on.

Carl spent the night in and out of consciousness, sometimes fainting from the agony, other times nodding off from exhaustion. In the darkness, it was hard to tell what was real. He heard voices and saw faces: Kathryn, Captain Newman, his mother, Anna, Lathan. His eyes popped open with the crackle of musketry. How far away, he couldn't tell. He couldn't make out if anyone was even around him. Had they forgotten him? He struggled to loosen his bonds, but couldn't move his body. It was numb, tickled by a thousand needles. He tried to cry out for help but his dry, gagged mouth could make no sound. He was completely powerless, alone, and terrified.

He woke again to the sound of horses. He blinked hard to clear his tear-crusted eyes. Were those his guys? Carl shook and tried to call out to them. Panic rushed through his paralyzed body. It was the 2nd Michigan Cavalry and they were heading into battle. They were leaving him behind.

The sounds of battle grew with the morning light. Kyle and Kathryn sat on their cots trying to decide what to do.

"I can't run. I've given them my word as a gentleman," Kyle told his sister.

"But if they decide you're a prisoner and not a deserter, they might return you in a prisoner exchange. You'll be back in front of a firing squad. That is if they don't hang us as spies first," Kathryn said.

"They're not going to hang us. That Gilbert's full of hot air," Kyle tried to soothe her. "A man's got to do what a man's got to do."

"Then be a man, damn it!" Kathryn blurted. Kyle blinked at her with surprise. "Kyle," she said, softening her voice and squeezing his hand, "you're going to be a father."

Kyle's eyes widened with shock, "What…?"

Kathryn sniffed and smiled as her eyes welled with tears, "I wasn't supposed to tell you. You're going to be a father. Your child deserves to know you. Liza is going to need you. None of this stupid war matters." She gestured with her arm. "Your own side turned against you. These Yankees don't care about honor. What matters is your family. What matters is your child."

The sounds of fighting increased as artillery crews began to fire upon each other. The sounds of men outside their tent became more frantic. Suddenly a soldier carrying a rifle burst into their tent. "Come on, everyone has to move back from the line. The Rebs are pushing hard."

"What about the 2nd Michigan? Aren't they holding your forward position?" Kyle asked.

"They moved forward at dawn but are pinned down now. We've got infantry moving this way to relieve them, but for the time being, we've got to move back. Reb skirmishers are pouring in on our flank," the soldier replied.

"What about the man that was bucked and gagged? Did he go with them?" Kyle asked.

"Probably not…look, I can't be answering these questions right now. We've got to move!" the man said.

"I see," Kyle said, turning his back to the man and looked at his sister.

Kathryn shrugged her shoulders and motioned with her eyes as if to say, "It's now or never."

Kyle spun around ramming his fist into the side of the man's head. The man fell to the ground dropping his rifle as he clutched the spot Kyle hit him. "Ow, fuck! Why'd ya go and do that for?" he protested.

Kyle quickly snatched up the rifle, drawing it back like a club, "I'm trying to knock you out."

"Wait! Just wait, God damn it!" the man threw his hands in the air trying to block the blow. "Stop hitting me! You're going to fucking kill me with that! Just tie me up and gag me! Jesus!"

The siblings obliged him. Kathryn squatted and lightly touched the man's swelling face. "We're truly sorry," she said. The man just rolled his eyes and said something unintelligible from his under his gag.

The world outside the tent was a whirlwind of activity as headquarter staff scurried off with whatever they could carry. Few took notice of the man in a Confederate captain's uniform and the red-headed woman dressed as a boy. "Just act like we're doing what we're supposed to," Kyle whispered.

"And just what is it that we should be doing?" Kathryn whispered back. They looked at each other and the answer was clear.

Carl tried wiggling his hands free the best he could. The bounds were so tight he could barely move them. He was sure he had been forgotten. Left alone to die, tied in a ball. He stopped wiggling for a moment to collect his thoughts. A stick broke nearby, then the sounds of soft footsteps came to his ears as bodies moved quietly through the brush.

"Well, well, well," a distinctly Southern voice made Carl's eyes pop open in terror. "What do we have here?"

Carl looked up to see a Confederate soldier in a ragged uniform standing before him. Soon several others stepped into his field of vision. They were all gaunt and hard-looking men. Carl tried to talk but only managed a panicked garble from his gag. The men laughed. "Looks like this one got left behind," another man quipped, poking him with his bayonet. The sharp point broke through Carl's paralysis that had settled in overnight.

"Leave that one alone," a strong but seemingly familiar voice broke through. "He's already captured, Sergeant. The enemy is on the run that way. Keep your skirmishers moving. We'll take care of this one."

"Yes, Captain!" the sergeant replied. Carl could hear the men moving off.

He heard one of them say, "Officers get all the damn credit for our work."

Another said, "Was that a lady with him?"

Kyle squatted and started untying Carl's gag. Kathryn worked on his bounds. "My God, Carl, are you okay?" Kyle gasped.

"Water…" Carl croaked once the gag came off. Kathryn pulled the rod that held his arms under his knees causing him to roll clumsily to his side with a painful groan. Soon, they had him completely untied. He groaned in withering agony on the ground, still unable to move his muscles.

"Come," Kathryn said to her brother. "We've got to get the blood moving back into his limbs." The two rubbed his arms and legs while Carl whimpered in pain.

"Carl, we've got to get you up and moving. We're in peril from both sides," Kyle pleaded, looking around for soldiers from either army to appear. Moments later they had him on his feet. Carl still couldn't straighten his back fully. Instead, he quivered in pain, hunched over like an old man.

"You came for me…" he croaked.

"Of course," Kyle said, "I had to even the score."

"I think you still owe me one more," Carl wheezed.

"You Yankees are never satisfied," Kyle laughed softly.

"Come on!" Kathryn hissed. "You can kiss each other later!"

The siblings helped Carl hobble along as they moved through the heavy brush. They flinched at the sounds of cannons that seemed to surround them.

"I can't even tell where the fighting is," Carl said. His muscles were starting to wake as they walked.

"It's these hills," Kyle said, "the sound is bouncing around like a tennis ball."

Carl was able to stand up straight by the time they got to the corral. It was a circle of wagons tied together to fence the horses in. Only a few horses remained. No one was in sight.

"It looks like the regiment is out in force. I don't see any guards either," Carl said.

"The guards must have fallen back in the confusion," Kyle answered. "Quick, let's find mounts and get before either side finds us,"

A large black man came screaming from behind the carts brandishing a pitchfork. The startled friends fell backward to the ground, screaming in terror as the enormous man towered over them.

Kyle was the first to recognize him, "Elijah…?"

The fury seeped from Elijah's eyes and was replaced with kind warmth.

"Master Kyle…Miss Kathryn…?" he said, lowering his pitchfork.

"You don't have to call me that anymore," Kyle said getting up and throwing his arms around the big man. "My God, it's good to see you!"

Kathryn patted the big man on his shoulder, "You're going to be an uncle, Elijah. Liza is with child."

"I'm…an…uncle…?" he stammered wide-eyed.

"Yes! It's my child…our child…heck, we're going to be family!" Kyle bubbled over.

"Come with us, Elijah. Come back to Memphis," Kathryn said.

Elijah's smile fell. He looked away at the sounds of battle. "They all left. They done run off. No one's here to look after the horses. I gotta stay. I have to watch over them."

The four stood in silence for a moment. "We understand," Kyle said at last.

"Won't you please come and visit," Kathryn looked up at him, "when you are able, of course. Liza misses you so."

"Sure, Miss Kathryn," Elijah looked shyly at the ground. The raging artillery fire grew with intensity. "Y'all need to get, quick. I can give you a horse. His feller died yesterday and his horse is yet to be given to another. I suppose a lot of fellers are going to die today. I suppose nobody will notice one horse missing." The roar of cannons continued, followed by the crackle of muskets. Smoke drifted and swirled around the friends. "Bessie's here for you too, Carl. I've got your saddle and everything."

Soon their horses were saddled and ready. Carl was relieved to find his saber still in its saddle scabbard. He had left his pistol and carbine behind when Klaus had come to arrest him. There was no telling where they were now. The booming of cannon made Carl turn his head towards the battle. Kyle, sensing his friend's thoughts, spoke up, "You're going to love Memphis, Carl. You can stay with us."

Carl turned to his friends. The answer was in his eyes, "God, I would love to…" The four were silent for a moment.

"You don't need to die here, Carl," Kyle said softly, then dropped his head.

"Who said anything about dying?" Carl said, gaining a light chuckle from his friends. "I've been… avoiding things all my life. No one takes me seriously…" He paused for a moment, "I don't know how to say it but…I can't leave. I can't run away…" he dropped his head.

Kathryn lifted it up delicately and looked into his eyes. A tear fell from one of hers, "You're the bravest man I know," she said shaking her head and smiling.

"I'm scared all the time," Carl smiled back with sadness.

"That's why you're so brave," she said and then kissed him. Elijah's eyes bulged at the two lovers. He turned to look at Kyle who merely shrugged his shoulders and then looked away as if to give the two some privacy.

"Maybe in another life," Kathryn smiled bittersweetly.

"Maybe someday in this one," Carl said.

"You've got to live then," She said, turning away.

Kyle took her arm and helped her up onto the horse he had mounted, "Stay alive, Carl. I still have one more favor to return."

"I'm satisfied. Be safe," Carl said in return.

"No promises," Kyle said with a smile and gave their horse a light kick, sending them on their way.

Carl tried to mount Bess but failed with a hiss of pain. Large hands wrapped around his waist and hoisted him up. "You take good care of her, Mr. Carl. She don't like to work too hard."

"Me either," Carl smiled at the big man. "If they break through, get somewhere safe. There's no telling what they'd do if they got you."

"I be fine," Elijah smiled back. Carl gave Bess a light kick and she began to trot towards the battlefield.

Chapter Seventeen: Into Darkness

The overnight fighting that started at Doctor's Creek continued eastward as Sheridan's division pushed the Arkansans out of the creek and then off of Peter's Hill on the other side. After several attempts to retake their position on the hill, the Arkansans fell further back into the woods on the other side of the valley below. Acting Brigadier General Gilbert sent Ebenezer Gay's 3rd Cavalry Brigade to clear the woods of the Arkansan sharpshooters who were threatening Sheridan's new position. The horsemen didn't make it far past their own pickets before the Arkansans let loose a volley, stopping them in their tracks. Gay ordered six of the 2nd Michigan companies to dismount and press forward into the woods. He hoped the volume of fire from Colt revolving carbines would be enough to counter the accuracy of the Arkansan rifles.

"Okay, boys, slow and low. Keep your eyes open for puffs of smoke. They're hiding in the trees," Newman hissed quietly to his men. Sergeant Barth squinted at the trees ahead as they made their way to the woods crouching low in the high grass.

The Arkansans revealed themselves at once with a crackle of fire and a line of smoke puffs that spread from left to right in front of the Michigan men. Several of the Michiganders fell to the ground, some already dead before they hit, others screaming and clutching their wounds.

"Take cover!" came the shout that was repeated along the line. It was a command hardly needed as men threw themselves to the ground and found protection wherever they could. Several failed to do so sufficiently, and the sharp eyes of the Arkansans made them pay by finding targets among the exposed arms and legs.

Chucky pulled the hammer back on his carbine, rotating the cylinder with a satisfying click. He sighted a gray hat peeking out from behind a tree. He pulled the trigger, and through the puff of smoke, he saw the hat come tumbling down. "I think I got one!" he yelled.

"Shut up and keep firing!" Sergeant Barth yelled back. The revolving rifles did their job, overwhelming the single-shot, muzzleloading rifles of the Arkansans. Soon the Confederates began to fall farther back into the hill behind them. The 2nd Michigan moved forward into the woods, firing and taking cover among the trees to reload their cylinders as they climbed.

Gay watched nervously from the brigade's rear position as the battalion of dismounted Michigan cavalry disappeared into the trees. He sent the 9th Pennsylvanians around the left to flank the hidden menace, but Rebel artillery had found a good elevated position to counter the Federal advance. Soon they started dropping shells and solid shot on the dismounted Pennsylvanians, sending them reeling back to the safety of their lines.

Gay then moved the rest his brigade forward to support the Michiganders, who were now completely

245

out of sight in the trees. But the Rebel artillery pounded them as soon as they tried to advance across the valley, causing a quick retreat. The 2nd Michigan was alone somewhere in those woods, and there was no way to get to them. Gay ordered his battery of Minnesotans to unlimber their brass 12-pounders and to start contesting the Rebel guns. He sent a rider back to the divisional command asking for help.

All he could do was wait for reinforcements to arrive while listening to the firefight in the woods before them. A sole rider approached. "Hopefully he's bringing news of our reinforcements," Gay said to no one in particular. The rider approached in a gallop. He was unkempt and hatless. His black wavy hair bounced with the rhythm of his horse. His green eyes were wide with fear and purpose.

"Where's the 2nd Michigan?" he gasped as he pulled his horse to halt, not bothering to salute.

"They're pinned down in those woods, Private. Who the hell are you?" an aide asked, astonished at the rider's impertinence.

"Arrest that man!" Klaus pointed at Carl with his brass claw. "He's supposed to be under punishment!"

"You left me to die, Klaus!" Carl shouted back with a fury that even surprised himself.

"Arrest him!" Klaus barked.

Two orderlies moved forward to seize Carl's reins.

"Now's not the time," Carl said kicking Bess into a run across the valley.

"Wait, you'll kill yourself!" the aide shouted. Carl rode off without looking back.

"Tell them we're sending help!" Gay shouted after him, and then mumbled to himself, "God help them…"

Klaus shook his head and gritted through his teeth, "*Dummkopf…*"

Bess galloped through the field spread out before the woods on the rise of the next hill. She avoided the craters and mangled bodies that littered the ground. Wide-eyed terror drove her forward as Confederate shot and shells tried to find their mark. The explosions and showers of dirt were deafening to the point that she could only sense the dull thud of her footfalls. Suddenly a cannonball buried itself into the ground under her feet causing her to stumble and fall. Carl instinctively leaped from the saddle and tumbled onto the ground to avoid being crushed. Bess floundered for a moment before finding her balance and getting to her feet. Carl ran to her and removed his saber from the saddle.

"Get! Hyah!" he shouted, slapping her on the rump. Bess bolted off toward safety and away from the noise. Carl watched her go and then turned and sprinted the rest of the way to the woods. He was sure one of the gunners would tag him. But he was too little of a target for the Rebel artillerymen, who had given up on the sport of the single rider to concentrate on the Federal guns that were beginning to return fire.

The dark woods brought a peaceful quiet as the colorful early October leaves blotted out much of the sun and damped the sound of battle outside. Carl leaned against a tree, catching his breath and orienting himself to his new surroundings. The crackling of musketry farther up on the hill brought him back into focus. They were up there somewhere. He pushed himself off the tree and started climbing in a crouch, finding cover as he went.

The 2nd Michigan had pushed the Rebels all the way to the top of the hill. There, the Arkansans made a stand using the brow of the hill and a fence that ran along it as cover. The Michigan men found cover below among the trees and traded shots with their enemy above.

"I'm out of ammo!" Chucky called out.

Captain Newman scoffed as he shook his head and rolled his eyes. "That's great, Chucky," he called back. "Do you got any other announcements you'd like to make to the enemy?" A round of chuckles came from the men.

Newman cocked an eyebrow as he detected some of the laughs came from the hilltop as well.

"Hey, Billy Yank!" a voice came from above. "You can have some of ours!" Newman instinctively cringed behind his tree as the Confederates let loose another volley. The Minié balls pelted the tree and ground around him. He was beginning to worry. They wouldn't hold out much longer if they didn't get help soon.

His hopes rose as he saw a figure climbing towards them, but soon sank as he realized it was a solitary, disheveled-looking soldier with no hat or jacket. The man was carrying only a sword. Then, he recognized him with stunned disbelief.

"Good God, Smith! What the hell are you doing here?!" he gaped.

"I got free…I came to help," Carl gasped for breath.

Newman shook his head, "With that?" He pointed to Carl's saber. "Where're your guns?"

"I don't know…sir…"

Newman looked at him incredulously for a moment, then broke into a laugh, "My God, son, you have to be the dumbest kid I know! At least you're here in time to die with the rest of us. Are there any reinforcements coming?"

"I think I heard of some…but I had to run to keep from being arrested. The Rebels are blasting away at the valley blocking any advance, sir. I think we're bringing up our own guns now to clear the way."

"I see," Newman said grimly. "Boys, our only chance is to overwhelm them with a charge before we completely run out of ammo. Otherwise, they'll just wait till we stop shooting and charge us. We'll wait until they give us a good solid volley. It'll then take them a moment to reload their muskets, that'll be our window. Be ready and look to your buddy…even if it's Bates," a low chuckle spread among the men. Newman looked at their grim determined faces. A bitter-sweet smile formed under his mustache. "I'm not asking you to fight for your country, the Union, or whatever fool reason you signed up for…you need to fight for that man next to you because he's the only one who can carry you through." The men looked at him silently.

Newman dropped and shook his head with a scoff. He looked back up at them. "It was my hope to bring each and every one of you home safely. I dreamt of marching you through the streets of Detroit in triumph. Well…we might not get the chance, but perhaps our souls will. When they write up the official report of our actions here…let it be known that the boys of Company H…the 2nd Michigan stood up, fought like fiends, and bled our cold Michigan blood all over this God-forsaken hill."

The men, wide-eyed in anticipation, nodded, some patting the shoulder of their neighbor. Newman beamed with pride, "Who knows, maybe some fool will write a book about us someday. Regardless, I'm proud of every one of you. It's been an honor to serve with you." The men nodded, murmuring in agreement.

"Okay, get ready. Pass it along the line, hopefully the boys in the other companies will follow. I think some of them have already lost their captains."

The men waited in anticipation for an organized volley to come from above. The Arkansans only obliged with occasional potshots. Newman started to worry that the full volley he needed would never come. That's when, much to his surprise, Bates stood up, put his hand to his mouth and yelled, "So are you guys just cousin-fuckers…or do you fancy your mothers too?!"

Newman's eyes bulged with shock at Bate's audacity. Bates dropped to the ground. A torrent of lead came pouring down upon them as the men cringed behind their cover. Newman shouted, "Now!" Like a wave spreading out along either side of the line, the men of the 2nd Michigan jumped to their feet, and then screaming like banshees, charged the men behind the fence. The Arkansans, having just unloaded their guns, could do nothing more than fall back down the other side of the hill.

The Michiganders who still had ammo fired into the backs of the fleeing Rebels as they overtook the fence and crested the hill. Carl ran along with his saber held forward feeling somewhat foolish. The sprint up the hill weighed heavily on his legs that so recently spent the night tied in a ball.

The charge came to a stumbling halt as the men came over the top of the hill only to find the Arkansans had reformed into a line with their muskets at the ready.

"Get down!" Newman screamed. The Arkansans unleashed a volley of hot lead as the Michigan men threw themselves to the ground. Some of the companies had already started to retreat.

"Fix bayonets!" a distinctly Southern voice roared over the din. A rattle of clicks spread out along their line.

Newman spat out the leaves that found their way to his mouth and clung to his mustache as he looked up from his prone position. "Fuck! Fall back! Fall Back!" He yelled as he sprang to his feet and fired the last of his pistol into the Rebel line.

The Rebels gave off a high shrill yell that made the hair on the back of Carl's neck stand on end. He struggled to get up onto his heavy legs as the men around him scattered back over the hill. The sounds of artillery intensified as shot and shell began to descend around them, adding to the confusion.

The gray line of men approaching was a blur as his sore and weary arm lifted his saber to defend himself. It was knocked away easily, the shock of it hurting his arm. Carl looked up just in time to see the fury on the face of an Arkansas man as he thrust his bayonet forward.

Sharp pain seared the blurriness from his eyes. Carl clutched the barrel of the man's rifle. He crumbled to the ground, trying to pull out the bayonet that was now stuck in his hip bone. The Rebel soldier obliged by sticking his dirty barefoot on Carl's chest and yanking the gun free.

Carl howled in pain. He could see through his now tear-blurred eyes the man drawing his musket back to stick him again. With one hand on his wound, Carl reached out with his other to stop the blow. "No, please…" he whimpered.

The fury on the man's face changed to horror as he looked up from Carl's pleas. In a blurry flash of steel, the man's head came tumbling to the ground. His headless body fell on top of Carl and started dousing him with blood and gore.

A riding boot kicked the corpse off of him. Carl saw a gloved hand wipe a saber off on the dead man's ragged uniform before hearing it slide into the sheath. The man squatted down next to him, grabbing Carl by the collar and lifting him high enough to swing his other arm under Carl's shoulder. Carl felt the cold brass claw pressing against his skin.

"Get up!" Klaus barked at him.

"You came for me…" Carl said softly.

"I keep my oaths," Klaus said flatly as he got Carl up onto his one good leg, propping him up with his shoulders. Then it came in a blur. Carl saw the bounding ball, skipping along the ground towards, and then past them, spraying them with a mist of blood. Carl looked down to find the source of the blood. Klaus was missing the lower part of his left leg.

Klaus didn't seem to realize it at first, only wavering with surprise as they teetered and fell over.

"Gaaaaaaaaaaaa…!!!" Klaus reeled in agony, clutching at his bleeding stump.

"Klaus! Oh, my God! Your leg! Are you okay?!" Carl screamed clutching his own wound.

"Shut up, you idiot!" Klaus screamed. "You must tie my leg off, quickly!" he said, then screamed as he arched his back in searing pain.

Carl frantically pulled Klaus's belt off of him, freeing the holster and pouches that were strapped to it before cinching it tight around the end of his bloody stump.

"Look out!" Klaus screamed.

Carl pulled the pistol from Klaus's holster, turned and shot. A butternut-clad man dropped his bayonet and fell on top of them, hitting Carl in the head with his own. Carl tried to blink away the stunning blow. More men were coming. They were nearly upon them when an exploding shell tore them to shreds, adding them to the pile of men.

Carl blinked as fresh blood dripped down into his eyes from the dying men above. He felt more bodies fall onto the pile with a thud. The sounds of battle raged on but became more muffled as the bodies blocked out sound and light. He started to panic. He couldn't move from the weight on top of him. He struggled for air. He couldn't see. The world started spinning. The sounds became dimmer. He was now falling, falling deeper into blackness, and then there was nothing.

What started as a retreat turned into an all-out run for their lives as the 2nd Michigan dashed down the hill, some carrying wounded men, some losing their balance and tumbling down the slope. The panic soon turned into exhilaration as below them came into view, hundreds of men in blue climbing towards them. The 2nd Missouri and the 44th Illinois Infantry regiments had arrived.

Newman panted heavily as he entered their lines. Captain Barrows's arm was wrapped over his shoulder as he helped him make the retreat with a wounded leg.

"You've done enough for this morning, boys," an officer called to them. "Get yourselves to the rear."

This new threat convinced the stubborn Rebels to abandon the hill. Soon the fighting in front of III Corps, which held the center of the overall Federal force, tapered off as the Rebels fell back. Having orders to not provoke a major engagement until the next day, acting Major General Gilbert pulled his men back to their position on Peter's Hill. Then he traveled even farther to the rear himself to have lunch with his commanding general, Don Carlos Buell.

But the Rebels weren't on Buell's schedule, nor were they done fighting for the day. The Confederates found the Federals' extreme left flank, miles to the north. They started throwing regiment after regiment at it, hoping to roll up the entire Yankee line. At first, McCook's I Corps' big guns held off the attacks, littering the hillsides with Rebel corpses. But the Rebels persisted, pouring most of their troops at the Yankees' far left. By mid-afternoon, the men of I Corps were getting desperate. They looked over the horizon, waiting for the reinforcements that had yet to arrive. The Rebels were pushing in their flanks and soon they'd be crushed if help didn't come soon. McCook sent a messenger to Buell to plea for assistance.

Having postponed the attack until the next day, Buell and Gilbert were enjoying a delightful lunch. Buell hoped the one day delay would also give him some time to heal from his fall. The home he had chosen for his headquarters sat in a peaceful valley. It was easy to forget the hot action that occurred just earlier that morning that was due to General Sheridan getting a little too feisty for his own good. Now, only the occasional booming of the big guns some three miles away penetrated their otherwise calm pastoral setting.

Buell let out a sigh as another boom distracted him from the conversation. "I really wish they'd save their powder for tomorrow," he lamented.

"A cock-measuring contest for sure among artillerymen, sir. Do you want me to ride out there and hush them?" Gilbert asked. He wanted nothing more than to please his commander who had ignored the fact that he had only recently been a captain. Now he was an acting major general in command of a corps. Gilbert desperately wanted to prove that his rise in rank was well warranted.

"No, no, please stay…eat! But send a messenger to find out the meaning of this and to tell them to stop unless there's something going on that we should know about," Buell said lightly.

"I hardly think so, sir. Not after the trouncing we gave them this morning," Gilbert chuckled.

Buell endured the annoyance of the distant booming for the next two hours as he tried to make himself comfortable on his cot and get some reading done. Once again, his peace was interrupted as a rider came barreling in, his horse lathered with sweat. Buell sat up with some effort, "For God's sakes, what is it now?"

The officer blinked for a moment, surprised by Buell's reception. He saluted and spoke breathlessly, "Sir, General McCook pleads for assistance in the strongest terms! I Corps is on the verge of collapsing!"

"What?! We're not supposed to attack until tomorrow! Those were my orders!" Buell exclaimed.

"Sir…" the man looked at him in confusion, "the Rebels have been attacking us in force. We've been fighting all day. Couldn't you hear?"

Buell was silent for a moment. The blood drained from his face. "My God…"

Help finally did come as Buell ordered units from III Corps in the center to shift to the left and relieve the thoroughly battered I Corps. Still, the Rebels fought ferociously well into the evening. Finally, badly bruised themselves, the Confederates withdrew from the stalemate and settled into town. Skirmishes still lingered in the streets until the Federals also pulled back after a punishing day of combat.

Realizing that only about a third of his army had been engaged that day, Buell decided to send his two relatively fresh corps into town at daybreak to finish off what remained of the Rebel army.

The Federals crept into Perryville in the early morning light, waiting for the first shots to come from the hidden Rebel force. Those shots never came. Soon it was quite apparent, the Confederates had slipped away in the night.

Chapter Eighteen: Home

Elijah was sick with worry. From the sound of it, hell itself had opened up somewhere over the hill to the east and Carl and Bess had ridden straight into it. The heavy cannons shook the ground all morning. Elijah tried to sooth the few horses left in the corral. Then the brigade returned. Several of the men were leading riderless horses. He looked for familiar faces among the worn and dispirited men. Soon he started seeing the soldiers from the 2nd Michigan Regiment. They looked a lot worse than the others. Elijah asked about Carl as the dusty dead-eyed men passed by. Most of them ignored him or mumbled, "I don't know…"

The fighting to his immediate front faded as Elijah kept himself busy tending to the weary and hungry horses. He looked up at every approaching rider, hoping it'd be Carl. The fighting kicked back up to the north by mid-afternoon and raged on for the rest of the day into the evening. Eventually, that too died off and still no Carl.

The rest of the contrabands left for the evening. Elijah stayed. He ate dinner with the horses and then crawled into his little spot under one of the carts which he had made into a little home during the campaign. He slept little, and when he did sleep he was running, running from the gray horsemen, running from their clean-shaven, cruel leader with the green eyes. "Lathan" Elijah's friends called him. Elijah's legs were thick and could barely move as he tried to run. The sound of horses and Lathan's laughing followed him. Elijah fell to the ground and struggled to get up. He could hear the horse nicker and paw the ground.

He opened his eyes. He heard the horse again. It was not in the corral. Elijah sat up, bumping his head on the cart. "Ow…" he hissed, mad at himself for having done it again. Then he saw the legs on the other side of the cart. A hoof impatiently pawed the ground. "Bess?"

Bess backed away as Elijah crawled out from under his cart. She still had her saddle on. She had strips of dried blood covered in dust on her flanks. "Come here, Bessie," Elijah tried to grab her reins. She jolted back a few steps. "Come on, girl," he whispered to her. Bess turned and walked away. Elijah followed her.

Carl was pretty sure he was dead. Somewhere in the darkness, he became conscious. He had no body. There was no light. There was no sound. *So this is death*, he thought. He wondered what he was going to think about for the rest of eternity. Then it occurred to him that he could smell. He smelled blood and body odor. He struggled for breath and fought the urge to vomit. Waves of nausea washed over him. He fought to free himself with wild panic, then fainted.

He woke again. He felt the pressure on his chest lifting away. Then a blinding light broke through the darkness, searing his eyes. *The angels have come for me*, he thought. Cool morning air rushed over his blood-crusted face. The angel's face moved in front of the light. "Anna…" he gasped weakly. Two large black hands reached down and pulled him from his dark pit.

He groaned in agony as the large hands placed him over the back of a horse.

"Don't worry, Carl. I got you," a deep baritone voice assured him. Carl began to cry. His body ached with each shuddering sob. "Take it easy, you safe now," the voice said. Then another body was slumped over the horse next to him. It was Klaus, yet his harsh demeanor was gone. As his head bumped with the gait of the horse, Klaus no longer looked like the terrifyingly furious warrior Carl had known. He looked more like a slumbering blond-headed, child. Carl slipped back into unconsciousness.

The days, perhaps weeks that followed were a blur in which Carl could not discern reality from dreams. He remembered screaming as nurses held him down during surgery. He saw faces, many faces. Some sat next to his bed, like Captain Newman, Chucky; some crept up on him in the night. *How did Lathan get in here?* he wondered. Kathryn crawled on top of him. He longed for her. She was gone.

He heard Captain Newman speaking, "Is there anything you can do for him?"

"He's survived the surgery all right, but he's succumbing to fever. Best send him home and let him die there," another voice answered.

Carl was being loaded onto a train. Elijah's face was there, wiping the sweat from his brow.

"No negroes in the hospital car," a harsh voice broke the moment of peace. Elijah was gone. The train was moving.

Elijah was back again, carrying him. "Where are we?" Carl groaned.

"Oh, you alive," Elijah's deep voice was soothing. Carl could feel it reverberate in his chest as he carried him. "We changing trains. You be home soon." Elijah was gone. Carl woke. He lay there rocking with the motion of the train. He leaned over and vomited. Nothing came out. The retching sent waves of pain through his body. He fainted.

They were lifting him. The air was cold. "Careful with him."

Was that Anna?

"Good God, does he stink!" Francis's voice broke through the haze.

"I tried to keep him clean, sir, when they let me," Elijah's voice answered.

"Who are you?" Francis responded. Carl slipped back into darkness.

The air was cold. The bed felt familiar. A woman dressed in black sat at the edge. "Mom?" Carl said wiping the sleep from his eyes.

"I am here, my child," Claudette said, wiping a tear from hers.

"This is the first time you've spoken to me since the duel…you didn't say goodbye, you didn't write…why, mom?" Carl said, feeling his own tears brimming in his eyes.

"Oh, child," Claudette let out with a sob and then composed herself, "because I couldn't bear the pain of losing you like I did your father." She gripped his hand, looking down at it and then back up at him. Her large blues eyes contrasting wildly with her gray-streaked black hair. "I have lived my life waiting for the angels to take me to him," she shuddered and then dropped her face into her hands and gave herself over her tears.

Carl sat up in the bed, watching uncomfortably as his mother cried. He put his arm around her. She collapsed into his chest, "Oh child, I love you so…" she sobbed.

"Then, please, tell me the truth, Mom…am I black?"

Claudette stopped sobbing. She lifted herself from his chest to regard him for a moment seriously before bursting into laughter. "Oh, my sweet child! You're so silly. Where in the world did you get that?"

"I've had a lot of people question my breeding," Carl said, wiping his own tears away, "I've been through so much, Mother. I deserve to know." His mother's smile was like a beam of sunshine after years of rain. She had never looked so beautiful to him in his life.

"Your father was not black, child," she patted his hands and smiled warmly, "although, I certainly would not have been ashamed of that." Carl blinked at her blankly. "Ah, if you would have known my sweet Alexandre back in France," she swooned, "I still have some of his writing. If you had studied your French better you could read his "Three Muske…"

"Mother, please…"

Claudette stopped her reverie and turned to him. She looked up at the ceiling as if seeing an imaginary person there and smiled, "Your father was the son of an hidalgo of Spain and an Aztec princess, but he proudly called himself Mexican."

"What…?"

"David, or Diego really, was a beautiful man, just like you, my child. He was a brave and dashing swordsman who fought for love, honor, and his country…"

"Country? You mean he…"

"Yes, my love," she squeezed his hands, "my sweet Diego, died defending his beloved Mêxico from the American invaders."

Carl stared at his mother with his mouth open. "Is that his sword on the wall, then?" he finally managed.

"Oh, *mon Dieu*, no," she laughed, "I took it off a dead soldier…I've kept it to remind me of what I had to…listen, now's not the time. You must rest, we'll have plenty of time to talk now that you're home safe."

"But, Mom…?" Carl whined. A knock came from the door. Claudette's eyes brightened with delight, "Oh, I think you have some visitors, and one is a very pretty young lady, I must say!"

"By the angels above, he lives!" Francis exclaimed as he burst into the room with his top hat and jacket cradled in his arm. Anna and a very self-conscious looking Elijah followed. Carl knew Elijah was a big man, but it occurred to him he had never seen him indoors other than a stable. Now he seemed to fill the room with his size as he clutched his cap with both hands and walked sheepishly behind the ever exuberant Francis. "We thought we'd never see that handsome face of yours again," Francis pinched Carl's cheek and gave it a wiggle.

"Stop it already!" Carl shoed his hand away, "I've been up for five minutes and you're already exhausting me."

"We brought you some soup," Anna stepped out from behind Francis. She had a small crock in her hands. Carl stared at her, stunned. Anna let out a nervous giggle, "…Ah, what is it?"

Carl couldn't believe his eyes. In the year he had been gone, the cute chubby girl had grown and blossomed into a beautiful woman who still held on to her excruciatingly thick curves. Her gray-blue eyes fluttered as she let out another nervous giggle.

"…Umm, nothing…ah…thanks!" Carl replied drawing the covers around his growing arousal. "Sorry, I'm still trying to get my head together. How did I get here?" Carl asked as his mom took the crock and the visitors' coats and hats.

"This big galoot carried you all the way home, it seems," Francis had to reach up to pat Elijah on the shoulder. Elijah dropped his head in embarrassed humility.

"You came for me, Elijah. You pulled me from that pile," Carl said with reverence.

"You came for me, sir…I mean Mr…Um…Carl… and you didn't even know me," Elijah said.

"I know you now," Carl said with conviction. "I know you to be a friend." Elijah smiled and looked back down at his hands, not quite sure what to do with them now that Claudette had taken his cap.

"This big fool was sleeping outside of your house," Francis broke the moment.

"I tried to get him to stay inside," Claudette said from outside the room, throwing away the pretense of not listening in.

"She did, she did…" Elijah was quick to defend her, "It just didn't seem…proper."

"Well, he's staying with my family since apparently, he's too good to stay with white people!" Francis chimed in.

"That's not it at all…!" Elijah protested, "It's… I…"

Francis cut him off, "My man, I'm joking! You're going to have to get accustomed to Yankee humor."

"Well, I suppose," Elijah said sheepishly, first looking at the floor and then back up at his new friends with a boyish smile.

The friends chatted for a bit. There was so much to say and so much to tell, but after an hour, Carl was showing signs of fatigue. "Well, we best get going and leave you to your rest," Francis said giving Elijah a look beckoning him to follow.

"We come check on you tomorrow, Carl," Elijah said. The two men left, but to Carl's delight, Anna stayed.

"I'll heat up the soup," Claudette said, moving toward the kitchen.

"Let me check the bandages," Anna said, sitting down on the bed and gently moving the covers aside. Carl immediately clutched the blankets to his lap, terrified that the sudden surge of arousal would be detected. "It's okay, I'm just looking at your wound," she giggled, moving the blankets just enough to reveal bandage. Carl hissed as she removed the gauze that was stuck to his skin. "I think its proper color is returning," she called out to his mom.

"Wonderful, child! His fever seems to have broken, too," Claudette returned with the soup, bread, and a little bit of wine. The smell filled the room making Carl realize he was famished. Soon, he was full with his wound clean and bandaged once again. His mother gave him a spoonful of laudanum to calm the wound's agitation from the cleaning. That, combined with the wine, and his full belly weighed heavily on his brow as Anna read the paper to him. Don Carlos Buell had been fired for failing to destroy the Rebel army at Perryville and allowing them to slip back into the mountains of East Tennessee. Now, there were many calling for the removal of General George McClellan in the east as well. McClellan had also allowed Lee's army to escape back into Virginia after a punishing battle at Antietam. Now, it seemed he had very little interest in pursuing them.

"I'm just going to close my eyes for a minute while you read," Carl said.

"Of course, sleep, Carl," she soothed.

His feet were stuck in the mud. They were coming. As he sloshed forward, his feet sunk farther into the quagmire. He could hear their high-shrill yell. He opened his eyes. Anna was sleeping in the chair next to him. The newspaper held loosely in her lap. A line of drool hung from her full bottom lip and pooled onto her bosom. She was snoring softly.

Carl shifted and hissed in pain. His pelvis was on fire. He let out a groan. Anna opened her eyes, slowly at first and then wide. She wiped away the drool with her sleeve. "Oh, Carl! Are you okay?"

"Ahhgg…yes, it just hurts when I move," he groaned.

"Here," she got up, wiping her mouth again and straightening her dress. She went out of the room and came back in with a glass bottle and spoon. Carl gagged as he forced down the bitter laudanum. Anna handed him his cup that still had some wine in it to wash it down. He plopped his head back on his pillow and sighed. She lightly stroked his hair.

"I'm surprised you're still here," he said softly.

"I know, I fell asleep. My father's going to kill me. I should go." She made to get up. Carl reached out and grabbed her wrist.

"No, please, stay with me," he said softly. Anna bit her lower lip looking at the dark street outside the window. There was just enough moonlight to make her large, light-blue eyes sparkle in the gloom. "It's cold out there…and Detroit is no place for a young lady to walk at night." Anna looked back at him, now really pulling on her bottom lip with her top teeth. Her blond hair was now falling out of her bun and onto her shoulders in platinum locks. In that moment, Carl was sure he had never seen anything so beautiful.

"Look," he said, trying to sit up and then hissing in pain, "it'll be fine. My mom will vouch for you. You fell asleep and it was too late to go home."

Anna looked back out the window, then sighed, slumping back into herself. "Okay," she said softly.

"Here, lay next to me. I promise, I won't do anything." Carl reached out to her, "Honestly, I don't think I can anyway."

She allowed a smile at that and then rolled her eyes, "Okay."

Carl couldn't believe his luck as she lay down next to him. Her thick and firm body pressed against him radiated heat in the cold room. Carl suddenly felt awkward in the darkness. With some effort, he turned to his side and put his arm around her. She turned as well, snuggling closer into him, pressing her rear into the arousal he no longer could hide. Embarrassed, he waited for her to react. When she didn't, he lay there wide-eyed staring into the gloom, not knowing what to say, if anything. Suddenly it hit him.

"Your brother…" he whispered.

"He lives," she whispered back. Carl let out a sigh. "He says you saved him," she continued.

"Well, he was in the act of saving me when he was hit," Carl added.

"He said that too," she replied.

"Of course he did," Carl grunted. Anna smiled softly in the darkness and then snuggled closer into him. Soon she was breathing softly in her slumber. Having her pressed so closely to his arousal was excruciating for Carl. He thought he would burst at any moment. He tried to think of anything else: Klaus, Lathan, the pile of ruined men on top of him. The laudanum started soothing his thoughts. He saw her. Saw her red hair spilled out onto the men's clothing she wore. He wanted her to look back at him one more time as the horse carried her and Kyle away into darkness.

He saw him in the early gray light emanating from the window, an older man in a foreign-looking uniform. He was bald on top with gray hair that circled around his head and then protruded into large, bushy mutton chops that connected through a broad mustache. He held a coffee cup and a saucer daintily in his hand as he sat erect in a chair at the foot of the bed.

Carl blinked to clear his eyes. The drugs and fever gave him vivid dreams, but this seemed so real. Anna lay next to him, still in her dress, snoring softly. Carl looked back at the strange man who seemed to be whispering to someone, twinkling his eyes in delight. Carl lifted his head to see his mother in a chair next to him. She was also sipping coffee from a cup using the saucer as a shield against anything that might drip onto her black dress. Her eyes popped open when they met Carl's. She nudged the old man. "He's up…" she whispered.

"Oh…!" the man whispered back, then looked for a place to set his cup and saucer before deciding to set them on the floor beside him. He cleared his throat as he stood, pulled out an old muzzle-loading pistol and pointed it at Carl, pulling back the hammer with a loud click.

"How dare you defile my daughter!" he bellowed.

"Papa!" Anna exclaimed.

"Mr. Schmidt!" Carl yelped as he bolted upright, clutching his blankets to his crotch then hissing in pain.

Anna instinctively wrapped her arm around him, shielding him from her father's wrath. Mr. Schmidt quickly raised the barrel of his gun towards the ceiling, away from his daughter.

Claudette gently set her cup and saucer down on the ground before standing up. She clutched Mr. Schmidt's sleeve, "Please, do not shoot my son, Monsieur. He'll make it right, won't you, child?" The last bit she said as she turned to look at her son.

"Um…yeah…whatever I need to do…" Carl mumbled, trying to piece together what was happening.

"Are you then agreeing to marry my daughter?" Mr. Schmidt cocked a stern eyebrow at him.

"…Umm…" Carl hesitated for a moment. He looked at Anna whose big imploring blue eyes seemed to be just at the point of boiling over with tears. In this moment, he realized he could never bring himself to do anything to hurt her. "Yeah, of course…"

"Excellent!" Mr. Schmidt let out, the twinkle returning to his eyes. "I'll start making arrangements!" He smiled as he returned the pistol to his belt. The hammer fell with a loud clink. "Oops!" his eyes bulged comically.

Claudette was quick with a distraction, "Here, you must give her a ring." She handed him a gold ring with a simple diamond.

Carl looked at it for a moment, "Where'd you get this?"

Claudette looked to Mr. Schmidt and then back to Carl, "I've had it for a while…I've been saving it for you, my love."

"…and you just happened to have it with you now," Carl cocked an eyebrow at her.

"Go on! Give it to her! Ask her to marry you, child!" Carl paused for a moment, to give his mother a scrutinizing look before turning to Anna. Her eyes were wide, brimming with tears.

"Anna, will you marry me?" he said.

"Of course!" she threw her arms around him and now the tears came. Carl felt them hot on his neck. He held her as she shuddered while he grimaced in pain.

Chapter Nineteen: Two Ceremonies

Carl couldn't decide if it seemed like time was flying by or if his wedding had been suspiciously prearranged. Either way, the day was upon him. Mr. Schmidt had told him and his mother that he had pressing family matters in what he called "the Fatherland" and that was the reason he was in such a hurry to see his only daughter safely wed before he made the transatlantic trip. "You might want to learn some German, Carl," he said with a twinkle in his eye, "our family's fortunes are changing quickly over there."

Carl was surprised how quickly the warm and likable Mr. Schmidt had considered him and his mother family. Of course, he had to convert to Lutheranism in order to marry at the little Mariner's Church on the river that the congregation had recently purchased. "You should convert too, Mom. Maybe the Lutherans will be more accepting of your witchcraft than the Catholics," Carl taunted her on their way to the church.

Claudette held up her hand menacingly, "Do not think you are too old for me to hit you, child."

Carl was able to walk with the help of a cane. At first, he found it embarrassing, but quickly learned it was a badge of honor, marking him as a veteran and a war hero. Everybody seemed to want to buy him dinner or at least a drink. Politicians and recruiters wanted him to speak at rallies. Carl was enjoying the newfound celebrity. He hoped it would help him when he returned to school after Christmas and in his career thereafter.

    The candles did their best to add to the gloomy gray light that seeped in through the windows from the overcast skies. The organ played softly as the mostly German congregation chatted lightly in their native language. Francis, Carl's best man, beckoned him forward impatiently to stand with him at the altar. Elijah was sitting alone in the last pew among the German immigrants who tried to politely pretend they didn't notice his enormous presence. Claudette went to him and bade him to sit with her in the front pew. They were the only two in the audience representing Carl's family.

    "You'll be late to your own funeral," Francis hissed at him under his breath.

    "I sure hope so," Carl whispered back, taking his place at the altar.

    The music paused and the congregation began to hush. The doors opened with a whoosh of cold air that flickered the candles. Mr. Schmidt stood proudly in his Prussian uniform. Anna stood beside him in a white dress. A veil covered her face. A moment of silence persisted and then the organ began to play Wagner's Wedding Chorus. Everyone stood. Carl swallowed hard as the father and daughter walked stately to the altar. Mr. Schmidt removed her veil once they arrived. She was more beautiful than Carl could've imagined.

    "*Bitte setzen Sie sich,*" the pastor said. Everyone sat down.

Wait…is this going to be in German?! Carl wondered, suddenly feeling a wave of panic as the pastor continued in the forein language. He eventually began to feel at ease, even bored as the pastor droned on until the homily abruptly stopped.

The doors opened and a gust of wind carried dead leaves into the sanctuary. They swirled lightly above the heads of the guests. The guests started turning towards the door, some gasping at the figure that entered. The man wore an immaculate US officer's uniform with polished brass buttons. He removed his hat with his right hand and tucked it under his left arm which ended in a brass claw that he held tightly to his chest. He clanked the floor with his prosthetic brass leg as he marched stiffly down the aisle, his face stern and impassive. Carl was sure his nightmare was complete.

Klaus stopped just before the altar, glaring at Carl, then turned his gaze to the people in the left front pew. They immediately scooted over, making room for the terrifying man.

"Please continue," Klaus said, sitting down, "*weiter, bitte.*"

It was clear that the Schmidts' had money from the size of their home and reception they held in their ballroom. Carl wondered if much of it came from Europe, where Mr. Schmidt was eager to return for what he would only call "family business." The party was warm and splendid with plenty of food and wine for the guests. A string quartet played waltzes and even a few polkas which drew many of the Germans to the dance floor.

Carl wanted to talk to Klaus. He wanted to make amends but every time he approached him, Klaus was speaking German to his friends, ignoring Carl's advances the best he could. Finally, Carl caught him momentarily alone and took his opportunity. "I hope that we can be friends now, Klaus," he told him.

Klaus looked to him, knowing he could no longer pretend to not notice him.

"Do not make this any more difficult for me than it has to be," he said, then turned and raised his eyebrows in recognition of one of his friends, smiled and walked off to greet him, his false leg clanking on the marble as he went. Carl was left standing alone.

"Don't worry, my son is a dick," Carl heard Mr. Schmidt's voice behind him. Carl turned to face him. "Just not the kind that makes babies!" the old man bellowed with a laugh poking Carl in the gut. "Klaus would rather make war and lose body parts. I might have to depend on you to give me my grandchildren."

"Um...yeah," Carl offered, not quite sure if he were comfortable talking about the subject with Anna's father.

"Give them to me quick, Carl. Much is riding on my line producing heirs," he said, this time a bit more seriously before walking off to greet his wife who was now making her entrance. She looked a lot like Anna, but of course older and quite a bit plumper. Anna was with her. Anna took her place at the piano and her mother started to sing. It was a beautiful song, although Carl understood none of it as it was in German. It was obvious that Mrs. Schmidt had a trained voice that would not be out of place on an opera stage. Carl sipped his wine and listened, watching his new wife play the piano with dutiful modesty.

Elijah and Francis approached him after the applause. Both of them were bubbling with excitement. "What are you two fiends grinning about?" he asked.

"I got a letter from Liza. She had a baby boy. I'm an uncle!" Elijah beamed.

"That's excellent, Elijah. Did…um…Kyle and…ah…Kathryn make it back to Memphis?" Carl tried his best to say her name without sounding too interested.

"They sho' did! We going down there to see 'em!" Elijah said with boyish excitement.

"We…? Are you going too, Francis?" Carl asked.

"Sure, why not?" Francis smiled, "I need to see what all this fuss is about the South!"

Carl blinked at his friend for a moment, reading him.

"What is it?" Francis asked, reading Carl himself and feigning ignorance.

"Don't be a fool, Francis. This is not a game. That war is a human meat grinder. Please, for me, stay out of it."

"Look," Francis put his hands on Carl's shoulders. "You once said it was not your fight. You were right. Now Lincoln is talking about declaring all slaves in the rebellious states free at the start of the year. Don't you see? This is our fight, Elijah's and mine. You got to have your glory. Now it's time for us to carry on the fight."

"Francis, I forbid you to go," Carl said.

"Why, because you're my master?" Francis stood, blinking at him.

"Francis, please. You know I didn't mean it that way. Look, I'm sorry," Carl said.

Francis's eyes softened, "I'm sorry too. I just get so worked up over this. Look, you've got to let a man make his own decisions. Isn't that what freedom is?"

"Honestly, I wouldn't know," Carl said.

Francis burst into laughter, "Ha, I think there may be some truth to that!"

"Francis, do what you feel like you need to do, but please be careful. If something were to happen…I would never forgive myself for not stopping you when I could."

"Don't worry, Carl," Elijah said. "I'll look after him."

"Pffft!" Carl scoffed, "I worry more about you, you big ox!"

A solemn snare drum rhythm accompanied Lieutenant Michael Davis as he marched from the Murfreesboro jail to the parade field where a brigade of men stood in formation. He was jacketless but surprisingly comfortable in the damp but balmy mid-December air. His security detail halted at the stake set in the center of the formation. He stood with his back to it as a sergeant bound his hands behind him.

"Do you have any last words before your sentence is carried out?" an officer asked. Davis trembled as he looked at the captain, calmed himself, and then cast his eyes across to the officers there to witness the execution. Lathan stood among them, grinning with satisfaction.

"You animals have become the very tyranny you claim to despise," Davis spoke with a trembling voice. "I die proud knowing that I'm not one of you." He spat on the ground as a sergeant blindfolded him. He shuddered as he fought to keep his chin high.

"Ready!" the sergeant shouted. Muskets rattled as soldiers snapped them to their shoulders.

"Aim!"

The men squinted down their barrels. The officers there to witness shifted on their feet. The captain stood with his saber held high. A crow called out with impatient anticipation.

"What do you fear, man! Strike!" Davis shouted.

"Fire!"

The line of muskets crackled with flames and smoke. The shot echoed momentarily, then died out. Silence held for a moment until one of the privates in the firing line started retching up his breakfast onto the ground before him.

"Punishment detail, dismissed!" the captain shouted mercifully to distract the men from their vomiting comrade. Captain Lathan Woods spat on the ground and walked away. He had just seen an enemy vanquished, but there were more out there still.

To be continued in the next book: Blood for Blood at Nashville.

Historical Note

Thanks for reading my novel. Of course, the main characters and their stories are fictional, but much of the historical events and real people were as I described them.

The Battle of Shiloh, or Pittsburg Landing as the Federals called it, was the bloodiest battle in American history up to that point. Some say the over 23,000 combined casualties were more than all previous American wars combined, dating back to the Revolutionary War. It was certainly one of the Confederates' best chances of destroying the Federal Army in the West. Many debate whether Johnston's death and Beauregard's decision to call off the assault on the first day stopped them from pushing the Federals completely into the river. Others say that the Federals had finally retreated to a defendable line with ample support from the gunboats moored within shelling range. They say this position would have broken any further push by the Rebels.

I used many real quotes from Johnston, and one from Beauregard, in their pre-battle meeting. However, these were taken from several meetings they had the night before and in the morning of the first day. For the sake of fluidity, I consolidated those conversations into the one scene I described in the morning just before the battle.

Johnston was the highest-ranking officer on either side to die in battle during the war. Frankly, he had no business leading from the front. At that moment he was acting more like a brigadier general or even a colonel than a commander of an army. However, he is credited for reinvigorating the otherwise stalled Rebel attack. He had been shot behind his right knee and didn't even realize it. That bullet severed an artery causing him to bleed to death. The irony is he carried a tourniquet in his pocket for such a contingency, but no one could figure out was wrong with him as he died. He also had earlier sent his personal doctor to care for some of the wounded Federal soldiers that were now behind Rebel lines.

His horse, Fire-Eater did survive his wounds. He was captured at the end of the war by the 4th Michigan Cavalry along with Johnston's son Colonel William Preston Johnston and President Jefferson Davis. It's assumed that Fire-Eater lived out the rest of his life in the North.

Okay, I'm sure some of you bristled at General Daniel Ruggles saying, "That guy's a dick." Well, there's no evidence of him saying anything like that. I'm sure that line sounds suspiciously modern. I'll say this, you're probably right, however, the terms "guy" as in to refer to a man and "dick" to refer to his private parts have been around since at least the time of Shakespeare. So I took some liberty here. I assure you that I at least researched to make sure all of the slang terms I've used in this work would have been around during the mid-19th century. Historical fiction is always an exercise in historical plausibility.

Dan Ruggles is an interesting character. He was a Yankee born in Massachusetts and an abolitionist, but he married a Southern woman. So when it came time to fight, facing off against the Federal army probably seemed a lot safer than facing an angry wife. As a man committed in a relationship with a Southern woman, I can assure you that he probably made the right decision. I don't know if he had a sense of humor like I tried to portray in this book, but I feel like I see one in his eyes when I look at his pictures. He probably needed one being in the ironic position the war found him. He did survive and sold real estate in Virginia after the war.

There are several accounts of the "angel glow" that seemed to emit from the wounds of the men left in the field overnight at Shiloh. It was also reported that more of the men who reported having glowing wounds survived than those who didn't. In 2001, a pair of high school students along with one of their microbiologist mothers did a study and found that the wounds were most likely infected with microscopic worms that carry a bacteria that glows under the wet conditions found at Shiloh that night. That glowing bacteria eats other bacteria, which may account for those glowing wounds not getting infected and thus the higher survival rate of the men infected.

Pierre Gustave Toutant-Beauregard suffered from a throat ailment that got so bad he had to have surgery. Unfortunately, little is known other than speculation of what exactly the problem was. Some say it was tonsillitis. The problem most surely affected his performance, forcing him to travel at times in an ambulance and spend many days in bed.

After his brilliant ruse and retreat from Corinth, he decided to take a few weeks off and checked into a spa to recover his health. However, he didn't get permission to do so. Furious, President Davis removed him from command and replaced him with Braxton Bragg. Beauregard was later sent to Charleston, South Carolina to command the coastal defenses. There he uttered one of the most metal quotes of the war:

"But, my friends, I do not appear before you tonight to make a speech, and for several reasons -- first, it is a time for action, not speaking; and secondly, my throat has been left in such a condition by recent illness, that the only way in which I can speak now is through the mouths of my cannon."

I like Beauregard's panache quite a bit. I think it's important to point out that he had a change of heart later in life and advocated for racial equality.

The town of Monterey Tennessee, which I mentioned in Chapter 8, is now called "Michie." They had to change their name when they applied for a post office because another town in Tennessee had already claimed the name "Monterey." "Michie" is the name of a prominent local family that lived there.

The Colt revolving rifles, or carbines, used by the 2nd Michigan Cavalry gave them an immense advantage over most of their foes who were still shooting single-shot muzzleloaders. The joke going around was that they could, "load on Sunday and shoot all week long." However, they were susceptible to chain fire in which the firing of one cylinder would cause the rest to go off, often wounding or even killing the shooter. This is why the revolving rifle didn't become as popular as the Spencer repeating rifle, which was the forefather of the lever-action rifles we see in the westerns and used even today.

The Battle of Memphis happened pretty much as I described it, at least by the witnesses who tried to piece together the wild naval action through the smoke and early morning light. That "madman" that Kathryn sees riding on top of one of the Federal rams was Colonel Charles Ellet Jr. It was such an outrageous display of courage and panache, I had to include it in the story. Ellet was shot in the knee during the melee. Ironically, he died of the measles while recuperating from his wounds.

Munfordville was one of the largest surrenders of Federal soldiers in the war. It's also one of the great stories of honor among enemies that were so prevalent during that time. Colonel Wilder put quite a bit of trust in his adversary when he had himself smuggled into his enemy's camp blindfolded to ask advice. To this, General Buckner later remarked, "I wouldn't have deceived that man under those circumstances for anything."

Both men survived the war. Wilder was paroled after two months. He distinguished himself at the

Battle of Chickamauga and rose to the rank of Brevet Brigadier General. He was born in New York but settled in Tennessee after the war and eventually became commissioner of the Chickamauga and Chattanooga National Military Park. Simon Bolivar Buckner also fought at the Battle of Chickamauga. Years after the war he later became the 30th Governor of Kentucky.

   The Kentucky campaign of late summer and early fall of 1862 was the Confederates' last chance of pulling the state into the Confederacy. Kentucky was a slave state but it had its share of both Union and Confederate sympathizers. It voted to stay in the Union. Kentucky declared itself neutral at the beginning of the war, however, but that neutrality ended when Confederate General Leonidas Polk occupied Columbus on the Mississippi River. Both sides recruited heavily in the state. The state was immensely important strategically. President Lincoln said, "To lose Kentucky would be to lose the whole game."

   The Battle of Perryville was the biggest and bloodiest battle fought in Kentucky in known history. There were roughly 7,500 casualties between the two armies. Some may say that Bragg had won a tactical victory that day, having pushed the Federals back, but the end result was that the Confederates had to retreat from Perryville overnight and then from Kentucky altogether.

   Buell won a strategic victory despite nearly having his entire left wing destroyed while foolishly failing to realize he was in the midst of a major battle. The reason given is that his headquarters was tucked away a few hills back from the action. This hilly terrain and the weather conditions created what some historians call an "acoustic shadow." In this shadow, Buell and his staff claimed they couldn't hear the battle raging just a few miles away. His failure to crush the outnumbered Rebels at Perryville, coupled with his reluctance to chase them afterward, led to his firing later that month. He'd never command an army again.

If you feel like you saw some Star Wars references in this and in *Rampage on the River*, you're absolutely right. They're intentional. I'm a big fan and I like dropping Easter eggs from the original trilogy in my work. You may also find a few Shakespeare, Alexandre Dumas, and Sir Walter Raleigh homages, as well among other things. What can I say, I'm a fan of history and great writers. I hope you stick with me. I have a lot more planned. This story will continue in my next novel, *Blood for Blood at Nashville*.

A Preview of *Blood for Blood at Nashville*, Now Available for Pre-Order on your E-Reader. Coming July 1, 2021

Chapter One: Here They Come

April 12, 1864: Fort Pillow, Tennessee

They came through the woods in the pre-dawn darkness like ghosts passing through the ravines and slipping between the trees. Unaware of this impending danger, men of the US 13th Tennessee Cavalry fought their own heavy eyelids as they sat in the rifle pits of the forward picket positions of Fort Pillow.

"Judgement Day, you traitorous son of a bitch!" a Rebel soldier hissed as he leaped into a pit and drove his knife into a nearly slumbering Federal soldier. He covered the dying man's mouth with his other hand and glared into his eyes until the man slumped to the muddy floor.

"You picked the wrong side," he spat at the corpse.

The Rebel cavalryman popped his head up from the rifle pit. All around he could hear the rustle of similar scenes: a whimper from a dying Federal solider, the sound of a knife plunging into flesh. Satisfaction spread across his dirty, blood-spattered face. These home-grown Yankees and their damn negro runaways dressed as soldiers had no idea what was about to happen to them. He waved his hat over his head, signaling the rest to come forward.

More men from the Confederate 2nd Missouri Cavalry, the "Missouri Mongols," emerged from the shadows. They crept forward, clutching their carbines, pistols, and knives. Alarmed by the sudden surge of the butternut-clad cavalrymen, two of the surviving Federal pickets sprinted from their hiding place towards the fort.

"Shoot 'em!" Captain Smith called out. A blast of gunpowder and the flash of muzzle fire split the darkness. One of the runners cried out as he tumbled to the ground. His companion stopped briefly to look back at the man rolling on the ground in agony before turning back to his all-out dash for safety.

"The Rebels are coming!" he screamed in terror only to be met by another volley of hot lead from behind.

Dr. Charles Fitch's eyes popped open at the sound of gunshots. He lay there for a moment in the darkness of his tiny cabin, wondering if he were dreaming. A second volley caused him to bolt upright. It seemed frighteningly close. Dogs began to bark.

"Good God, they're here…" he gasped, clutching his blanket to his chest. A woman screamed somewhere outside.

"Dear God…" he said, scrambling into his clothes. Manic yelping from the woods caused goosebumps to ripple across his skin.

"Ow!" he hissed, as he banged his head on the low ceiling of his hut. The morning air was cool but fear warmed him as he ran down the bluff towards the river to where the provost marshal's cabin lay. Without bothering to knock, he burst in and started shaking the man sleeping inside.

"Captain Young! Captain Young! You must get up! The Rebels are attacking."

"Jesus!" Young let out as he reached for his pistol next to his bed. He blinked at Fitch for a moment, gathering his thoughts, then focused his eyes. "Start alerting the contraband camp. We need to get the women and children to the landing. Hopefully, we can get the *New Era* to evacuate them. I need to alert Major Booth if he isn't already. This could get ugly fast," he said, turning to put his feet on the floor while he shimmied up his trousers.

Panic was beginning to stir as people popped their heads out from their tents and cabins in the little contraband town that had sprung up outside of the fort's earthen walls. "What's happening, Doctor?" a woman asked as Fitch passed her hovel.

"It's alright, Rosa." He tried to sound calm. "It's just some skirmishers. Major Booth has everything under control. Get your children to the launch so we can get you to safety."

A woman screamed. Droves of people brushed against him as they dashed down the slope towards the river. "Stay calm, everyone!" Dr. Fitch called out. "Get yourself and your families to the launch. We have a coal barge there to whisk you away. There's plenty of room." The sound of crackling wood began to blend in with the tramping of feet. He could smell wood burning. Smoke wisped through the crowd. Dr. Fitch looked up to see the glow coming from the far end of the camp as black smoke rose into the air like a flag climbing a pole.

"Good heavens, they're firing the camp…" he gasped, then to a couple of boys who weren't quite teens yet, "You two! Help me get the sick out of the hospital tent!"

"Are we gonna die?" one of them asked. The whites of his eyes contrasted with the early morning twilight.

"No, not if we stay calm and use our heads, Seddy," Fitch smiled at the boy patting his soft curly black hair.

A crackle of musketry brought a screech from the women trying to find places for themselves and their children on the largest of the three coal barges docked at the river. Dr. Fitch waved his arms frantically at the *New Era*. The timberclad gunboat sat impassively in the mist on the river. Fitch sighed in frustration. She showed no signs of movement.

"Stay here and stay calm, everyone. I have to go to the fort to signal the boat to come get you. We'll have you away soon!" With that, he ran back up the slope to the little earthen fort that commanded the heights over the Mississippi River. Behind him, the *New Era* finally woke with an eruption of fire and smoke, eliciting more screams from the civilians huddled on the barge. The shells whistled overhead and crashed in the woods on the other side of the fort with a deafening percussive roar.

Dr. Fitch was winded and sweating when he got to the fort. He was relieved to see Major Booth already dressed and giving orders with the confidence of experience.

"Major Bradford!" he called to his second in command. "Get your men to their forward gun pits and hold your position! If we let them get too close they'll get under our cannons and we won't be able to tilt down enough to shoot them!"

"Of course," Bradford replied, Booth's command snapping him out of his wide-eyed paralysis.

"Don't worry, Bill," Booth put his hand on Bradford's shoulder. "With your boys holding those positions, these raiders will be nothing more than target practice for my artillery boys. I trained them myself." Then turning to the newly arrived surgeon, "Dr. Fitch, are the civilians loaded aboard the barge?" Booth called to him.

"Umm…yes, sir. I tried to signal the *New Era* to come get them," Fitch stammered.

"No worries, we'll do it now." Booth said, and then turned to one of his officers, "Lieutenant McClure, signal Captain Marshall to retrieve the civilians! Once they're away he can continue to fire on Ravine No. 1, just as we planned. There's no place those Rebels can hide that we can't hit. Let's give them a warm welcome!"

"Yes, sir!" the young man replied and ran off to the signal station. Soon coded flags shot up the poles causing the *New Era* to stop firing and start steaming towards the landing.

For the first time since he woke, Fitch was beginning to feel relieved. Major Booth was a man who had started his career as a private and rose to the rank of Sergeant Major before accepting a commission to lead the newly formed 6th US Colored

Heavy Artillery Regiment as well as two companies of the 2nd Colored Light Artillery. Now at the rank of Major, he had assumed command of the fort from the well-meaning, but inexperienced Major Bradford. Just weeks before, Bradford had commanded the fort alone with his 13th Tennessee Cavalry. They were a white regiment full of Tennesseans loyal to the Union, although many of them were Confederate deserters who still resented serving alongside the black men they had once known as slaves.

Those white troops were now trotting out to their positions, leaving Booth with his staff and artillerymen in the fort. A crowd of wide-eyed black troops formed around him. "It's alright, boys. Just a little live-fire exercise for us this morning. Get to your guns. Listen to your sergeants. Remember the drill." Then to his officers, "Lieutenant Hill, McClure! Get your men to their guns! I want every man not directly involved in a crew to man the wall with a rifle. Make sure they're ready to replace any crew member shot down!"

Booth then turned to the lithe and well-groomed freeman who had come from Detroit with his oversized friend and enlisted a little over a year ago. These were two he had learned to depend on. "Francis, Elijah, take the rest of these men and go bring those two Parrot rifles back into the fort. Our gunners will be too exposed out there among the rifle pits."

"Yes, sir!" Francis snapped. "Come on, fellas," he turned to the group of men around him. Together they dashed out from the earthen walls to where the newly arrived 10-pound rifled cannons had been placed. They had planned on building earthen works around them to protect the crews, but it was too late now that the enemy was upon them.

"We finally get to try out the new ones!" Elijah huffed with excitement as they ran.

"That's if you don't get shot fetchin'em first, you big dummy," Jerry quipped. "They won't risk a horse to get they guns, but they'll sure spend the life of a nigga on them."

"Come on, Jerry," Francis gasped as they slowed their run just in time to avoid slamming themselves into the cannons. "By the time we fetched horses and rigged them, we'd all be shot to pieces and you know it." A bullet pinged off the barrel of one of the guns causing the men to cringe.

"I guess you right, Frenchie," Jerry looked up from his crouch behind the gun. "Let's get out, quick!"

The two 6-pound James rifles and the two 12-pound mountain howitzers in the fort began firing, scattering the Rebels who were just beginning to take positions in the wooded ravines out beyond the earthen walls, wood cabins, rifle pits, and abatis of felled trees. The white troops of the 13th US Tennessee Cavalry began to fill those rifle pits and answer the potshots that came from Rebels.

Major Booth beamed with pride as his artillerymen wheeled the two iron guns back into the fort with stoic determination just as the intensity of fire from the Rebels began to increase. The 10-pound Parrot rifles had tapered barrels that were a little over 6-feet long. They were made from cast iron with a ring of wrought iron wrapped around the breach to keep them from bursting upon firing. Using less powder than their smoothbore counterparts, the Parrot rifles fired a conical shell nearly two thousand yards with far more precision. That came from the spiral grooves, or "rifling," cut into the inner wall of the barrel that caused the shell to spin.

"Good job, boys! Wheel them into the embrasures here on the south end and commence firing!" Booth commanded.

The men went to work ramming powder charges and shells into the muzzles with well-rehearsed precision. Soon the guns were alive and kicking, bucking backward with jets of fire and smoke. Francis ran to one of the smoking barrels with his worm pole, which was an iron corkscrew-shaped tool attached to a pole. With it, he pulled out the leftover debris from the barrel. Jerry followed by plunging a wet sponge inside. It sizzled and steamed as it cleaned the barrel. Francis then did so with a dry sponge before they reloaded and wheeled the gun back into firing position. Sergeant Weaver squatted to sight it and set the elevation once more.

"By the numbers, boys, just like we drilled!" Major Booth yelled over the thundering cannons. Then to his nearby subordinate, "Lieutenant Hill, take a volunteer and set fire to those cabins outside our walls! They're giving the enemy too much cover!"

"Yes, sir!" Hill answered.

Dr. Fitch watched as the young officer and a civilian volunteer ran down to the cabins with torches in their hands. He flinched as bullets kicked up dirt around them. Soon the first row of cabins was burning. Fitch let out a breath of relief but then suddenly sucked in his next breath with a hiss, cringing as he watched Lieutenant Hill and his companion tumble to the ground and then lay lifeless.

"Do you think you can hold them, Major?" Dr. Fitch asked nervously.

"Certainly, as long as everyone keeps their heads together," Booth assured him. Fitch suddenly dropped to the ground clutching his thigh.

"Good God, Doctor, are you alright?" Booth squatted next to him.

Fitch patted his bleeding leg before looking up, "I think it's just a scrape. I have no idea where the bullet came from."

"Well, we need to get you out of the line of fire," Booth said helping him up. "Isaac, Billy!" he shouted towards the troops manning the wall. "Help Dr. Fitch to the rear. Doc, set up a hospital and prepare to receive the wounded."

A young man about to drive his wet sponge into a barrel suddenly collapsed. His lifeless eyes stared at the sky as blood began to surge from the hole in his head. The gun crew halted for a moment, regarding the corpse.

"Drag that man away! Johnny, take his place!" Booth called to others on the wall. "Keep firing, men don't stop!" The crew restarted their work swabbing, loading, and firing. More of them were dropping. More and more, men were dragging the bodies away and taking their places with stoic determination.

"Well, you wanted to see some action, Frenchie. Here it is," Jerry quipped as they labored.

"Shut up and keep moving," Francis shot back. Both of them cringed as a bullet pinged off the barrel. "They must have sharpshooters up high somewhere firing down on us!"

"Never mind that, men. We'll spot 'em and drop some shells on 'em, keep firing!" Booth exhorted, stepping over the tail of their gun. "We can't let them get any closer. We can't let them take the colors...!" he shouted, then collapsed. Blood began to pool around his body. For a moment, the sounds of battle seemed far away as the men looked down at their leader bleeding out his lifeblood at their feet.

"...Oh, shit," Jerry mumbled, resting on his rammer.

"Don't just stand there gawking like a bunch of hens, God damn it!" Sergeant Weaver snapped them out of their trance, "Keep firing!" Then to Francis, "Frenchie!"

"Yes, Sergeant!" Francis shouted back.

"Put them dancing legs to work and run down to Major Bradford. Tell him he's in command!" Weaver shouted. "Bobby! Off the wall and take his place!"

Francis crouched low against the inside of the fort's wall, calculating his timing. The crack of a sharpshooter's rifle from one of the high knolls was his cue. With a burst of motion, he was over the wall, out of the ditch, and sprinting towards the log cabins. He slammed himself against a cabin wall just in time to hear the rattle of musket balls pepper the other side. He drew long breaths trying to calm himself. He scanned the rifle pits, looking for Major Bradford. There he was! Once again, Francis waited for a volley before dashing off to Bradford's position. Just as the Rebels had sighted and tracked him he dropped to his hip and slid into the trench feet first, bullets kicking up the dirt around him.

"Jesus Christ, Private! You damn near scared the ghost out of me!" Bradford gasped.

"Sir, Major Booth is dead. You're in command. What are your orders?" Francis blurted over the swelling noise of combat.

Bradford stared at him, blinking, the blood rushing from his face. "We've got to get out of here…" he mumbled.

"Sir…?" Francis prodded.

"Captain!" Bradford called to his subordinate, "Order the men back to the fort! Pass the message along the line. Everyman, back to the fort! We need to consolidate our forces!"

"Sir, shouldn't we leave a line of rifles forward of the fort? The Rebels will get under the tilt of our guns if we don't hold them here."

"Are you questioning my judgment, Private!" Bradford grabbed him by the arm.

"Of course not, sir!"

"Then get back to the fort and tell whoever is in command to cover our retreat!" Bradford shoved him back.

The guns of Fort Pillow opened up in a coordinated volley, cueing the men in the forward pits to make the dash back to the fort. The Rebels made sport of the fleeing men, dropping several of them in their tracks. Soon the men of the US 13th Tennessee Cavalry were finding places along the walls with their counterparts from the 6th US Colored Heavy Artillery and the 2nd US Colored Light Artillery.

"Never thought I'd be fightin' alongside a nigger," one of them protested.

"This nigga may be the one to save your life," the man next to him answered.

The white cavalryman regarded his black comrade for a moment before returning eyes to the sights of his gun, "May God save us all, then…" he mumbled.

Sources

This book is a work of fiction. However, there are many historical accounts in it. I tried to stay as faithful to real history as possible. Below are some of the sources I used in my research. I highly recommend them if you want to learn more about the real history that this book is based on.

Thatcher, Marshall P. (1884) A Hundred Battles in the West: St Louis to Atlanta, 1861-65, The Second Michigan Cavalry. Detroit, MI: self-published.

Sam Watkins (1999) Company Aytch or, the Side Show to the Big Show. New York, NY: Plume (Original work published in 1882).

Daniel, Larry J. and Bock, Lynn N. (1996) Island No. 10: Struggle for the Mississippi Valley. Tuscaloosa, AL: The University of Alabama.

Dr. Ranney, Geo E., Surgeon 2nd Michigan Cavalry. (1897) War papers read before the Michigan Commandery ... v.2. Military Order of the Loyal Legion of the United States. "Reminiscences of an army surgeon." Detroit, MI: James H. Stone & Company.

Engle, Stephen (2001) Struggle for the heartland : the campaigns from Fort Henry to Corinth Douglas. Lincoln, NE: University of Nebraska Press.

Woodcock, Marcus (2001) A Southern Boy in Blue : the Memoir of Marcus Woodcock, 9th Kentucky Infantry. Knoxville, TN: University of Tennessee Press.

Chester G. Hearn, Baton Rouge (1995) The Capture of New Orleans 1862. Baton Rouge, LA: Louisiana State University Press.

Noe, Kenneth W. (2001) Perryville: this Grand Havoc of Battle. Lexington, KY: University Press of Kentucky.

Smith, Timothy B. (2012) Corinth 1862: Siege, Battle, Occupation. Lawrence, KS: University Press of Kansas.

Toutant-Beauregard, Pierre Gustave (1862) THE BATTLE OF SHILOH, Official Report. Corinth, MS.

Hurst, Jack (2012) Born to Battle: Grant and Forrest-- Shiloh, Vicksburg, and Chattanooga. New York, NY: Basic Books.

Hurst, Jack (1994) Nathan Bedford Forrest: A Biography. New York, NY: Vintage.

McCaul, Edward B. (2014) To Retain Command of the Mississippi: The Civil War Naval Campaign for Memphis, Knoxville, TN: University of Tennessee Press

Coombe, Jack (1998) Thunder along the Mississippi: the River Battles that Split the Confederacy. New York, NY: Bantam.

Kidd, James Harvey. (1908) Personal Recollections of a Cavalryman With Custer's Michigan Cavalry Brigade in the Civil War. Ionia, MI: Sentinel Press.

Volo, Dorothy Denneen and Volo, James M. (1998) Daily Life in Civil War America. Greenwood Press.

Miles, Tiya. (1970) The Dawn of Detroit: a Chronicle of Slavery and Freedom in the City of the Straits. The New Press.

Woodford, Arthur M. (2001) This is Detroit, 1701-2001. Detroit, MI: Wayne State University.

civilwarpodcast.org

civilwartalk.com

historicalemporium.com

Works by Cody C. Engdahl

Novels:
The 2nd Michigan Cavalry Chronicles Trilogy
- Rampage on the River: The Battle for Island No. 10 (Book I)
- The Perils of Perryville (Book II)
- Blood for Blood at Nashville (Book III)

Mexico, My Love

Nonfiction:
The American Civil War WAS About Slavery: A Quick Handbook of Quotes to Reference When Debating Those Who Would Argue Otherwise

How to Write, Publish, and Market Your Novel

Printed in Poland
by Amazon Fulfillment
Poland Sp. z o.o., Wrocław
26 November 2022

22a6bcbe-1f95-4583-852e-a0750ecde819R01

Drown Her!

© 2021 Juliana Lilley

Contents

1. Jenesis
3. To Change
4. Your Garden of Eden
5. July
6. Pink
8. The Night Fits You Well
10. Everyone Hated Me
11. Forbidden Love
12. Innocence
13. Moonself
15. Anthropogenic Relic I
16. Anthropogenic Relic II
17. The Dream Trapeze
18. Raised Vegetarian
19. Forgetness
20. I'm on TV!
22. The Square-shaped Trap
23. Sleepers

24.	My God is an It
25.	Copywrong
27.	Hold Me Tight
28.	The Unmasking Poem
30.	Minotaura
32.	Cemeteries
34.	Juli and Ana
36.	When Your Mind is Dark
38.	Bodywaves
39.	The Thing About Drowning in a Glass of Water
40.	In the Silence
42.	Home

Jenesis

This is the creation story of my world.

It was always the good that turned out to be bad, never the bad that turned out to be good. There was evil to be discovered, but nothing to be discovered in evil; no love. No lesson.

If goodness were an orange, then evil would be something that resembled an orange, but with an infinite number of peels, that would reveal itself an infinite number of times. There would also be oranges with four or five peels. All three fruits would grow from the same tree; not a tree of knowledge, but rather, a tree of fickle fruit. A tree of doubt.

Adam picked an orange. Satan picked one with five peels. But no matter how many times Eve peeled the fruit she had picked, there was only more peel. She finally smiled as she thought she had gotten to the juice; it turned out her hands were just bleeding. She mistook her own blood for orange juice and her own detached fingernails for orange seeds. She knew she must have been getting closer.

She starved to death, the fruit still cradled in her lap. They called it the Original Sin.

To Change

To write would be to confess. To let go of something I'd gotten quite comfortable holding onto, like the handlebar of a bicycle

Sweating palms cohered to rubber,

One body, one single creature.

To write would mean I'd cease to be that thing. To write would be to change; or, maybe, to admit that

I am changing?

All of me has become ink in a cocoon of paper; all of me has become imprisoned in what I refuse to say.

I picture a butterfly with secrets printed small on its wings, opening and shutting like a notebook left outside in the wind. Could I become that? Could I stand to?

Could I stop myself?

Your Garden of Eden

The heart of me is a bulb

My veins aflower

With love; with longing to reach you,

To wrap myself around your soul

Until we can't get any closer

And to bloom around you beautifully,

To turn myself into your garden of Eden

From the inside out,

To be tranquillity

With a touch of

Temptation.

July

I should write more, but you've hollowed me;

I want only you.

You in the space between my heartbeats;

You in the darkness, in the silence,

Like a dream.

I want only your arms, your smile, your closeness

Your breath on my hips.

To soak in your shadow,

Let it blacken mine.

Let me disappear.

Pink

Snap of a big branch
Sun is pink and all is sky
Hiss of laughtering

Sprig of willowherb
The same colour as your hair
Stuffed between my breasts

Half becomes a whole
How better to fill a hand
Than with another?

Night is white as milk
And rumbles like the noises
One makes during sleep

You say I'm perfect

But I can't freeze time.

Still,

For you,

I'll always try.

The Night Fits You Well

The night fits you well

Starlit haze

Eyes wild as the sky

See me reflected

Between blinks

In glimmering black

Perfect mooncrescents

Contour your

Muscles in the dark

Strong arms around me

Soft small kisses

Symphony on skin

Calmly as the moon

Waning off

Knowing he'll be back

Everyone Hated Me

I could never understand why I always got the feeling everyone hated me. I used to mistake the absence of love for hatred, because I survived on the belief that the absence of hatred was enough to be love.

Those who didn't outright love me must have hated me, because those who didn't outright hate me must have loved me. I needed to believe in that. I needed to, or else I would have had no love to live on.

But I don't need to anymore.

All I needed was love. One love was a thousand; one love was all it took to make me see the thousandfold love that had been there the whole time, eclipsed by my belief in hatred, when all I needed was to believe in love; and all I needed to believe in love, was love.

Forbidden Love

To love with courage is

To love in spite.

To love with courage is

To cross every line.

The forbidding of love

Is merely the test of it;

The beauty of love

Is that love never fails.

Innocence

I dreamt I was trying to make tea from garden daisies

But they kept on bleeding.

I dreamt that she held me by the jaw

Putting poisoned lipstick on my lips

And that when she was finished,

I immediately kissed her.

I dreamt I pulled the hair of a gorgon

I felt her venom in my organs

I tried every trick in the book,

Anything just to make her look,

But she preferred to hear me cry

Than let me turn to stone and die.

Moonself

You make me feel like the moon as a girl

Queen of all stars,

Light in the dark;

Only

Ever so lonely.

I just can't forget that

I'm part of the night,

Locked in her ribcage

Between sharp black teeth

A trembling heart, a pounding lung

Wondering how I look from beneath.

Double-edged swords flung

From the earth

And eyefuls of contempt

From the sea,

A mirror gilded with the gold of tears

If only it would loosen its grip on me.

Anthropogenic Relic I

They planted cherrystones in the soil of the moon

And soon picked the fruits,

Dark and glistening

With the juice of sunbeams

Although, they were hard as rocks,

And entirely inedible;

Little black moons that would orbit the heart

And drink it slowly to pieces.

Anthropogenic Relic II

They felled the trees of heaven

To make bibles to write of its beauty in;

They left it bare

And took the wings of angels home to wear.

The mine don't shine when the gold is gone,

Cyanide salt

Smelted smooth to spilt milk,

Mopped up with rags in the rush.

Heaving hollow chests

From which roasted hearts were torn

And brokenness was born

Have no blood to spell violation

With all the wounds in the world for an alphabet.

The Dream Trapeze

You saw me two-dimensional, paper-thin

Cut me up and stuck me back together wrong

You couldn't change me, only rearrange me

Into something ugly

Like the shards of a mirror.

Lie to hear them say it back,

Sew your doll and burn it black,

But now every splinter of bone is creeping back

Into its proper place,

Light returning to my face

Triangular scars coupling into stars

I hang from a night sky pearled, I cling to the top of the world

Black-haired giant's blind hands seize the dream trapeze,

She's swinging like a winter gale

She's beaming like a comet-tail.

Raised Vegetarian

"What would be the most satisfying animal to kill?

Probably a crab, right?

Because of the crunch."

"Probably."

The light goes out and I dream of an animal,

Its ribcage stuffed with the bones of another,

An ostrich with a slot in its back

In which the skeletons of piranhas collect, a vast sum,

Or perhaps a dog filled to the brim with mice.

Why am I doing this?

I'm playing.

Am I playing?

The sun comes up.

Forgetness

It was written on a girl's hair

Then a breath of wind shattered it

To hair-thin splinters,

To needles for haystacks.

It was written as a river

Rushing its sentences undone

The letters all scattered minnows swam

Forgotten: /fəˈgɒtn/

Written in white on white,

Not quite 'written, erased'

But written, illegible.

There, imperceptible.

True, not known.

I'm on TV!

My window has become

A television-screen

My daily life, a spectacle

I'm stuck inside a scene.

Why do you only like me

When I'm really far away?

Why do you make me feel

Like I am always on display?

Even without windows,

Would you watch me through a crack?

Why do you only listen

When you know I won't talk back?

Why do you discuss me

As if I don't have a heart?

Why let me just sit there

If you won't let me take part?

You don't see me

As one of you,

You don't see me

As human too,

You want me doll,

You want me dead,

To whisper to

My sleeping head,

Is it so hard

To say hello

To someone you

Already know?

The Square-shaped Trap

Ceramic person

Earth and fire

Kiss of flames on clay

Gives her hollow porcelain skin for a body.

She is caught in a square-shaped trap

That is as much a symbol of infinity

As any ring or figure-eight,

Only, she will prick her finger on the same four corners

Until they are sanded flat

By the microscopic ridges of her fingerprints;

Only, she will burn.

Sleepers

It sleeps unquietly on the palm of my hand

Harsh humming, wet tickling

I make a fist;

Unexpected glistening crunch

Insect-blood like black syrup provokes

A desperation to get clean;

At least the humming stops,

Or is it just that

The sound of the water drowns it out

Momentarily?

My God is an It

My god is an it

For what is the difference

Between he-gods

And the most vulgar kind of men?

Don't you love both?

Don't you fear both?

Don't both kill and kill and kill,

Demand your heart

Demand your blood,

Don't both tell you they love you

While they hurt you

Over and over again;

And don't you believe them?

Copywrong

You're as hollow as an echo

You're as hollow as a drum

You're as human as a shadow,

A photograph of someone,

You have built quite a collection

You have cut me out with scissors

You have stolen my reflection

From inside of every mirror,

Like a strange man following me

On a quiet street at night,

Something slowly swallowing me

Like a greedy parasite,

Like a black sky without a moon,

Like a smile with no teeth,

It's uncanny, like a costume

With nobody underneath,

You have glued me on so tightly

It'll hurt to take me off

But I'm asking you politely

Because I have had enough.

Hold Me Tight

Dismembered parts, I wonder
If you can see them too.
If they catch your eye,
If you like the view
When you happen to catch sight
All I can do
Is hold you tight.

Dismembered parts of better girls
Are strewn all across the bed
They keep on catching my eye,
They keep on turning my head
Like sudden bright light
But all you do
Is hold me tight.

The Unmasking Poem

I didn't think I was real

I thought I'd just invented me

Made my own synthetic soul

To fill the hollow doll of me,

'Cause I was having no fun

Being no-one.

I used other peoples' words

Without knowing what they mean,

Copied peoples' gestures

Like a choreographed routine,

'Cause I was getting no thrill

Just sitting still.

I've realised self-invention

Can't replace self-discovery,

So I will chase my own heart

Relentless in recovery,

'Cause I will never make it

If I fake it.

Minotaura

First I was a bull in a china-shop.

In retrospect, I don't know if I ever was a human being.

I thought so at the time,

But it was inevitable

That I broke everything, anyway.

I didn't ever mean to.

I would always get a terrible fright when it happened.

I hear the sound of it in my nightmares:

The smashing of the plates,

And the peoples' voices booming.

When there was nothing left to break,

I broke myself. Gradually.

I learned to speak, to walk on my hind legs. I bit off all my fur.

One day, I turned human.

Or at least, I thought I did.

I thought that would be the end of it,

Until I knocked one of the shelves down again;

Then came

The smashing of the plates,

And the peoples' voices booming.

Cemeteries

They say

Bury your hurt in graves

Let it die and leave it dead

In the green open fields of freedom,

But what if the hurt is inside of me

And I must make myself its coffin

Without having meant for,

Deserved for

Something inside of me to die in the first place?

Why must I bleed headstones

Like big sharp kidney stones

From my little tear ducts?

They say

Bury your hurt in graves

Let it die and leave it dead

In the green open fields of freedom,

But why must my green open fields of freedom

Be cemeteries

While others do not mourn?

And why must my green open fields of freedom

Be minefields

While others frolic in white gowns without a care?

Juli and Ana

I get so cut off from myself

With all these interrupting voices.

I want silence.

Silence,

So each part of me

Can fall in love with the other,

Tenderly synchronising our breath

Braiding ourselves together by the hair

Feeding our common belly,

Guarding our common heart

With twelve white talons.

The kind of things

You can only really do with yourself;

I want to think a thought together,

Heal a wound together.

Decide on the colour

Of something that's almost-purple,

Almost-pink together.

I want to hear my point of view.

I get so cut off from myself

With all these interrupting voices.

I want silence.

When Your Mind is Dark

When your mind is dark

You mustn't rush to find your way.

It isn't wise to try to find your way by moonlight,

By the glimmer of perceptions of cold, distant orbiters.

You'll end up lost in regions of black

That'll have you start believing the earth is flat

And falling off the edge.

They'll have you racing to consume it

Before it consumes you,

They'll have you trying to bottle it

And drinking god-knows-what

Was really in the bottle.

When your mind is dark

You mustn't rush to find your way.

Lay still as a corpse

And let the night wash over you.

Don't breath

The darkness in.

When your mind is light again

You must consider it a dream.

Bodywaves

Purple lips

Snow-for-bones

But nothing else stays the same.

Now my hair is black.

Now my shoulder-blades are hidden,

Now my breasts reach my belly,

Now my thighs are curved

Like the bodies of doves.

My skin turns from something like milk

To muscle;

Milk to muscle, milk to muscle.

And inside:

There is a seashell of a skull I inhabit,

There is a murmur of an ocean,

There are gentle waves,

And a mirror

That never stills.

The Thing About Drowning in a Glass of Water

The thing about drowning in a glass of water is that you still die.

And everyone just laughs about it, but you're gone. And they say, well

I once swallowed a bit of water down the wrong way

And you don't see me laying there dead

Because I just fucking breathed. And they say

I'd love to see her drown in the sea,

Then she'd see

Then she'd see what it's really like to drown, they say.

And you can't explain it to them, because the thing is,

You still die.

In the Silence

Edinburgh city centre.

Only,

You haven't heard the sound of bagpipes

For a half an hour or so;

You pay it no mind until you come across a red-faced man

In a kilt and a bonnet

On the phone to the suicide hotline on the corner of the street.

Then, you wonder:

What else is missing,

And

Why?

For missing things are all around you

Lurking in the silence,

In the empty spaces

Of the backdrop,

Only tending to bob to the surface

Once lifeless.

Home

I rest in peace, piece

Of another world, whirled

Around inside death a while while

They're waiting there, they're

Rocking back and forth, fourth

Hour of the morning, mourning

Far too soon; soon

I'll return, turn

Back, the blue of ambulance lights lights

My way home.

Printed in Great Britain
by Amazon